# THE LAST LAUGH CLUB

## KATE GALLEY

Boldwood

First published in Great Britain in 2025 by Boldwood Books Ltd.

Copyright © Kate Galley, 2025

Cover Design by Lizzie Gardiner

Cover Images: Adobe Stock and Shutterstock

Map designed by Boldwood Books. Images: Shutterstock.

The moral right of Kate Galley to be identified as the author of this work has been asserted in accordance with the Copyright, Designs and Patents Act 1988.

Every effort has been made to obtain the necessary permissions with reference to copyright material, both illustrative and quoted. We apologise for any omissions in this respect and will be pleased to make the appropriate acknowledgements in any future edition.

A CIP catalogue record for this book is available from the British Library.

Paperback ISBN 978-1-83533-883-4

Large Print ISBN 978-1-83533-884-1

Hardback ISBN 978-1-83533-882-7

Ebook ISBN 978-1-83533-885-8

Kindle ISBN 978-1-83533-887-2

Audio CD ISBN 978-1-83533-877-3

MP3 CD ISBN 978-1-83533-878-0

Digital audio download ISBN 978-1-83533-881-0

This book is printed on certified sustainable paper. Boldwood Books is dedicated to putting sustainability at the heart of our business. For more information please visit https://www.boldwoodbooks.com/about-us/sustainability/

Boldwood Books Ltd, 23 Bowerdean Street, London, SW6 3TN

www.boldwoodbooks.com

*For Richard*

THE SHETLAND ISLES

MUCKLE FLUGGA •

UNST

YELL

MAINLAND

SANDNESS •

LERWICK •

BRESSAY •

SANDWICK •

ST NINIAN'S ISLE •

SUMBURGH •

# PROLOGUE

My dearest friend,

If you are reading this, then I am dead!

A little melodramatic, but please indulge my dear deceased heart. And it's not as if we didn't know it was coming.

I thought I'd be sad writing this to you, but actually, I'm not. The last ten years have been 100 per cent more tolerable because of your friendship and that is no small thing, believe me. Your visits have boosted me more than you could possibly imagine and I will take my gratitude with me into the next life – or certainly with me into the flames at the crematorium. I know! You don't like to talk about the mechanics of death, but there it is and it is done.

I will ask one more thing, if I may? Two things, actually.

Please wear the last garment I knitted for you to my funeral. I can't bear the thought of a lot of dismal colours, and if I thought you would be a beacon of hope in a sea of darkness it would make me so happy.

The other thing is a bigger request. I wish to take one last trip – a journey I wasn't able to make while I was still alive.

*Would you consider scattering my ashes for me? You know I wasn't blessed with a family in my life and I look to you to fulfil my wishes. All of the details are with my assistant and she will seek you out after the funeral.*

*And that is all. I have had a good life. I hope you know that.*

*A fond farewell to you.*

*Your ever-loving friend,*

*Norman*

# 1

## GOODBYE, NORMAN

### *Bridget*

Bridget drummed her fingertips against the steering wheel, the pace increasing with her irritation while she waited for her husband, Graham, to appear. She had her eyes on the rearview mirror and watched the open doorway to their 1930s semi-detached. She'd left it open to remind him they had somewhere to be. Graham always thought he had all the time in the world, which for a man in his seventies was optimistic. It wasn't that Bridget was a pessimist, though, she just knew *she* wouldn't be around forever.

Eventually he appeared wearing his corduroy jacket, which Bridget thought made him look a bit like an ageing geography teacher, but she knew he would have chosen it because it wasn't black. Norman had expressly asked for them to be colourful. The jacket was tan, but it would have to do as time was moving at quite a pace. There could be no fashionably late to a funeral.

Graham patted his pockets, glancing in the hallway mirror at his newly cut hair before disappearing back inside the bowels of the house. Bridget ceased the drumming, leaned her head back, closed her eyes and tried to quell the rising tension in her body. Then she began to bite furiously at the skin around her thumb.

The driver's door opened and Graham appeared beside her. She noticed it had begun to rain.

'Wrong side, sweetheart,' he said.

'But I was going to drive,' she said. 'I thought you could have a drink at the wake.'

Graham looked at her with that expression she saw a lot of lately. It was a patient but sad smile and Bridget knew that if she didn't remember what it was that was wrong here, he would have to tell her. On this occasion, she had no recollection of why she wasn't driving them to the crematorium.

'You don't drive any more,' he said. 'You decided.'

She was about to say, *Don't I, did I, are you sure?* but there was one of those little nudges, as she'd come to call them. A memory seemingly buried that was unlocked with a couple of words from her husband. The memory itself was her behind the wheel and the car embedded in the hedge at the bottom of the road when she'd become flustered and forgotten which pedal was the brake.

'I know that, of course. I was just warming the seat for you,' she said as she slipped back out of the car and walked round to the passenger side with her handbag over her head to keep her hair from getting wet.

'Is that what you're wearing?' he asked as his eyes slid over the knitted cardigan she'd pulled on. It was a riot of raspberry, fuchsia, hot pink and bubblegum-coloured wool in a busy pattern across the knit.

'Yes,' Bridget said. 'It's what Norman wanted.'

Graham hesitated before he switched on the engine and the windscreen wipers.

'Well,' he said as he plugged in his seatbelt and began to

reverse out of the driveway, 'it's a nice contrast with your silver hair, I suppose, but I have to say that I think Norman is taking the piss.'

Graham pulled out of their road onto the seafront and Bridget watched seagulls swooping low over the golden sands of Bridlington South Beach. Then he cut back onto the main road towards York. Norman had chosen the crematorium near where he lived in Bishopthorpe because it had ample parking and was only a short hop to the Rottweiler and Bunny. The pub was actually called the Hound and Hare, but Norman always did have an odd sense of humour.

Bridget and Graham used to live near Norman in Bishopthorpe when she still worked at the factory. But that was ten years ago, before they retired and moved to Bridlington to be by the sea. Bridget had wanted to move back to where she was born and raised in Cambridge, but she and Graham both agreed that Norman needed them and it was just too far to visit. It had been a while since Bridget had made this journey on her weekly trips to see her old friend as Norman had spent his last few weeks in a hospice, which took her on a different route. At the very end, he hadn't wanted to see her at all. His decision was to slip away without an audience and Bridget had to respect that.

'Are you okay?' Graham asked her and Bridget realised she was gripping her handbag tightly in her lap.

'Yes,' she said, loosening her grasp. 'I will miss him, but I suppose he's at peace now.'

She wondered about that. Was Norman at peace? Was Norman anything any more? She could feel a sob building in her throat and she took a couple of steadying breaths until it subsided.

Bridget thought back to the man she had visited for the last ten years of his life. The poor man in his wheelchair with his beloved computer and his knitting needles. Her heart constricted at the image of who he'd been before: vibrant, active and full of plans for his retirement.

'Poor Norman,' she said, reaching into her bag for a tissue.

'I wish you wouldn't call him that. He wasn't a poor man. He led a very full life.'

Bridget looked sharply at her husband and was about to ask him how he would know, but Graham was speaking again.

'He was my friend too, you know,' he said.

'Yes,' she said, quietly, but it wasn't comparable. Graham didn't have the same history with Norman. Graham didn't live with that agonising guilt.

She actually felt uncomfortable in her lurid cardigan, whatever she'd said to her husband. It was the last thing Norman had knitted for her and she'd not known what to say as she'd taken the gift.

'Do you love it?' Norman had asked her and, of course, she'd said she did, but this was the first time she had worn it, because she didn't like it at all. Perhaps Graham was right and Norman was having his last little bit of fun – and that was okay, why shouldn't he? – but she really hoped she wouldn't see anyone she knew, not looking like an ancient pink Barbie doll.

'Norman will live on in his knitwear,' Graham said, and they shared a grin as he pulled into the car park.

\* \* \*

### Derek

The place was surprisingly packed for a man without family. All the seats were now taken and there was barely any standing room either. Derek was perspiring quite profusely. He was wedged between a large man in a wool overcoat and a woman with a huge fluffy sweater and matching scarf. He tentatively moved his head towards his left armpit to see if he was whiffy, but it would only go so far before his neck protested with a sharp twinge and he had to give it up as a bad idea.

He should have stood at the back, but he'd been so early that most of the seats were free and he'd felt awkward standing around. He'd chosen to sit right in the middle of the row as he didn't presume to sit at the front and Derek was a man who wanted to cause as little fuss or irritation as possible. If he sat in the middle then others could easily access the seats from each side. Now though, as he felt a trickle of sweat working its way down his back, he sorely wished he'd just hovered in the open doorway instead.

He hadn't anticipated as many guests as there were. Was it guests to a funeral? It didn't seem right. Perhaps it was attendees, but that sounded far too formal for Norman. Dear Norman, what a lovely chap he'd been. A great friend he'd become, a good laugh, a sounding board and confidante. Derek would miss him.

Derek also missed his job at the factory, where they'd met. He'd really been part of something there. Taylor's Fruity Sauce had enjoyed a moment in the limelight when it had been launched by Timothy Taylor back in the 1930s. It successfully plugged that gap between red and brown table sauce with just a hint of chilli and six secret spices. It had experienced another surge in popularity in the seventies when old Mr Taylor died and his son took over. Derek had joined the ship at that point and had loved every minute of the journey.

Retirement didn't really suit him, he'd discovered. His garden and home were immaculate and, yes, you could make a full-time job out of domestic chores, but would you want to? He had his allotment too, but that wasn't the mindful place it used to be. The nice couple that would chat with him had moved away, old Martin had sadly passed on and since Alec had taken to bringing his radio down along with a packed lunch to keep out of his wife's hair, Derek's gentle afternoons had disappeared. Alec liked to listen to people droning on about football and politics, and when Derek had suggested headphones would offer him a better sound quality, Alec had said he couldn't possibly, it would be rude not to share.

So, Derek was spending less time with his vegetables and more time at home where his sister could more easily reach him. And yes, it was nice to talk to Sally, but it came with a large dollop of expectation and suggestion that he never felt he could step up to. Most of their conversations ended with her saying things like *So, you'll really think about that, won't you, Derek*, or *Let me know how you get on with what I suggested.*

He pulled his sweater out at the waist and tried to waft a bit of air up inside, but there didn't seem to be any air and he was worried that if there was a whiff, he'd only be sharing it with everyone around him. He'd worn the last thing Norman had knitted for him, as requested. It was a traditional Fair Isle sweater that he'd not worn before. It was as beautifully crafted as all of Norman's knitwear was, but the colours were a touch brighter than Derek would have chosen. Greens and purples weren't really his colours, but he'd have done anything for Norman. He didn't know why he'd been singled out in this way, because as he looked along the lines of chairs he could see that everyone else was in black. He decided to believe it was because he'd been a particular friend to Norman, but in truth, he wondered if it was Norman having one last laugh at Derek's expense. He smiled to himself and ignored the odd glances from the woman next to him. Norman could have his last laugh because, quite honestly, Derek owed him that.

* * *

*Gloria*

Gloria Taylor's heels clicked against the concrete path as she strode across the car park. She was late. Nearly ten minutes late. She wasn't sure she'd locked the car either, but she couldn't turn back now.

It had been Paul's fault. Gloria had been set to jump in the shower, but he'd enticed her back to bed with that seductive smile of his. She didn't think she'd have him for much longer and needed to make the most of him while she could. By the time he'd finally pulled on his trousers and reluctantly gone home to his wife, Gloria had less than forty minutes to get ready. Her shower had been brief and she'd not had the time to run the straighteners through her hair, so her new highlights weren't as sleek they had been when she'd left the salon the previous day. Paul had seen to that.

Paul was becoming a bit of a problem. He had started to hint that he'd like to make things permanent with Gloria, but she didn't want that – why on earth would she? Gloria was financially independent, happy in her own company, and enjoyed what she wanted, when she wanted it. It was a long time since she'd had to cook a meal for anyone or pick up after someone. The washing machine held only her own clothes and she liked it that way. Paul needed to stay with his wife, and that meant she was going to have to give him up.

It was Norman's funeral, though. She'd worn the knitted tank top he'd asked her to, so it didn't really matter that much about her hair. With a canary-yellow top flecked with orange and silver threads, she certainly wasn't looking to impress anyone and it wasn't likely to be that well attended anyway. Poor Norman. He really had been the one seriously good thing in her life and he was gone. Poor Gloria.

She pushed open the door as quietly as she could and was immediately met with a wall of people. Being only five-foot-three in her heels, she couldn't even see down to the front of the crematorium, even though she could hear that the service was in full swing. The celebrant was talking about something called Norman Knits and its huge following, what a life-changing experience it had been for Norman. Gloria was confused. She knew very well that Norman had had a life-changing experience; it had happened on her watch. She knew he knitted, of course; it had been a life saver in the preceding years with him being at home all the time and not as mobile as he had been before, but she didn't know what Norman Knits was. Did he have a club? She'd like to think of him with a group of people, all knitting together, but he didn't really have any friends other than her. But then the celebrant was talking about his followers and the number she used was over eight hundred thousand! Gloria knew Norman's sitting room wasn't that big.

She used her shoulders to push through the crowd. It felt imperative she was properly present at his funeral. He didn't have any close family and he needed her. But as she made her way to the back of the seating area, leaving a few disgruntled noises in her wake, it was clear that he didn't really need her specifically, because he had all of these other people. Who on earth were they all? She didn't recognise anyone from the factory, but to be fair it had been a number of years since she'd sold it and right now she was only getting the backs of their heads.

The celebrant stopped talking and a screen above her head lit up with the face of Norman, smiling and looking relaxed, happy and very much alive. It made Gloria feel choked as she glanced down at the coffin resting on the stand, covered in a floral knitted blanket. She thought it was a recording of him for a moment and prepared herself to see him talking for one last time, but it was just a series of photos and everyone was quiet while they watched a few choice moments of Norman's life running in a loop.

Some were from before his accident and showed him in the factory, hard at work. Norman had been an engineer, and there he was, head bent over one of the machines, wielding some large tool or other. A couple of them Gloria remembered taking herself for promotional shots. When her husband, Tim junior, had died and she'd taken over the business, she was keen to push the ship harder, with herself at the helm. Taylor's Fruity Sauce would be in its third moment of glory. Unfortunately short-lived, but fun while it lasted.

But she'd not taken the photos of him at home after that tragic day. She had been a consistent visitor to Norman over the last ten years, but she'd not taken pictures of him; she didn't think he'd have liked it. But someone had, because there he was with his knitting needles in front of his computer screen and with a large grin on his lovely face.

Gloria turned her head away from the images and wondered how long the service would be. She was badly in need of a drink.

# 2

## THE ASHES

*Bridget*

Glasses of sherry were lined up along a table in the far corner of the bar with rows of sandwiches and sausage rolls. A huge bowl of steaming chips sat to one side next to a large plate of what looked like spring rolls, but Bridget wondered if someone might have sat on them, as they did look rather squashed.

She decided to relinquish her driving responsibility in favour of a drink. Graham wouldn't mind; he did most of the driving now anyway.

'Do you mind, love?' she asked him, as she rummaged in her handbag for the keys.

'Do I mind what?' he asked, just as she remembered she wasn't actually supposed to be driving.

She pulled her hand from her bag and zipped it back up. 'Do you mind passing me a glass of that sherry?' she said, thinking on her feet. This was something she seemed to be doing a lot lately.

'Not at all,' he said, leaning around her to pick up a glass before pressing it into her hand. 'You're a much better passenger when you've had a couple. Less inclined to stamp on that imaginary brake of yours.'

She rolled her eyes good-naturedly as she lifted the glass. She'd forgotten it was Norman's favourite tipple. He'd usually follow up a hefty swig with the words, 'I'm going to get legless,' which she knew was supposed to make her smile, but it never did. How could it? It was always the most enormous elephant in the room – Norman's wheelchair. He seemed to be able to make fun of it, but Bridget couldn't.

Just as she got the glass to her lips, her eyes caught the sight of a figure walking in through the door. A man in a green and purple Fair Isle sweater with a brown jacket over his arm. He was both instantly familiar and also oddly unrecognisable. Like seeing someone you think you know but out of the context of their day job. Like when the woman from the local garage started working behind the bar in the pub at the end of the high street. It took Bridget ages to work out who she was. Then again, these days it usually took Bridget longer than normal to work things out, full stop. She drained the glass, realising a little late that alcohol probably wasn't going to help but deciding that perhaps, just for today, it was a crutch she needed. She placed it on the table and reached for another, while Graham helped himself to a sausage roll.

'Derek Maywood!'

She didn't mean to say it so loudly, but his name slipped out as soon as it had appeared in her mouth. It was the only way to be sure to keep hold of a memory – share it as quickly as possible so that someone could remember it for her. She turned around, but not before she had seen the Fair Isle man look up.

He'd lost weight, a lot of weight. Derek had never been what you'd call obese, but he'd certainly been a very big man with a quite a tummy. Now, though, he'd lost that and actually looked toned – if it was possible to look toned through a knitted jumper. His face was thinner and his neck less thick. It made him look older, as if the wrinkles had been stretched out before and were now able to sag freely. But then she hadn't actually seen him for ten years, so he would be older. They were all older.

She nudged Graham with her elbow and offered him a jerking of her head in Derek's direction. He looked confused at her for a moment, but then a dawning overcame him.

'Looks like you weren't the only one Norman was having a laugh with,' he said, and he left her side and strode off towards their former colleague. Bridget hovered for a moment, unsure what he meant, and then she realised it was the sweater: brightly coloured, out of place. Exactly like her cardigan. She finished the second sherry and then, before she could talk herself into a third, she scuttled after Graham.

'Well, I never did. Derek Maywood, how on earth are you?'

The two men were shaking hands in that slightly overly dramatic way people who hadn't seen each other for a while did. Bridget wondered what would happen when they stopped – how that might leave them with the physical equivalent of silence.

'I'm well,' Derek said. 'I'm actually very well.'

Bridget noticed that, even though he'd lost almost a third of his body weight, he still spoke in the small and apologetic voice that he always used to. Was Graham going to make mention of the weight loss? She hoped not. It would be better not to draw attention to it.

'And you've slimmed down amazingly,' Graham said, and Bridget winced. 'I don't think I'd have recognised you if it hadn't been for Bridget.'

Graham looked round then to find his wife standing next to him and he reached an arm around her shoulders.

'And you remember Bridge, don't you?'

Bridget wanted to lift the keys from Graham's pocket and leave then. She wanted to get in the car and drive straight home.

\* \* \*

### Derek

Derek looked at Graham as if he might be mad rather than just a bit old. Did he remember Bridget Scott? He remembered her like he remembered to brush his teeth. Like he remembered to put the bins out on a Wednesday evening after eight so as not to bother his neighbour who worked night shifts. He remembered their time at the factory. He remembered *that*, because it was ingrained in the darkest part of his brain.

'Lovely to see you, Bridget,' he said quietly, and swallowed, hard. It wasn't lovely; he felt a bit nauseous but at the same time thought he could really murder a pint. She didn't lift her hand in greeting and Derek was grateful. His arm had only just recovered from Graham's overenthusiasm.

'Hello, Derek,' Bridget said and thankfully she left it at that.

There was an uncomfortable silence for a moment until Graham filled it.

'I wonder why more people didn't come back,' he said.

'No one really wants to hang around after the funeral service,' Derek said. 'To be honest, I only did because I'm meeting someone.'

'Can I get you a drink?' Graham asked him. 'Perhaps a pint?'

Derek opened his mouth to say that, no, he'd like to get it himself otherwise he'd be stuck making small talk with Bridget, not a prospect he relished. Graham was already walking towards the bar, though, and Derek had no choice but to say that, yes, a pint would be nice and could it be real ale and not lager.

'How have you been, Derek?'

Derek looked at Bridget and thought about how best to answer her. He could tell her he was lonely, how he'd taken to reading out loud just so he could hear a friendly voice. He could say that mostly he was just bored with his own company and terrified of reaching out to fill that huge void in his life.

'Pretty good, you know. How about you? You and Graham moved, didn't you?'

'Yes, we did. How did you know about that?'

Derek thought of all the times he'd cycled past Bridget's house, trying to pluck up the courage to knock on the door and urge her to discuss what had happened at the factory, until that last time when the removal van had been there with the contents of their house in the back.

'I think someone in the library mentioned it,' he said, vaguely.

'Here you go, pal.'

Graham was back with the pint and Derek took it, gratefully.

'So why are you both wearing such colourful clothing?' Graham asked.

'I told you, Graham, it was what Norman asked me to do in his letter.'

'He wrote to you too?' Derek said, surprised that Norman had been in contact with Bridget.

'You don't think I would have chosen to wear this voluntarily, do you?'

Derek noticed a slightly scathing tone to Bridget's voice. He thought back to the contents of his letter.

'Was that the last thing that Norman knitted for you?' he asked her, but she didn't respond, because her head was turned away and she was staring at the person who had just walked through the door. Derek's legs seemed to liquify as he took in the form of Gloria Taylor.

His first thought was how little she had changed. Her hair was still golden blonde and turned into gentle curls that caressed her shoulders. Her face was bright and couldn't possibly be wrinkle free – at what was she now? Seventy-one, seventy-two? – but from this far away it certainly appeared that way. She was wearing a horrible yellow jumper, but even in that she looked amazing. Derek hadn't seen Gloria for years, but she still managed to turn his stomach to a mushy mess.

He tuned out Bridget's words beside him as she whispered to her husband. 'Facelift – trying too hard as usual – typical American – honestly, who does she think she is?'

Bridget could think whatever she wanted, because there was no denying it: Gloria was glorious.

* * *

### Gloria

The smell of fried chips hit her as soon as she closed the door. It made her mouth water, but not as much as the sight of the line of sherry glasses. How quaint. Norman had always loved it. He took after his old mom, bless her. Gloria had a sudden image of Norman and his mother laughing at something on the TV, always so happy in each other's company. It was Ida who had taught Norman to knit. Gloria remembered him showing her the first holey attempt at a hat, how they had laughed at the time, how Norman had said Ida wanted him to keep his hands busy and his mind on gentle things after his accident. She was now beginning to see how much Norman had got out of it and how much he offered to others. Who else knew how entrepreneurial Norman had become? About eight hundred thousand people if the celebrant was correct. Sadly, Ida hadn't seen how far his knitting had taken him as she'd died a year after Norman's accident.

Gloria took a glass from the table and poured the contents into her mouth, then headed to the bar, because sherry was all well and good, but a large glass of red would be better. She'd just had a run-in with a Scottish woman who seemed to think that Norman was some sort of public property. Gloria had been a little rude, she now realised, when the woman had begun touching the knitted blanket covering the coffin and Gloria had wrestled it out of her hands.

'Back off, lady,' she'd said. 'This is nothing to do with you.'

Gloria now felt a bit ashamed of her reaction as she remembered how upset the woman had looked.

'Medium Merlot,' she said, changing her mind about a large glass when she ordered as she remembered her Mercedes coupé in the car park and it was a fair drive home.

Gloria leaned her back against the bar and surveyed the room. Most had left now, which surprised her. Didn't people want a free sherry and a sandwich? But if she didn't have this meeting she'd have gone herself, to be fair. She'd been singled out as Norman's particular friend and the very least she could do was to fulfil his wishes. She was about to leave her glass on the bar and ask for a coffee instead – a clear head might be needed and the sherry had just struck home – when her eyes fell onto the face of Bridget Scott. My goodness! There was a face she'd never expected to see again. She clutched her glass a little tighter, she was going to need it for moral support. Then, as her gaze moved across those people Bridget was talking with, it fell on Derek Maywood and her heart gave a lurch.

\* \* \*

It felt a little like parents' evening. Gloria thought back to the one she'd turned up to when her stepson was in his last year of primary school. She'd misunderstood when her husband, Tim, had said *they* had parents' evening. Of course he meant his ex-wife. Gloria hadn't made that mistake again.

Now, there were the three of them sitting on one side of the table and Norman's solicitor sitting on the other. Norman had used the word assistant in his letter, but surely he'd meant solicitor. Bridget's husband sat to one side as if he wasn't really part of the group.

Gloria knew the three of them looked ridiculous in their multi-coloured knits, but she could only imagine Norman's grin from wherever he was right now. He'd be loving this. He wasn't exactly a practical joker, but he certainly liked a good laugh.

The solicitor was a young woman of about twelve in Gloria's eyes, but then she had reached an age where everyone else seemed to be a lot younger than herself. She looked smart enough in black trousers and a cream blouse, but surely she could only just have passed the bar exam, or whatever exam they had to pass in England. Even though Gloria had left the States over forty years ago, she still wasn't sure on some of the finer points of Englishness.

'Thank you all for staying behind,' the woman said. 'My name is Charlotte Jackson and I'm here at the wish of Norman Knits – oh, sorry, I mean Mr Norman George.' She blushed then and looked down to her notes. 'I'm actually Norman's assistant.'

'Assistant? Is this legally binding?' Bridget asked. 'I mean, is it official? I thought you'd be a solicitor or something like that.'

'I'm Norman's neighbour and I've been his assistant for a few years,' she said, and Gloria noticed her eyes begin to swim with tears that she blinked away. 'He needed help with his YouTube channel and with his knitting patterns. I give support to knitters that have bought his patterns. He couldn't have done it on his own; he was a big deal, you know.'

'I don't think any of us realised how big a deal he was,' Derek said.

'I didn't even know he had a YouTube channel,' said Bridget.

'Perhaps it suited him to keep us in the dark for his own amusement,' Gloria said.

'I don't think that's fair,' Charlotte said, indignant. 'Maybe you didn't ask him about what he was doing with his life.'

Gloria had to concede that this could be true. All she ever thought about when she visited him was how guilty she felt. She looked at the other two and wondered if it had been the same for them.

'So, to business,' Charlotte said. 'This is all fairly straightforward. Norman left all of his money to the hospice that cared for both his mother and himself before they died, so this isn't anything to do with an inheritance, apart from a small amount to cover your expenses.'

'Expenses?' asked Bridget, but Charlotte just said she'd get to that.

'I wouldn't have taken any of his money, anyway,' Gloria said, decidedly. 'I was his boss and in the habit of giving him money, not taking it.'

'He earned his money,' Bridget cut in. 'You didn't just give it to him.'

'Of course, I realise that,' Gloria said with a hint of a glare in Bridget's direction.

'Well, anyway, this is about his ashes,' Charlotte continued.

'Yes,' Gloria cut in this time. 'He wrote to ask me to scatter them and I'm very happy to do it.'

'He wrote to me!' Bridget said.

'And me,' Derek added.

'Perhaps you could all just listen to what Miss Jackson has to say,' Graham interrupted from the corner. 'And save that bickering for later.'

'So, I have his instructions here. I've got three sets printed off for you to take away, but for now I'll read them out to you.

'"My dearest friends, you will all have received a letter from me after I died and I do hope that you are sitting in the Rottweiler and Bunny with a glass of sherry and looking dapper in my knits. I truly would give anything to see your faces. It was a little joke to lighten the day, but I hope you'll forgive my indulgence."'

Gloria looked across at the others to see if it had lightened their day, but Bridget appeared stony-faced and Derek just looked bewildered. Bridget's husband was watching Miss Jackson with a look of expectation on his face. Perhaps he hadn't been listening when she said there was to be no inheritance.

'"As I said in my previous letter to you all, I wish to ask you to scatter my ashes and it would give me great comfort to know that the three of you would do it together."'

'Together?' Gloria said. 'I see no need for that. One of us can do it. I'll do it and send you both a photograph.'

'And why should it be you?' asked Bridget. 'I could just as easily do it. I've been a good friend to Norman over the years.'

'It seems we've all been his friend,' Derek said, quietly.

'I'm the boss, I'm used to being in charge, it makes sense for me to do it,' Gloria said, and Bridget scoffed.

'You're not the boss any more,' she said, coolly. 'I'm sure we can all walk up a hill together, or across a beach, or into some woodland to do as Norman asks.'

'May I just continue, please,' Charlotte said, pushing her glasses back up to the bridge of her nose. Everyone stopped talking and she gave a slight nod of her head.

'"Since I started on my knitting journey there has always been somewhere I would have loved to have travelled to, but never got the chance. That place is the home of knitting, somewhere I hold very dear to my heart and I wish to have my ashes scattered there. It might sound strange to you three, but to me it would be like coming home and I know I would have peace if you could do that for me.'"

'The home of knitting?' Gloria said. 'Where on earth is that?'

'Wherever it is, we must do as he asks. Now is not the time to shirk our responsibilities,' Bridget said.

Gloria turned sharp eyes on her, but Bridget remained facing forward, one eyebrow raised and with her lips pursed. Gloria always observed that Bridget thought too highly of herself. She clearly hadn't changed.

'"There is a lighthouse on an island that I have developed a great affection for. It is serendipitous, I feel. That is where I would like you to scatter my ashes.'"

'But where is it?' Gloria said. 'I always assumed he'd want to be near to his mom. And anyway, I don't do small boats. Can we scatter them somewhere close, but on dry land?'

'We wouldn't have to go up inside the lighthouse and throw them out the window, would we?' asked Derek.

'If it's somewhere I could pop in a day, I don't mind the boat or the lighthouse. I'm just not very keen on being away from home for too long,' said Bridget.

Charlotte placed the paper down on the table in front of her and steepled her fingers.

'The lighthouse is called Muckle Flugga and is off the north-ernmost point of the UK,' she said.

'Scotland! I can't do that in a day,' Bridget said, but the others remained silent.

Charlotte raised her eyebrows. 'The northernmost point of the UK is in the Shetland Islands.'

# 3

## EMAILS

### *Bridget*

'Well, I won't do it. I don't care what Norman's wishes were. This is an ask too much.'

Bridget had been pacing the kitchen since they'd returned from the funeral and now she was banging pans about in pursuit of making dinner.

Graham lowered the blind on the window above the sink and pulled two wineglasses out of the cupboard. The sun hadn't quite set, but the rain had increased throughout the afternoon and there was more cloud than sky. Certainly not worth hoping for a last burst of daylight.

Bridget opened the fridge with the hand that wasn't holding a pan and contemplated the options for dinner. They'd been shopping only the day before and the fridge was well stocked with everything they'd need for the meals they'd planned for the week. The only trouble was, Bridget couldn't remember what any of the meals were. Had they bought minced beef for a chilli or a Bolognese? Were the chicken thighs for a casserole or had they thought about a tray bake? Was the chorizo for a paella or was that going in the chilli? Having a memory problem was so damn tiring. Graham leaned past her and took a bottle of white wine from inside the door. And that wasn't going to help.

'Let's just get a takeaway,' he said, taking the saucepan from Bridget's hand and putting it back in the cupboard. 'Why are you so angry about this?'

'Norman knows I'm a home person, why would he expect me to suddenly want to go on a trip like this? It's miles away. We'd need to fly or get a ferry or something. I don't like flying. And what about when we're there? We'd have to hire a car or take ours with us.'

'Bridget,' Graham said gently. 'I wouldn't be going. It's you, Gloria and Derek he wants to scatter his ashes. It's nothing to do with me.'

Bridget turned to her husband with wide eyes.

'You can't think I'd be able to go without you? Of course you must come. Norman would never know.'

Graham smiled then before handing her a glass of wine and beginning to rummage in the kitchen drawer for the Chinese takeaway menu.

'What are you smiling about? I can't imagine what's so amusing.'

'You went from being adamant you wouldn't consider the prospect, to negotiating your terms of travel.'

'Oh,' she said, sitting down at the table.

'I think this will be really good for you, Bridget. Derek is a good man; he'll see you're okay. We know Gloria can be bossy, but I expect she could be good fun too. You might enjoy yourself.'

'We'd be scattering Norman's ashes, it wouldn't be a holiday,' she said.

He smiled again and she realised she *was* actually considering it. If it could just be her and Graham it would be easy to think about, but the thought of travelling there with Gloria and Derek made her feel a bit uneasy. It had been ten years since they had last been together and she was perfectly happy to have forgotten that time completely.

'Why don't you take the bull by the horns and email the other two? Get in there quick before Gloria takes over; you remember what she's like, don't you?'

Bridget remembered Gloria. She'd been the boss and, unlike her husband, Tim, who'd kept himself removed from the staff as much as possible, Gloria had been into everyone's business. She had a sudden memory that Gloria had always favoured Derek Maywood for some reason. Bridget had been Tim's secretary and then, after he'd died, she'd become Gloria's and remembered full well how her new boss could be. Could she send an email and let the other two know that she was fully on board with this trip? She could feel a bubbling energy inside her suddenly. She could book the tickets, plan the itinerary. It was what she was good at, what she used to be good at. But what if she forgot something? What if she couldn't be the secretary she used to be?

'You're overthinking,' Graham said with his face buried in the menu. 'It's just a trip with some ex-work colleagues to scatter the ashes of an old friend.'

'And you're oversimplifying,' she said. 'It's a lot more than that.'

Bridget hesitated in the middle of her kitchen for a moment. The truth was that she didn't really have any choice in the matter. She could be as unhappy as she liked about the idea, but she would still be going. It really was as simple as that.

'Can you order me sweet and sour chicken and a mushroom fried rice, please. I'm going to send an email.'

Bridget went upstairs and into their spare room where the PC sat on an old desk. Their daughter lived in Germany and it was their one source of face-to-face conversation. Bridget loved seeing her two grandsons bouncing into view on the screen when they connected. With Bridget not keen on flying and their daughter busy with her work, her husband and the children, they didn't see nearly as much of them as Bridget would like.

She blew the dust from the top of a dried flower arrangement on the windowsill next to her as she switched on the computer. Thoughts of how she'd word her email come to her mind. The travel, the hotel they'd need, the extra layers for the poor weather they'd likely experience. Bridget felt a sense of purpose as her fingers found the keys, but Gloria had beaten her to it.

From: Gloria Taylor
Subject: Norman's ashes trip
To: Derek Maywood, Bridget Scott

To both,

It was interesting to see you again, it's been a long time!

Now, I do realize we all have our reservations about doing this. I'm sure we are all busy people, but I do feel that we owe it to Norman to fulfil his wishes. Perhaps the least said about that the better, though.

It isn't the best time of year to be in Shetland, weatherwise, but I don't feel inclined to have this hanging over my head into next year. I suggest we aim for the first week in December. So, that's the week after next. Does that give you both enough notice? It's not going to take too long; I think a couple of days should do it, island ferries permitting. I plan to fly from Aberdeen, but you should both travel however you see fit. We can meet in Lerwick where I'm going to hire a car and book a hotel room. I suggest you both do the same.

I have no intention of taking the money Norman left us for this trip, but of course, you must both do what suits you.

Having said all of this I am still more than happy to do this alone, so if you don't feel as if you can manage to come, then that is fine, also.

I will be in touch when I've booked things my end.

Regards

Gloria

No bloody way was Gloria going to take this away from her. Bridget was Norman's dearest friend. She blithely ignored the fact that Norman had sent the exact same letter to all three of them and began to furiously tap out a response, but before she'd finished, another email pinged into her inbox.

From: Derek Maywood
Re: Norman's ashes trip
To: Gloria Taylor, Bridget Scott

Dear all,

Lovely to see you both today.

I will be very pleased to fulfil Norman's wishes.

I await your command, Gloria.

All best

Derek

Bridget rolled her eyes. Of course Derek would await Gloria's command, he always did. She didn't know why it miffed her so much to be the second recipient on both of their emails. Bridget Scott, surplus to requirements as per usual. She finished her message and pressed send. She would not be left behind on this trip. She was Norman's dearest friend!

From: Bridget Scott
Re: Norman's ashes trip
To: Bridget Scott

To you both,
 Of course I will be there. Norman was such a good friend
of mine, I wouldn't miss it for the world!
 All best wishes
 Bridget

And then Bridget resent the message again after discovering
she had originally only sent it to herself.

# 4

## RESERVATIONS

### *Derek*

Derek was washing up his lunch dishes and looking out of the kitchen window as his hands plunged in and out of the hot, soapy water. He'd finished off the tuna he'd opened on Saturday with a jacket potato, which meant that was one less thing to have to clear out of the fridge before he left for Scotland.

A thick mist was settling over the back garden. It gave the space an eerie feel, reminding him of the horror movie he'd made the mistake of watching the previous evening. He'd never had the stomach for frightening films. He blamed it on his cousin who'd locked him in the attic room of his childhood home after a particularly savage retelling of some gruesome ghost stories. It had been the Christmas after Derek's ninth birthday. Later, his cousin said it was only supposed to be a joke, but it hadn't been funny for Derek when the entire family had gone out for midnight mass, forgetting he wasn't with them. Those few hours stuck in the cold and dark loft space with the wind howling through the rafters had left him with a deep-seated avoidance of closed spaces and anything terrifying.

Years later, his nephews were watching the film *Home Alone* where a child is left at home while the family go on holiday. His sister had scoffed and said how unlikely that was. *Who could forget their own child?* Derek reminded her.

He pulled the plug and looked out into the garden while he waited for the water to disappear. He could just make out the shape of next door's cat stalking something through his rose border. Not that there were any roses now; it was the end of November. Bonfire night had been and gone a few weeks back and talk was mostly about Christmas now. It was all over the television and had been in the shops for what felt like months. Derek always went to his sister, Sally's, in Kent for Christmas. It was a busy house with his nephews, an oversized shaggy dog and the big presence of his brother-in-law – an oversized shaggy Bert. He'd always been made welcome since the kids were small and they'd shared a room so he could pinch one of theirs. Now their kids had left home, it was just Sal and Bert, and Derek slept under a duvet of chintzy flowers in their spare room rather than whichever superhero was in favour back in the day. Those kids now brought their own kids and he was looking forward to another whirlwind three days in Pembury. What stood between him and that time was Shetland, though. He couldn't even imagine how that was going to go.

There'd been a few emails back and forth between the three. Gloria's were organisational, Bridget's were confrontational and his, well, his were short, even though he strove for conversational. They'd met up at Norman's house with Charlotte Jackson again, but she had really just reiterated the same information about where Norman wanted his ashes scattered. They'd chatted briefly about Norman's choice of the Shetland Islands for his final resting place. Gloria said she couldn't understand why, given how close he was to his mother in life, he'd choose to be so far away from her in death.

'He's being scattered,' Derek had said. 'It means he can be everywhere.'

It was quite simple as far as he was concerned – when you were dead, you were dead. This was something that Derek knew very well indeed.

But Bridget and Gloria had begun to go through a box of photos, letters and personal effects that Charlotte gave them to see if they could uncover anything further. They had left Norman's house none the wiser, but Charlotte gave the box to Gloria and suggested she took it with her on the trip, much to Bridget's annoyance. Derek felt that Charlotte had been unnecessarily forceful as she pressed the box into Gloria's hands, really insisting it went with them. If Gloria had been surprised she hadn't shown it, but Derek had been.

Then they switched their talk from email to WhatsApp after Gloria set up a group chat, and Derek's phone kept pinging with updates on their travel arrangements.

Much to Gloria's irritation, she couldn't secure a car for hire in Shetland, so her plan to fly had gone out of the window. They were now all booked onto the NorthLink ferry leaving Aberdeen in a couple of days' time and Derek wasn't looking forward to it. It was an overnight crossing of about fourteen hours and it could be rough. Gloria had hired a car near the port in Aberdeen and thought it might be best if they all travelled together, so they'd be meeting on the ferry. Derek would have preferred to fly, but in truth, he'd be happy to go along with Gloria's plans. She had been his boss and doing what she wanted seemed to run through his blood.

Of course, when Derek first took the job in the warehouse of

Taylor's factory, Gloria had been the wife of the boss, but she came in occasionally to see her husband and chat to the staff. Derek still remembered the first time he saw her. She breezed into the warehouse like a golden breath of fresh air and his own breath left his lungs in one sharp exhale. He'd been about thirty-five years old at the time and feeling very much on his own. Gloria's visits were both pain and pleasure for him. This woman he became infatuated with, but who was completely out of his reach. Certainly at that time.

His thoughts went to the reality of fourteen hours on a ferry. If Derek survived that, then surely he'd manage a few days with his old workmates. It wasn't Bridget that was the problem, though. The big question was whether he could manage a few days with Gloria Taylor.

Once he'd finished at the sink he went to the fridge and organised what he'd eat over the next couple of days, making sure not to have anything hanging around while he was away. His cheddar would be okay, but the ham would definitely need to be consumed. He counted out how many slices of bread he had in the bread bin and luckily it was just enough to have a ham and cheese sandwich for his tea, two slices for toast in the morning and two more that he'd save for a packed lunch on the train up to Aberdeen. The crusts he crumbled and took to the bird table to share with his garden friends.

He was about to settle with the crossword and a cup of tea when his phone pinged and he snatched it out of his pocket, keen to see what Gloria had planned now. It wasn't her, though. It was the dating app his sister had set him up with – Mature Companions. A plain-looking woman called Meryl had left him a message saying he had a nice face and would he be up for long walks in the country and did he like French. The message ended abruptly and Derek was left wondering if she meant food or kissing. In truth, if pressed, he'd have to say neither. He left the phone on the table in case Gloria messaged and then set about the crossword.

# 5

## SETTING OFF

*Gloria*

Her flight to Aberdeen was nearly two hours late in the end and it was a slightly flustered Gloria Taylor that opened the door to the car hire place and tried not to lose complete control when the woman on the reception desk calmly told her that the nice and compact car she'd booked wasn't available. Instead, an ugly brown minivan arrived outside the front.

'What on earth do I need seven seats for?' she demanded, and the woman shrank under her glare.

'They fold into the floor of the vehicle, so you'll have lots of luggage space or if you're feeling tired you could have a lie down.'

Gloria opened her mouth to let out a sharp retort, but she noticed the clock on the wall behind the woman's head and closed it again. She had just under two hours to find the ferry, get on board and check into her cabin, so all she really had time to do was take the keys and leave the threat of a strongly worded email in her wake.

The Beast, as Gloria decided to call it, didn't have satnav and she had to shove her phone into the cradle stuck to the middle air vent so she could see her way to the ferry. It had the unfortunate double problem of meaning that the hot air she needed to warm her chilly body was being blasted into the back of her phone instead of onto her. She set her jaw into a tight grimace and followed the path to the port.

Her phone began to buzz and Paul's name flashed across the screen. She sighed and pressed to answer, switching to speaker phone.

'I've done it,' he said. 'I've gone and done it. I've left my wife. I've left Janet.'

Gloria wasn't sure why he felt the need to clarify with his wife's name. She was pretty sure he only had the one.

'Right,' she said, wishing she'd had the wherewithal to give Paul his marching orders before this unfortunate change in circumstances.

'I wonder if I can—'

'I'm not at home at the minute,' she interrupted.

'I know that. I'm on your doorstep, darling.'

'Paul, you know I said that I liked things the way they were with us.'

'But – but I've always said I was going to leave her, we talked about this.'

'No, Paul, *you* talked about this and I repeatedly told you that I liked things just the way they were. The trouble is, you were never listening and I assumed you were never going to leave her. Men don't tend to leave in the long run.'

'I have, though, isn't it great? I've got my things in the car and I'm just here waiting for you to get home. Where exactly are you?'

Still not listening, Gloria mused as she pulled into the line of traffic waiting to board the ferry.

'I'm on my way to Shetland,' she said. 'I won't be home for a few days.'

'But, darling, I'm on your doorstep. Do you leave a spare key with a neighbour? I could make myself at home until you get back...'

'No, Paul,' she said sharply. 'I don't want to share my home with anyone. Not even someone as lovely as you.'

She thought adding this might soften the blow, but she was pretty sure she could hear a strangled sob on the end of the line.

'I'm sorry, but I think it's best if we say our goodbyes.'

'But I left Janet a note in the kitchen saying I was moving in with you.'

'Paul,' Gloria said in her best commanding voice. 'What time is Janet due home?'

'Err... she's at her sister's for their bridge afternoon. She's usually home about six to start my tea.'

'Well, I suggest you get back in your car, drive home and destroy that letter before Janet sees it.'

'Oh, shit,' he said and then, after an anguished noise, the call disconnected.

Gloria leaned her head back against her seat and let out a long sigh. The truth was she had always seen Janet as a spectral figure, someone who didn't exist in her world or the world that she and Paul created during their brief *visits*. But she was a real-life figure and Gloria didn't like herself all that much in that moment. Imagining poor Janet rushing back from her sister's in time to cook her husband's tea only to find that note. She shuddered and then shook off the thought as the line of cars in front of her started moving. Gloria did what she did best for self-preservation in these situations: pretended it had nothing to do with her. And quite honestly, it wasn't really her problem, was it?

* * *

Gloria left her suitcase in the vast boot of The Beast once she'd parked it on the car deck and found her way up the stairs into the main area of the ship. She just had an overnight bag with her essentials: make-up, silk pyjamas, extra-firming super-restorative hydra-luminère night cream and her eye mask. Once she'd located her cabin and taken a moment to marvel at how tiny it was, she lowered the blind, dropped her bag onto the bed, used the compact loo and left her room to find the others.

She headed to the front of the ship, expecting to find them in the bar, but apart from a young couple, a handful of singletons and one incredibly old man with a Father Christmas beard and a thick gansey that made him look as if he'd just stepped off a fishing trawler, the place was empty; Derek and Bridget were nowhere to be seen. Gloria wondered if they were relaxing in their cabins and did consider doing the same, but then she decided to have a wander instead.

Her ticket entitled her to the use of an exclusive bar and lounge, but after she popped her head around the door, she decided that in all honesty, as nice as that room appeared, the rest of the ship was pretty decent anyway, even for Gloria Taylor's standards. In fact, she rather wondered at how well appointed it was for a ferry. It certainly wasn't the cross-channel experience of her distant memories, back when she and Tim used to go on booze cruises to France.

She bypassed the cinema, the gift shop and another bar until she was at the back of the ship and in the main restaurant where a few passengers were beginning to get some food. The ship hadn't left yet and it was a long journey ahead, but perhaps these people were keen to eat and then get to bed. That seemed like a sensible plan to Gloria. However, Derek and Bridget were not among them.

There was a door to a viewing area and she decided to have a quick look before she headed back to her cabin. They had the next couple of days together; it wouldn't be the end of the world if they didn't spend every waking minute with each other.

But there they were, on the upper deck standing against the railing, a distance apart and silently looking out over the Aberdeen city skyline. The sun had set and it was only a quarter to five. The sky was a clear inky black with the first stars appearing. The city skyline was a solid granite grey with its own twinkling stars. The lit windows of the buildings, the cars' headlights and the streetlights glittered their reflection in the harbour water.

'There you both are,' Gloria said, and they turned around, surprised. She wondered for a moment if they had been talking about her, but their body language suggested they hadn't been talking at all. They still had their coats on and their bags were at their feet. Gloria shivered and pulled her cashmere cardigan closer. She walked over to the railing where the others were leaning just as the ship started to move, and all three watched as they began to leave the safety of the harbour and the solid stone city into the unknown of the cold, dark waters of the North Sea. 'Haven't you been to your cabins yet?'

Bridget gave her a sharp look and Derek just shuffled his feet.

'I didn't book a cabin, I booked a pod,' Bridget said. 'They have reclining seats in a private room and they do look very comfortable, but I just don't want to leave my bags in there if I'm not with them. I thought that if it was rough, I'd not want to be confined to bed, I'd rather be upright. Have you seen the number of sick bags everywhere? It's notorious for being a rough crossing.'

'I'd rather not be reminded, thank you, Bridget,' Gloria said. 'I shall probably take a sleeping pill and knock myself out for the duration.'

'I didn't bother booking anything. I'll just slink into a corner somewhere,' Derek said. 'Didn't want to waste the money, to be honest, and I certainly wasn't going to use Norman's. Those cabins are double dear.'

He turned his head back to the view and Gloria just caught a glimpse of something before he did. Was it embarrassment? Defiance? Unlikely the latter. The Derek she used to know didn't have a defiant bone in his body.

'Well, I do have a cabin and if it's any comfort, it's tiny,' Gloria said, with the intention of making them feel better about their choices, but as the words left her lips she could hear how crass she sounded. 'It's perishing up here, shall we get a drink? My round.'

Derek and Bridget glanced at one another and then dutifully followed their former boss back inside the ship.

# 6

## ROLLING IN THE DEEP

### *Bridget*

Bridget had chosen the fish and chips, but it was sitting heavily in her stomach as the ship began to roll. It had started as a gentle movement but was fast becoming an experience akin to a trip to a funfair. She looked at her watch; it was only nine o'clock and hours until they would hit dry land. Gloria had consumed two large glasses of red wine and Derek a couple of pints of beer. Bridget's lime juice and soda had seemed like a more sensible choice and yet she seemed to be the only one complaining of feeling queasy.

It didn't help that Gloria had plonked Norman on the table between them. In his urn, of course, but Bridget had gasped when Gloria had pulled it from her bag and even Derek had raised both of his eyebrows. It was a ceramic black pot with golden wings hand-painted on the front. Not Norman's style at all, but when Bridget asked about it, Gloria said she'd had it made especially. Of course she had.

'I don't like to think of him stuck in the cabin on his own,'

Gloria said, and put like that Bridget could hardly complain, although it did seem a little disrespectful to see him wedged between a salt cellar and the plastic-covered menu.

From the start, Gloria had claimed Norman as her own responsibility and Bridget had been openly irritated by it. Privately she had actually been relieved not to have to be in charge of him. The idea of carrying her friend around was a little morbid to her. Derek was going with the flow, as he put it. Typical Derek.

Talk was perfunctory and limited to subjects such as pets and holidays, books they'd read and television programmes they'd watched. There was no mention of their shared history and oddly no mention of the task ahead of them. Bridget decided to rectify that.

'So, is the plan to get to Lerwick and drive up to the northern-most point as quickly as possible?' she asked, her eyes firmly on Norman's urn.

'Yes, well, I'm not intending to hang around for too long. We'll get to the hotel, drop off our bags and get going. With any luck the weather will be with us,' Gloria said with her fingers crossed. She lifted her glass to the urn. 'Cheers, Norman. We'll do this for you, but honestly, couldn't you have just chosen a rose bush on a hill closer to home?'

Derek chuckled and finished his pint.

'I've never been further north than Durham and certainly not over the border into Scotland, so for me, this trip is a bit of an adventure and I don't mind at all.'

Bridget watched as Derek seemed to catch himself in a moment of honesty and clamped his lips together.

'I'm here for the quick trip, personally,' she said. 'Norman meant a lot to me. I wouldn't want to let him down, of course, but I do prefer to be at home these days.'

'And what of the box of photos and letters?' Derek asked. 'Did you uncover anything useful?'

'I've had a bit of a further look through,' said Gloria, 'and of course I've brought it with me. I didn't seem to have much choice, the way Charlotte insisted. There are a few photos of Norman's mom. She was really quite beautiful back in the day. I didn't read her letters; it didn't seem right. There's also a ring in a box at the bottom. I'm not sure what he wants us to do with that. We could sell it and give the proceeds to the hospice charity, maybe.'

Bridget rested her head back against the glass partition between them and the next table and closed her eyes, only to open them again immediately as the roiling in her stomach intensified.

'So, we've all been visiting Norman over the last few years?' Derek said. 'I wonder why he didn't tell us that the others were visiting too?'

'I wonder why he didn't tell us about his YouTube channel and phenomenal following,' Gloria said. 'Why all the secrecy?'

'Perhaps he wanted something that was just for him,' Bridget suggested, and Gloria scoffed.

'It wasn't just for him, though, was it? It was for hundreds of thousands of people,' she said. 'It seems it was just us three out of the loop for some reason only known to Norman. I've been looking at his YouTube channel and I have to say he was brilliant behind the camera. He's so engaging and his followers clearly loved him. He has loads of comments underneath each video. Obviously I didn't read them all, because there are so many. It's nice to see him receive so much love from people. It made me wonder if we should document his ashes being scattered and share it with his followers. What do you think? We could get Charlotte to do it, as I wouldn't imagine we could access his channel. I've just added her to our WhatsApp group chat so we can keep her up to speed.'

'Video ourselves?' Bridget asked. 'I'm not sure about that.'

'Well, it's not really about you, it's about Norman, so I'm sure you could manage to smile into the camera,' Gloria said.

Bridget opened her mouth to retort but closed it again. She couldn't really be bothered with an argument, not with the way she was currently feeling.

'Have either of you two looked up the channel?' Gloria asked.

'No,' Derek said. 'I didn't think to.'

'I don't think I'd know how to,' Bridget said. 'I don't know anything about YouTube.'

'When did you become an airhead?' Gloria asked her. 'You were always very savvy in my office.'

'That's a bit uncalled for,' Derek quickly said.

'Well, you know Gloria, always saying whatever she feels like with little regard for anyone else,' Bridget said, blinking back a tear that had appeared in the corner of her eye.

'I didn't mean anything by it,' Gloria said, looking offended, as if she was the one who'd been slighted.

Bridget had little memory flashes of Gloria then, back in the factory, back in the day. Always a sharper word than necessary, a longer stare than needed, an ill-thought jibe at someone's expense. Most said she was an excellent boss and if she was harsh it was because the job needed doing and, in a man's world, a woman should always be that little bit tougher. Bridget just thought she was a bit of a bitch.

'I think I'm going to find my pod and settle down for a gentle read. And try to keep my dinner down,' Bridget added as she got up from the table with all of her belongings.

'Can I help you with your bags?' Derek asked.

'Kind, but no, thank you, I'll be fine,' Bridget said, lifting her holdall onto her shoulder, sniffing for effect and throwing her coat over her arm. Then she hesitated while she tried to orientate herself. Was the room with the pods at the back or the front? She'd seen the map of the ship on the wall by the reception desk. She could ask a member of staff. But she'd dithered too long and both Derek and Gloria were watching her. Gloria with a smirk on her face, or that was certainly how it appeared to Bridget.

'The pods are at the rear of the ship,' Derek said. 'I think there are three rooms, so you'll have to check your ticket to see which one you've booked.'

'Thank you,' she said, and then was about to ask something else but it had gone clean from her head and, anyway, Gloria was asking Derek if he'd like another drink. She got to the door of the bar before glancing back. She wasn't sure, but it looked as if Gloria and Derek were laughing, probably about her. The word *airhead* was clearly still in her mind, she hadn't forgotten that.

The rolling of the ship continued as she made her way to pod room two. The rolling of her stomach matched it wave for wave. Using her key card, she opened the door and found her seat. It was actually quite roomy and had sockets for headphones and a charging port for her phone. There were only a couple of other people in the room even though there were about fifteen seats. She pushed her bag down by her feet and settled into her seat with her coat on her lap. She wasn't cold, but it would give her a cosier nest. She tested out the recliner and found it was just back enough for her to rest her head on the edge without falling forward. She thought about cleaning her teeth but decided for now to stay still, close her eyes and see how comfortable she could be.

Five minutes later, her eyes snapped open again, she reached for a sick bag from the rack in front of her and emptied the contents of her evening meal inside.

# 7

## ARRIVING

*Derek*

It was the single most awful night of Derek's life. Well, the second most awful night of his life. He did recognise that.

The beer had been a mistake. Not because of the rolling ship, not because he'd been sick, because he hadn't. He had remarkably good sea legs for someone who generally never sailed. The reason the beer had been a mistake was because it had made him relax and then, after Bridget had gone to her pod, he'd let Gloria talk him into joining her in a large whisky and then another. Derek didn't usually drink that much at all and now, at five-thirty in the morning, after hardly any sleep, he had not only a thumping headache, but also little recollection of what he and Gloria had talked about. He had a niggling idea that he might have said she was beautiful.

Derek perched on the edge of the seat he'd spent the last few hours on and buried his head in his hands. He willed more memories to come to him, but he couldn't distinguish between what he might have said and what he thought he'd like to have said. He let out the longest of sighs and went to find the toilet so he could put his head underneath a cold running tap.

* * *

He found Bridget up on the viewing deck after he'd restored some of his faculties with a toothbrush, a comb and a spritz of the cologne his sister had bought him last Christmas.

Lerwick was coming into view through the mist that had descended, although the sun had yet to rise. There was enough light coming from streetlamps and some of the buildings to make the shape of the town just about visible. It looked grey and flat and eerie.

'Morning, Bridget,' he said as he approached the side of the ship. She was leaning on the railing just as they had both done the previous evening leaving Aberdeen. 'Did you get any sleep?'

Bridget turned and the pallor of her skin told him the answer to his question. She looked a little grey, a little flat and possibly a little eerie.

'The pod lounge was a mistake and a waste of money, although it didn't cost as much as Gloria's cabin, of course.'

'Sorry to hear that. We can catch up on some sleep later at the hotel, hopefully.'

'It would have been fine if the man near me hadn't been snoring. The seats were very comfortable, but that noise was not conducive to sleep. Well, it must have been for him. If it had been Graham, I'd have dug him in the ribs. Not really appropriate in this case. I should have brought earplugs. In the end I sat in the recliners next to the bar at the front of the ship. No one was around and, to be honest, the seats were fine. I just couldn't settle because of the waves. What about you?'

Derek leaned his arms on the rail and breathed in a lungful of cold air. He didn't ask Bridget if she'd been sick – he didn't need to; it was obvious.

'Similar, to be honest. I must have been in the recliners around the corner from you. Not that I slept much. It was too rough.'

'I'll bet Gloria was all right in her cabin. I'm surprised she didn't offer you a bed for the night,' Bridget said, and Derek looked at her, appalled. 'I just meant that those cabins must have two beds and it would have been nice of her to offer. Actually, I could have offered you my recliner, but I didn't think and, anyway, you would have had to put up with that terrible snoring man.'

Derek kept his eyes firmly on the shapes of Lerwick as they became clearer and tried to push the fractured images of the previous evening from his mind.

'It was a shame it was still dark as we hit land. I saw the glow from a lighthouse and could just make out the shapes of the landscape but not the detail. After such a long night, I'm just so happy to be arriving now. How steady and inviting Lerwick looks. Even in the dark it appears solid,' Bridget said.

Derek racked his brain for small talk, but coming up with nothing suggested they gather their things and make sure Gloria was okay and awake. Bridget gave him a long hard look that he couldn't quite understand. He took his phone from his pocket and sent a message in the WhatsApp group.

'I've sent her a message to say we're up and going for breakfast before we dock, although I'm not sure I can handle anything to eat. Maybe a coffee, though,' Derek said.

Bridget took her phone from her handbag and stared at the screen with a frown on her face.

'I didn't get that message; did you message her privately?'

'No, I sent it in the group,' he said. 'Are you logged onto the ship's Wi-Fi? It's free. You won't get any data otherwise.'

'Oh,' she said. 'I didn't think about that. I tried to message Graham last night but it didn't go through.'

'Here,' he said, taking the phone from her and logging her on to the Wi-Fi. 'Make use of it while you can; I've read reports of sketchy signal across the Shetland Islands. You know, you used to be a dab hand at this stuff at the factory. You used to keep us all in order.'

Derek had meant this as a compliment, but it didn't seem to land that way and Bridget turned her head away from him.

'Things are different now,' she said simply, and he didn't push her to explain why.

He turned his attention back to his own phone and could see that Bridget had received and read his message, but for Gloria it didn't show as having been delivered at all.

'Let's go in, you look frozen,' he said as Bridget's teeth started chattering.

They took all their possessions to the restaurant and Derek considered the options. Now they were near land the huge swell had lessened and his stomach was more settled. He decided on a small hot breakfast and a coffee while Bridget opted for a cup of tea and nibbling the edges of a pastry.

'I wonder if we should try and get her up,' Derek said. 'She had a couple of drinks last night and she might have slept through the ship's announcements.'

'Lucky her,' Bridget said. 'I don't know what cabin she's in, though.'

'She said she was right in the end cabin, made a thing of having to walk all that way to bed.'

'Come on then,' Bridget said. 'As much as I'd like to, we can't go without her; she has the car.'

Back down in front of the reception desk, Derek was unsure. He did remember leaving her here before he went off to find his corner, but there were four corridors leading away from them and he just wasn't sure which way to go.

'We could ask someone which room she's in, but I'm not sure they'd tell us,' Bridget said.

'Maybe she's already up, and down on the car deck,' Derek suggested.

'Car deck won't be open until we're moored,' a voice behind them said, and they turned to see a member of the crew.

'We're worried our friend has slept through the announcement,' Bridget said. 'Can you tell us which cabin she's in and we can wake her?'

'Gloria Taylor,' Derek added, and the woman slipped behind the desk and looked at her computer.

'Room 225,' she said with a wink.

They set off down the corridor in front of them until they were outside door 225 and Derek was suddenly unsure again. He took a step back, not wishing to be the person to find Gloria in her pyjamas. Bridget clearly had no such worries and she rapped loudly on the door. When there was no answer, she called out Gloria's name and rapped again. After a third rap and another bellow the door opened and it was a slightly unkempt Gloria that stood in front of them. She was wearing pretty floral silk pyjamas and had an eye mask pushed up on top of her head. Derek was ashamed to think that she looked a little older without any make-up, but he still thought she was the most attractive woman he'd ever met.

'We're about to dock, I think. Didn't you hear the announcement?' Bridget asked sharply, and Gloria rubbed at her eyes.

'No,' she said. 'I was completely out of it. Had the best night's sleep ever.'

Derek, who was standing back from the door, watched as

Bridget turned with her lips pursed and began striding back down the corridor.

'You never used to be so disorganised,' Bridget said as she went.

Derek opened his mouth to say something just as Gloria closed her door. It was going to be a long few days, that was for sure.

# 8

## THE BEAST

*Bridget*

Bridget's outrage propelled her back to the reception desk where she kicked her bag into the corner and plonked herself down on top of it. Gloria's lack of self-awareness was staggering. She'd never read the room, always did or said whatever she wanted with little regard for anyone else.

Inconveniently, an image of the beautiful bouquet of flowers Gloria had sent Bridget when her father died slid into her head, but she pushed it out and took her phone from her bag. She was about to send a message to Graham but then decided it would take too long to type, so she phoned him through WhatsApp instead. He picked up after only a couple of rings, which impressed Bridget as it wasn't quite seven yet and Graham had never been an early riser.

'Hello, darling,' Graham said, and Bridget felt a bit tearful at the sound of his voice. 'How was the crossing? Are you in Lerwick yet?'

'No, not quite,' she said, her voice a little shaky. 'It was horrible, Graham. I was sick, it was so rough, I didn't sleep at all.'

'Poor you,' he soothed. 'Get some rest when you get to the hotel.'

'And Gloria, *well*, she's already driving me mad and we haven't even hit dry land yet.'

'What about Derek? How was his night?'

'Same as mine by the sounds of it. Gloria booked a cabin and slept like a baby.'

'We talked about this, Bridget. You wouldn't have wanted to be lying down. It would have made you more sick.'

'I should have flown.'

'But you don't like flying, the ferry was the best option and you'll feel 100 per cent better when you're standing on land and not on the rocking ship.'

'I wish you were here,' she sniffed.

'I think you'll be just fine.'

'That's not really the point, is it, but yes, I'm sure once we've scattered the ashes I'll be home very soon.'

'Well, yes, I'm sure I'll see you soon,' Graham said.

'As soon as I know what ferry we'll be coming home on, I'll let you know. Although the thought of that journey again is too much at the moment. I hope you'll be there to meet me, Graham.'

Bridget wondered if he didn't want to drive back up to Aberdeen again. Perhaps it was too far for him, but Graham had always loved driving. She had that sense again of him moving away from her and it gave her a chilly feeling. Her mother had done the same to Bridget's father after his early-onset dementia diagnosis. Their marriage hadn't been the smoothest and Bridget's mother decided she didn't want to care for her ailing husband. She had a lot of life still in her, she'd told Bridget as she'd packed her possessions and booked a flight to Spain, leaving Bridget to pick up the pieces. Bridget had moved her father in with her and Graham and she had cared for him until he'd died, although her lovely dad had long departed this world before his body had given up. It made sense that Graham didn't want to go through it again with her. But she was getting ahead of herself again. She was becoming forgetful and so far that was all it was. She'd not had a formal diagnosis and wasn't about to get one. Best not to know, she decided.

'Take care, darling, and I'll see you soon,' Graham said, and then he hung up before she could say goodbye.

Derek appeared first and he went into the shop to browse with some talk of buying his sister a gift. Bridget wanted to suggest he wait until they were in Lerwick as there was sure to be better shops and better gifts, but she wasn't feeling very generous and kept her mouth shut. Then, about twenty minutes later, Gloria arrived with her hair tamed and a full face of make-up.

'Right,' she said. 'Let's go and get The Beast.'

'The Beast?' Bridget and Derek chorused.

'You'll see,' Gloria said with what Bridget thought a very grim expression.

\* \* \*

Bridget saw immediately what Gloria was talking about. It was more of a minibus than a car and nothing like the sports car she'd seen Gloria whiz off in after the funeral. It was also a horrible muddy-brown colour and not very appealing.

'Not your usual style,' she suggested, and Gloria sighed.

'A mess-up at the car hire place,' she said and opened up the boot so they could dump their bags in the back. 'Right, get your bags in the trunk and jump in, you two. I don't want to be on this ferry any longer than I need to be.'

Bridget scoffed as she slid into the back seat. Gloria had slept all night while Bridget had vomited her way through the North Sea. Gloria, she felt, had a bloody nerve.

Gloria took her seat up the front and Derek chose to sit beside her in the passenger seat. The ferry was at a complete stop now and the swaying and rolling had ceased. Bridget found her stomach immediately settled and she stopped frowning into the back of Gloria's head. Once the cars began to roll off the ferry, Bridget felt a twinge of something close to anticipation for what was to come and she decided to be a little more benevolent towards Gloria.

'Thank you for driving,' she said. 'It's appreciated.'

'Goodness,' Gloria quipped. 'I'll take that.'

Derek was looking at his phone and giving Gloria directions she didn't need. At that point all the traffic was going the same way, but once they'd left the terminal, he pointed out the way into town.

'It's all very industrial looking,' Gloria said as she navigated past warehouse units and drab buildings. 'I thought the vibe here was supposed to be sort of bleak but pretty.'

'It's always like this near the docks,' Derek said. 'It's a working area. I'll bet it'll improve further along.'

And it did. Bridget leaned towards the window and watched as those drab units disappeared and attractive grey-stone houses came into view. They skirted the coast for a little while and the mist began to lift. That sea that had seemed so perilous the previous evening now looked quite calm and inviting. She could see an outline of land over the water, through the line of boats moored up in the harbour. The sun hadn't quite come out from behind the clouds, but it had risen enough to give them some weak December light.

'That's the island of Bressay over there.' Derek pointed to where Bridget had been looking. His voice was more enthusiastic than it had been on the journey so far, but Bridget understood; it was the joy of dry land.

'Peerie Shop and Café,' Bridget pointed out as they passed another stone building. It reminded her a little of the houses in Guernsey. Her aunt and uncle lived on the Channel Island and Bridget used to visit with her brother when she was a child. There seemed to be a similar feel, but then it was probably just coastal island villages. Maybe they all had similarities. 'What does peerie mean?'

'Sounds odd. Does someone peer in at you while you're having a coffee?' Gloria said, laughing at her own joke.

'I think it just means small,' Derek said.

Not for the first time, Bridget was glad he was here with them. She imagined for a second that it was a trip for just her and Gloria, and she shuddered.

'Are you cold in the back?' Gloria asked. 'I can turn up the heating.'

'I'm fine, thank you,' Bridget said.

They came to the end of the road running along the harbour and Derek suddenly squealed, causing Gloria to stamp on the brake, and Bridget to lurch forward in her seat before being winded by her seatbelt.

'What?' both women said at the same time.

'I know this,' he said. 'I know this place.'

'You said you hadn't been here before,' Bridget said.

'Do you mean in a former life?' Gloria asked. 'I'm fascinated by people who have lived lives before. I sometimes think I lived as a Victorian English lady. I have visions.'

Derek turned around in his seat and gave Bridget a look. Bridget instinctively lifted her finger to the side of her head and drew circles in the air around her ear before she realised that Gloria could see her in the rearview mirror.

'Um, I just meant that I remember it from that television series, *Shetland*.'

'Oh,' Gloria giggled. 'I see.'

'A Victorian English lady?' Bridget said from the back seat. 'How very unlikely.'

\* \* \*

Gloria searched for a parking space behind the hotel. There was a row of spaces underneath a line of flats, but there was a sign telling them they were for the residents only. Instead, Gloria found a couple of spaces near the harbour wall and pulled into one of those. No one seemed to be around. Bridget guessed that in the summer months it would be a different story. They all climbed out and there was a general stretching of limbs, not so much because of the twenty minutes in the car, but more the hours on the vomity ferry. Bridget took in a large lungful of the crisp air. The wind had dropped, the mist had lifted and there was the merest slip of lighter sky behind the clouds.

'What's the plan?' Derek asked. 'Check-in isn't until two at the earliest.'

'I booked my room for last night as well so I can check straight in. Did you not both do the same thing? It's a top tip.'

Derek looked rueful and Bridget scowled.

'No, I didn't think to pay for a night in a hotel that I wasn't going to be using. How silly of me,' she said.

'Well, look,' Gloria said. 'I'm not tired, but you must be, Bridget. Why don't Derek and I go and get some coffee and come up with a plan of action and you can have a sleep in my room.'

Bridget was torn between annoyance and utter gratitude, and sensibly, gratitude won.

'That's kind, thank you,' she said. 'Will you manage until two, Derek?'

'A large coffee and a slice of whatever the best local cake is and I'll be grand.'

## 9

### THE HARBOUR VIEW HOTEL

*Gloria*

The hotel was sold to Gloria online as a tranquil place to stay, with stunning views and great hospitality. What it didn't say was that the décor was so dated that Gloria thought she'd been transported to her grandmother's house and that she would have to share a bathroom, also much like her grandmother's house.

'I had my own bathroom on the ferry, for goodness' sake,' she told the young woman behind the desk.

'I'm sorry, but it is clear on our website that we only have a couple of en suite rooms and those were both booked. We're only a small hotel.'

'I assumed I would have my own bathing facilities, though; I didn't check. Who will I be sharing with?'

She couldn't bear the thought of going into the bathroom after someone else and finding unwanted smells and a wet bathmat.

'With Mr Maywood and Mrs Scott,' she said. 'There are three rooms together at the top of the hotel with one bathroom. Your room is available now, Mrs Taylor, and the other two will become available at two o'clock, once we've had a chance to clean them.'

Gloria turned to the other two and took in their expressions. Bridget looked slightly worried and Derek looked embarrassed, even though he hadn't even been in the bathroom yet.

'Well, I suppose it will have to do. We've booked for three nights but might not even be here that long.'

'Aye, well, here is your key and the other two will be here for you later.'

Gloria took the key and suggested they all went up and offload their bags in her room, so they trooped up the two flights of stairs together. At the top, Gloria could see the four doors at one end of the landing: three bedrooms and the lone bathroom. She opened the door to her room and stepped inside.

'I think you'll have to swap those silky PJs for a winceyette nightie,' Bridget said from the doorway, and Gloria surprised herself by laughing.

'I think you might be right,' she said, and the two women shared a small smile. 'Despite the chintzy décor and the velvet lampshades, it does have a gorgeous view.'

Gloria could see out over the water to that island Derek had been talking about earlier and it did look stunning. There were only a few buildings dotted about along the line of the land that Gloria could see from the window and she thought about how isolated they were all these many miles from mainland Scotland. What would it be like to live so remotely, she wondered, but her thoughts were broken by Derek suggesting he use the facilities.

Bridget took Gloria's place by the window after she'd vacated it to hang some clothes in the wardrobe. It occurred to her that her choices were not the best for the climate here. She'd been thinking about warm vehicles and cosy hotels. Perhaps a pub with a log fire or a restaurant with the same. She'd expected rain and she had a

light mac and an umbrella. In truth, the chill as they had got out of
the car had been telling. The wind had dropped, but it was
December, many miles north, and she realised that her sparkly
top, her cropped jeans and her thin sweaters were not suitable.

'I'll leave you in charge of Norman,' Gloria said, placing him
on the windowsill next to Bridget.

She closed the door while Bridget's attention was diverted by
the view. She could do without another smart-assed comment
from her. She'd leave Bridget to sleep while she hit the shops.

\* \* \*

Gloria and Derek left Bridget with the promise of returning at
two and they walked down the street in search of a café. Gloria
had missed breakfast and was in need of something to finish off
the end of her hangover.

'Let's head back to that Peerie place,' she suggested as she
pushed her arms into the sleeves of her jacket.

'Is that all the coat you've got?' Derek asked her. 'You wouldn't
have thought you've spent years in Yorkshire with a peerie jacket
like that.'

Gloria laughed. 'I'm still a Floridian at heart,' she said. 'But I
will need to get myself something a bit more substantial. Perhaps
we could go shopping after the café? What do you think?'

Derek looked a bit bemused, but he nodded all the same.

The café was indeed very *peerie*, but Gloria was sold with the
scrambled eggs with butter and Shetland cream served on Sandwick Bakery bread. Derek chose a slice of Bakewell tart to go with
his huge latte. They pretty much had the place to themselves and
chose a table upstairs as the seats by the counter looked more for
those hovering for food and drinks to go.

Gloria tucked in to her breakfast and Derek took small bites of his tart. She thought about asking him about his weight loss journey but decided against it while he was eating dessert. It just didn't seem the right time. He might think she was judging, which she most certainly wasn't, and he might feel awkward.

'So,' she began instead, and Derek seemed to tense on the seat opposite her. 'Look at us after all these years, sitting in a café in Lerwick. Who'd have thought it?'

He nodded and wiped crumbs from his mouth with his napkin in what Gloria thought a very dainty gesture for a man.

'Yes, well, I suppose it is all a bit strange.'

'Do you want to look at that map on your phone and see what the plan is for tomorrow? I don't think that after you and Bridget have checked in officially and she's had her rest that we'll have enough time to do too much today. We can get an early night and set off at first light.'

'First light,' Derek mimicked. 'You sound like quite the adventurer, Gloria.'

'You know me, always up for a challenge,' she said, using the last of her bread to mop up the ketchup she'd squirted onto her plate. 'Delicious.'

'Good cake too,' Derek said. 'Not that I eat much of it these days.'

Surely she could mention it now he'd made that comment.

'I have to say, Derek, that you are looking very fit. What's your regime been?'

'Regime?' He laughed. 'I got a good kick up the backside from my sister after I suffered a heart attack, and began to move my substantial arse,' he said.

'Ouch, a heart attack. Are you all okay now?'

'Yeah, I'm okay.'

'She bossy, your sister, then? Or just a caring sibling looking out for you and your health?'

'She told me I'd never meet a woman carrying all that weight around with me,' he said and then blushed. He cleared his throat to try and disguise the fact he'd said too much. And besides, they both knew that wasn't true.

Gloria had a flashback to when she'd first met Derek at the factory and it wasn't his weight that had taken her attention, it had been his smile and those lovely brown eyes. She noticed they were just as warm and inviting all these years later. Someone had told her that Derek had been married once, many years ago, and that his wife died in her early thirties. She then understood why Derek always seemed to carry so much pain on his broad shoulders and also why he didn't look after himself properly. He did now, though. She picked up her glass of freshly squeezed orange juice and pushed those thoughts back to where they'd popped out from. Derek moved the plates to one side and stretched out a paper map across the table.

'Wow,' she said. 'That's impressive.'

'I bought it on the ferry in the gift shop. Phones are all well and good, but the signal on a paper map never cuts out. So, we are here,' he said, pointing his finger along the east coast of mainland Shetland.

'Oh, we're already halfway up. I assumed the ferry would dock at the southernmost point.'

Derek drew his finger down the map to where Gloria could read the name Sumburgh Head. There seemed to be a lighthouse there and she could see the strip of runway that told of the airport she hadn't been destined to fly into. Derek traced a path all the way up to the top of an island called Unst and to Muckle Flugga Lighthouse on some stacks out in the sea.

'And that's where dear old Norman wants us to scatter him,'

Derek said. 'I must say it's quite a stretch to get out on the water to do that near the lighthouse. I don't think it would be safe. Surely it will be rocky, hence the lighthouse. We might have to be inventive.'

'I'm sure it would be enough to do it from here, where we can see the lighthouse,' Gloria said, pointing to the edge of the island. 'Let's decide when we get there. We've come so far already and yet we've only just arrived. That's an odd thought, isn't it?'

Once they had finished with the map, Derek folded it away and put it in the small rucksack he carried with him.

'Before I do anything else,' Gloria said, 'I'm going to need to find somewhere I can get a decent coat.'

'Let's ask the staff here where the best place to go is,' said Derek. 'I'm sure they have shops selling winter wear.'

'Let's just have a wander,' Gloria said. 'I'm happy to see where our feet take us.'

Derek wasn't sure, Gloria could tell. He was a man who liked a map and a plan. And she was someone who excelled at planning, but she also liked to live a little dangerously, if you could call a walk through the streets of Lerwick living dangerously.

There was bunting strung between the buildings along what Gloria assumed must be the high street or certainly the centre of town. It had a flavour of the seaside and nostalgic charm. It was unlike anywhere Gloria had been before. There were certainly a lot of shops selling knitwear, reminding her of why they were actually there. She liked the strong presence of Derek next to her as they made their way along the street. Gloria was glad to see that he hadn't changed at all in the years since she'd seen him. Of course he was smaller in stature, but fundamentally the same person. Gloria wanted to ask him if he was happy, but she thought that was a question for another time. Maybe when they'd had another drink. The memory of him leaning towards her with those brown eyes of his and telling her she was beautiful still hung in her mind. She wondered if he remembered saying it to her or if it was gone from his memory when the drink had worked its way through his system.

'Look, Gloria, how about that,' he suddenly said, breaking her from her thoughts. He was pointing to the window of the shop across the street which had a mannequin wearing a puffa jacket in a dark grey. It truly wasn't Gloria's style at all, but they crossed over to stand outside the shop window anyway and a very expensive-looking woollen coat caught her eye.

'Let's go and take a closer look,' she said.

# 10

## LERWICK

*Derek*

Derek hadn't ever been shopping for clothes with a woman, not his sister or even his wife. He might have been shopping with his mam, but he couldn't remember as he'd been four when she'd died. His aunt looked after him and Sally when his dad was at work, but she'd never taken them shopping for clothes. She'd either made them herself or turned up at their house with a bag full of generous hand-me-downs from the various neighbours who all wanted to do their bit for those *poor children*. Derek had been used to pulling on trousers with patches on the worn knees or school shirts that had dulled to a chewing-gum grey.

He'd seen the film *Pretty Woman* at his sister's one Christmas, but this experience wasn't like that. He didn't feel like Richard Gere with a platinum credit card, he felt like a chump.

Gloria tried on every jacket and coat in the shop and asked his opinion about them all. Unfortunately, he didn't have an opinion other than about one in particular that had a frilled collar and made him think about her saying she'd been a Victorian English lady in a former life. He'd just shaken his head at that one and she'd grinned at him, causing his knees to go a little bit weak. In the end he was pleased to see she chose a sensible, warm and showerproof coat with a fake-fur lining. He picked her a hat and gloves to match from the stand behind where he'd been loitering and she graciously donned them and then bought them all.

Once Gloria was kitted out, she looked far more comfortable in the chill air and Derek took a chance and asked her if he could visit a local beauty spot, and when she agreed, they walked round to The Lodberries.

'It's from the crime series I was telling you about.'

The stone house looked as if it had been hewn from the sea itself, the way the water slammed into the side of it as if it was a cliff face rather than someone's home. It gave Derek a warm buzzy feeling looking at the building from the series he'd watched so avidly. Detective Inspector Jimmy Perez's house. Derek looked over the harbour wall and down to the small beach below, where many a conversation had taken place between the cast members. He felt as if he was suddenly part of something big.

He glanced over to where Gloria stood with her hands on the wall, staring out at the sea, and thought about that first time she had come to find him at the factory, many years ago. How she had leaned in close and touched his arm, how no one else was around and he thought he was dreaming that this woman might be interested in him. Nothing had really happened, though, and Gloria never got to the point of why she had sought him out, but he had a lightness in him after that. Then Bridget had set him straight, reminded him she was married and not only that: Gloria had an agenda, apparently, and Derek should steer very clear of her.

He was about to reach out to her now, but she turned

suddenly and suggested they went back to the hotel to see how Bridget was doing.

**\* \* \***

Bridget was sitting in the lounge area of the hotel when Gloria and Derek headed back. She looked a little forlorn sitting by the window, gazing out at the harbour. Gloria went to sit with her while Derek approached the desk to check in. It was close enough to two o'clock and surely their rooms were ready.

There was a different person behind the desk now, an older man. He looked very smart in a tweed jacket and certainly more in keeping with the traditional décor of the hotel.

'Mr Maywood?' he said in an accent that was certainly Scottish but had a hint of Scandinavian about it too. 'It is lovely to have you with us and a warm welcome to the Harbour View Hotel. I'm Lachlan Jamieson, the hotel manager.'

'Thank you, it's good to be here,' he said and he meant it. After a morning spent with Gloria, he really was very happy to be here.

Lachlan gave him his key and got him to sign the requisite forms.

'I understand you're a group of three,' he said. 'I'd like to offer you all a welcome drink. I'll come and take your order in a minute.'

Derek was pleasantly surprised at such a welcome gesture. He wondered about them ordering some lunch and he asked Lachlan for a menu. It had been a long time since his Bakewell tart. He walked over to join the others and found Bridget admiring Gloria's coat. He hoped there was some sort of truce between them. He found it difficult when Gloria said the things she did and how Bridget reacted in response. He didn't really want to be stuck on an island with two feisty women, but, well, here he was.

'The manager has offered us a welcome drink,' he told them and took the remaining seat. It was nearest to Gloria and he found his knee grazed hers before he pulled his leg sharply away. He didn't look at her and didn't want to know if she was looking at him. 'I've got the menu too. I thought it might be a good idea to get some lunch before they stop serving.'

'Great idea, Derek. I'm starving,' Gloria said as Lachlan appeared.

They chose toasted sandwiches and soup. Derek ordered a pint and wondered if he ought to cut down. He was beginning to treat this like a holiday. Gloria asked for a large glass of house red and then, after Lachlan left, she quietly reprimanded Bridget for choosing a mineral water.

'When you're offered a free drink, Bridget, you go large and you go for alcohol.'

'You do you, Gloria,' Bridget said in return.

'Anyway, we've been looking at the map while Derek and I had coffee this morning and we know the route we need to take. I think if we get an early night and set off when it's light we can be up at the northernmost point by lunchtime. It's all surprisingly close. Back here for one more night tomorrow night and then perhaps the ferry home the next day?'

'That does sound like a good plan. I can let Graham know we're on track.'

'Maybe we should hold fire on that until we're underway with the journey,' Derek said, unfolding his map and laying it out on the table. 'We should check that the ferries are running. There's two to get between here and Unst.'

They'd only just arrived and he wasn't ready to talk about going home yet. This felt like a much-needed adventure. He pointed out the route to Bridget and then Lachlan arrived with their drinks. He also laid out some cutlery and napkins.

Just then Derek's phone made a loud pinging noise and he pulled it from the pocket of his coat that he'd left hanging on the back of his chair. Gloria's phone was also chirping, he noticed, but she was quicker than him and was already staring at the screen.

'It's a message from Charlotte,' she said. 'With a link attached.'

'I've got it too,' Derek said and noticed that Bridget began desperately rummaging in her handbag.

'Me too,' she said, looking pleased.

'Well, you would do,' Gloria said. 'It's come through on the group chat.'

'Oh, yes, of course.'

Derek couldn't bear to see how deflated Bridget seemed to look with a few seemingly simple words from Gloria, but he'd never really understood women and wasn't about to start trying now.

He opened the message and was about to read it, but Gloria had got there first and was reading aloud.

'"Firstly, I hope you've made it to the Shetland Islands in one piece,"' Gloria read.

'Just about,' Bridget interrupted.

'"Secondly, please don't shoot the messenger! Norman wanted you to be on the island before he put in his next request to you three. If you click the link I sent you, there's Norman himself to tell you what he wants. Hope you're having a lovely time. Charlotte."'

'What?' Bridget said, looking perplexed. 'What else does he want us to do?'

'There's only one way to find out,' Gloria said, tapping her screen. 'Oh, it's a video of Norman, God love him. Gather round and we can watch it together.'

Derek pulled his chair as close to Gloria as he dared and Bridget did the same. Gloria turned her phone on its side and leaned it against her glass of wine, and there on the screen was Norman. He was sitting in his dining room that he'd had converted into an office. All his many balls of yarn were on the shelves behind him, stacked in order of colour. He had piles of knitting books and jars stuffed full of needles. Knitted swatches were pinned to a cork board and he had a mannequin wearing one of his creations. Derek had always thought Norman had a nice little hobby, but looking with fresh eyes at the set-up now, he couldn't believe he'd not seen that his friend was running a business, a very successful business.

'Right,' Gloria said. 'Are we ready?'

She pressed play and Norman came to life before them.

'Well, hello, my lovely friends. If you're watching this, then I am dead. Sorry about that! I am delighted you decided to take me on my final journey. Really, I'm incredibly grateful to you. I won't blether on for ages, I don't really have the energy now, so I'll cut to the chase. Not long before my mother died, she told me my father was from the Shetland Islands. This came as a bit of a surprise to me as I was always led to believe he was a one-night stand from a party she'd been to down south and consequently of no importance and also untraceable. As a northerner, this always bothered me. I never fancied a southern softy for a dad.

'This new info actually appealed to me, even though I didn't embrace it straight away as such. In fact, I parked the idea for a long while, which I now realise was a mistake. I only had that one passing remark from my elderly mother and she was very much at the end of her life; I did wonder if she was delusional. The trouble with having no living family is you've no one to corroborate a story like that. She'd simply told me my dad was a Shetlander and he gave her a ring that belonged to his grandmother. She never told him she was pregnant when she left there. I assume she was up there on holiday, or a summer job or the like. She'd never once before told me that she'd visited the place.

'The thought that I had Shetland blood in me began to worm its way into my core, though. There was some sort of serendipity to it, because I'd just begun knitting with Shetland wool and my mother's words came back to me. It made more sense of how I felt about myself. I dreamed of making a trip up there for Shetland Wool Week. Charlotte was helping me with my business at this point and I began to make plans to go. She was going to accompany me. And then the pandemic hit and I wasn't the only housebound person in the country.

'The good thing was that everything went online and I was suddenly part of the Shetland knitting community. What a fabulous bunch of people. I still wanted to visit, of course, but you know what happened once the restrictions started lifting; I became ill. All chances of making that journey were lost. Are you all crying yet? I bet you are, you soppy sods.'

Gloria pressed pause on the video for a moment while they all collected themselves. Derek handed around a packet of tissues he found in his rucksack.

'Poor Norman,' Bridget said, blowing her nose. 'No wonder he wants his ashes scattered here.'

Derek tried to disguise his sniffs so he could be a man about it, but he wasn't very successful. Gloria was openly crying while using the tissue he gave her to save her mascara. Derek noticed the tissue had black streaks on it. She took a gulp of her wine, then re-positioned the phone and pressed play again.

'Anyway, you have taken me to the one place I desperately wanted to go, which is wonderful, but I'm now going to ask more of you all. I would love it if you could find my family for me. I don't have anything to offer you to go on. When I asked Mam questions, hoping she'd expand on what she'd told me, she just got confused and couldn't tell me any more. Charlotte has hopefully given you the box with photos and letters. Now you're on the island that may give you inspiration, hopefully. There's one of Mam, it's dated on the back and she would have been just pregnant with me. Look, I know it's an ask and it's sneaky of me to wait until you were there, but it would mean a lot to me if you could do your best to find any living family members. Tell them I was a good bloke and give them my mother's ring, it's in the box. It belongs to them now.

'And now I really will say goodbye to you. It's been a pleasure to know all three of you. I hope you know how important you are to me and also to each other. This is Norman signing off.'

'Blimey,' Derek said, sitting back in his chair and letting out a puff of air from between his lips. He glanced across at the two women and they both looked a bit stunned. Then Bridget gathered herself together.

'Well, bang goes our couple of nights on the island, then.'

Gloria stared at her for a moment and Derek braced himself for trouble, but their phones began pinging again and whatever Gloria was going to say was parked for now.

'It's from Charlotte again,' Derek said and he began to read.

'"Hope you're all still talking to me. I had to go with what Norman asked me to do. He was worried if he laid it all out, you wouldn't go at all. Anyway, there's more. I've finally been going through some of the comments from his followers on his Norman Knits YouTube page and I've noticed one account keeps popping up with suggestions that they meet up. I didn't think anything of it to start with, but I followed the thread of comments and it's over a few of Norman's last vlogs. I mention it in case it's linked to his family. It might be a member. The person calls themselves The Knitting Warrior and they do seem a bit demanding, but there's not much to go on. Norman wasn't reading his comments at that point. That was my job to do, but honestly, there were so many I often did a quick glance. Also, I've sent you a photo of the bucket list Norman wrote – things he would have done on Shetland if he'd made it there, people he would have seen. Perhaps you could do it for him. Take his ashes with you. Keep in touch and I'll do the same. Charlotte."'

A photo arrived in the group chat and Derek opened it up.

'The Knitting Warrior? Sounds a bit aggressive,' Bridget said, and Gloria laughed.

'I'm imagining someone charging around with their knitting needles primed and ready to attack,' she said.

Derek was pleased to see Bridget smile at this.

'But do you really think it could be a family member trying to reach out?' Bridget asked.

'Bit late if it is,' Gloria said.

'The thing is,' Derek started, 'it isn't too late. It will only be too late once we've scattered him. Would it be right to do that if he's got living family here?'

'That's all very sentimental,' Gloria said, 'but we don't know where they are and even if there actually *are* any family members here. Why has no one been in touch before? Why didn't Ida take Norman to Shetland when he was a child or even when he was an adult? Why didn't she tell him anything about his family before? I wonder if she had good reason. Maybe they're not nice people and we should leave well alone. I was kidding about The Knitting Warrior, but in truth, I don't really want to come face to face with a weirdo wielding sharp needles. I think we should travel north, scatter his ashes and then we go home.'

'She told him before she died. Whatever had gone on before,

she wanted him to know. And what about this new list?' Derek asked, reading it from his phone. 'It looks like a few tourist places we could visit en route. We could take Norman with us and get him to where he wanted to go.'

'I quite like Gloria's vision of scattering his ashes and getting home,' Bridget said.

'Then again, if we don't do this for him he might haunt us,' Gloria said, and Derek couldn't tell how serious she was.

He watched as Gloria leaned towards Norman's urn and he found himself leaning in too.

'Norman,' Gloria said in a frankly creepy voice, 'if we don't take you to the places on your list and try and find your family members, will you haunt us day and night until we're dead too?'

There was a moment of silence and Derek noticed that Bridget had moved herself closer even though it all felt ridiculous.

'Give us a sign, Norman,' Bridget said.

Suddenly, Derek felt a hand on his shoulder and at the same time there was an almighty crash from the kitchen. He jumped in his seat and knocked his glass over on the table. The beer spilled out and seemed to gravitate towards Norman's urn in some sort of poetic sign, although he did recognise that the table was on the wonk.

'Your food is ready,' Lachlan said, removing his hand from Derek and leaning forward to mop the beer with a napkin. A waitress was behind him with their lunch order and once the table was clean she set it out for them.

'Do you consider that a sign?' Gloria asked the others.

'I consider it a waste of beer,' Derek said, good-naturedly.

'I'll get you another,' the waitress said.

Derek turned his attention back to the list. He ran his eyes over the words but didn't take it all in at once. There seemed to be a lot to take in.

'What's on the list?' Gloria asked.

'Sumburgh Lighthouse, St Ninian's beach, Jarlshof and various tourist spots that I've already seen on the map, but there's activities too. Shetland pony experience, knitting classes, that I assume Norman would have been teaching rather than taking. Some of these things wouldn't be available in the winter. He's got sheep shearing here, we couldn't do that. There's a couple of people mentioned that I guess he was hoping to visit.'

'If Norman wasn't already dead, I'd kill him,' Gloria said, and no one laughed but her as the waitress returned with a fresh drink for Derek.

'The thing is,' Bridget said, 'he is already dead and would never know what we did or didn't do for him. Is this all a bit silly? I mean, who is this really for?'

'I think that if we don't do this, it will hang over our heads. I for one don't need anything else hanging over my head,' Derek said, and there was a stony silence. 'And I'm not remotely concerned he'd haunt us.'

He took a long gulp of his new pint, hoping this was true.

'I'd really like to go home sooner rather than later, though,' Bridget said simply.

'Well, we're here now,' Gloria said decidedly. 'This will be the only opportunity we will ever have.'

'You've changed your tune. Can I at least go and unpack my bag?' Bridget said. 'If Norman requires us to traipse around the Shetland Islands on his behalf I'd rather not do it in crumpled clothing.'

After they'd finished their late lunch, they all disappeared up to their rooms with a plan to meet up in the restaurant for dinner once Gloria had scrutinised the menu and deemed it reasonable enough. Derek lay on his bed and tried so hard to go to sleep, he was tired enough after all, but Norman's list sat in his head like a chore that needed completing. It was one thing to have a day trip with the other two, scatter the ashes and maybe enjoy a meal together before their return, but this list and family hunting meant days on the islands. Even though he'd been the one to push it, he just wasn't sure he could handle Bridget's sulks or Gloria's demands, no matter how beautiful he found her.

# 11

## THREE SKEINS OF SHETLAND WOOL

*Bridget*

The mood was sombre around the breakfast table, all three pushing their food around their plates.

'We're going to have to embrace this,' Gloria said. 'We've come all this way and I for one am not prepared to stop now. I mean, it won't kill us.'

'It might,' Bridget mumbled and picked up her cup of coffee. After an afternoon asleep in Gloria's room, she hadn't slept all that well through the night and now was feeling the effects like a hangover without the pleasure of drinking alcohol the night before. She hadn't joined the others in their red wine at dinner and wondered if they just thought she was a bit boring. The truth was, her memory wasn't great, so adding wine to the situation just meant it was less likely she'd know what was going on. 'It might have been better to wait until summer,' Bridget continued. 'Because *you* insisted on us all coming here in the depths of winter, Gloria, we now have to navigate the appalling weather to see some beauty spots we might not actually be able to see because of thick fog, lashing rain or hurricane-force winds.'

'God, you can be such a bore sometimes. How empty is your glass, Bridget?' Gloria said with not a small amount of gusto.

Bridget sank back into her seat, feeling like a reprimanded schoolgirl.

'At least the list starts off gently,' Derek said, just as gently. 'A trip to visit a wool shop and to meet Shona Johnson. We can do that and we won't have to worry about the weather inside, and we've got The Beast.'

Derek had the list in his hand and was reading from it. Bridget put down her cup and sighed.

'I do hope we're not expected to knit anything; I don't think I'd be very good at it,' she said. 'Also, if I had wanted to learn I would have asked Norman, for goodness' sake.'

'I can actually knit a little bit,' Derek said. 'I asked Norman to show me once, but I never really continued with it. I can remember how to cast on, I think, and to knit, but I wasn't very good at purling.'

'Well, I think I'd ace it if I tried it,' Gloria said, 'and if you chose the same attitude, Bridget, you'd probably ace it too.'

'What's the weather like on that silver-lined cloud of yours, Gloria? I imagine the whole world looks wonderful with those rose-tinted specs you wear. How does it measure up in reality?'

Gloria laughed. 'It measures up pretty darn good.'

'Unless we're planning to come back in the summer,' Derek said, 'I suppose we should just finish up here and get on with it. Everyone in agreement?'

Bridget slurped the last of her coffee and clattered her cup in the saucer.

'Is it walkable?' Gloria asked, turning to look out of the window.

Bridget did the same and could see rain rolling steadily down the windowpane. It looked windy too. Some of the drops, she noticed, were also working their way back up.

'I think it's a bit of a drive, but it's in the direction of Sumburgh Head, so we can go and visit the lighthouse there after,' Derek suggested. 'And wrap up. The forecast isn't great.'

'Is this the lighthouse where we scatter his ashes?' Bridget asked him. Now there was Norman's bucket list thrown into the mix, she found herself becoming a little confused about what was going on.

'No, Bridget,' Derek said gently. 'Muckle Flugga is where he wants us to scatter his ashes. That's in the north. Do you remember? The northernmost point of the UK.'

'Oh, yes,' she said, but really she couldn't recall it at all.

'I think we should take a selfie here by the harbour wall,' Gloria said as they left the hotel. 'We can start to document Norman's journey and I guess that's right here.'

Reluctantly, Bridget found herself being jostled into position, with Derek behind her and Gloria, and Norman's urn out in front. Gloria got her to hold it so she could take the photo with her phone. The hotel was in shot behind them.

Gloria took back Norman and tucked the urn under her arm. Bridget felt a little less uneasy about it now they were supposed to be taking Norman with them to fulfil his bucket list. It seemed just the smallest bit less odd. But only the smallest bit. She wondered very briefly if Gloria kept Norman on her bedside table at night, or left him on the windowsill, but stopped the thought in its tracks and turned her attention to getting ready to go out in what looked increasingly like a storm.

\* \* \*

They followed the road out of Lerwick with Bridget behind Gloria, and Derek in the passenger seat again. The rain had ceased momentarily, but the sky was threatening and moody. It was a bit like Bridget's current disposition.

She leaned against the window and watched the countryside pass by beside her. It was bleak and bare and beautiful. There was the odd stone property dotted about, some no more than ruins, others substantial houses and farms. She imagined what it would be like in the summer months. She'd read about the puffins returning to the islands, and Arctic terns, northern gannets and fulmars to name but a few. No chance of seeing them in December, thanks to Gloria, she thought, ungraciously. It did seem easier to blame Gloria, when in truth either she or Derek could have said let's leave it until the spring. Neither of them had spoken up.

'I've just realised there are no trees,' Gloria said from the front. 'I thought something was odd. The landscape is so flat looking but really isn't flat at all and it's because there aren't any trees. How strange. Is it because of the wind, I wonder? I can really feel the car being buffeted.'

Derek, who'd been tapping away on his phone, began reading out his findings about how the first human settlers cleared ancient trees for livestock, cultivation and firewood. How grazing sheep and rabbits can destroy sites. About acidic soil conditions, weather conditions. By the time he began talking about manage-ment and the Shetland Amenity Trust, Bridget could feel her eyes drooping and her lack of sleep finally caught up with her. The next time she was aware of her surroundings in the stuffy car, with low murmured conversation coming from the front, they were driving over a bridge and the rain had returned. She shuf-fled in her seat and looked out of the window. The water below looked choppy and cold. There were fishing boats moored and what looked like lines of something in the water. She wondered what they fished here and was sure Derek could tell her if she asked him. She didn't.

'There's a real Scandinavian vibe to the buildings,' Gloria said, her voice now louder. Bridget was sure they'd been whispering before. What was it they didn't want her to know? She was embarrassed to realise she'd been dribbling and wiped her chin with the back of her hand.

'It's not a huge surprise,' Derek said. 'We're closer to Norway than to London here and the Shetland Islands were part of Norway until the 1700s. I think this is it, Gloria. Does that say Fullridge House on the gate?'

Gloria stopped outside a white house at the top of the hill that looked stark against the gunmetal-grey sky. Bridget was reminded again about the lack of trees and that without them every building stood proud of the landscape.

'It doesn't look like a shop at all,' Bridget said. 'It's a house. I don't think we should just turn up unannounced to someone's home.'

Behind the property the view was breathtaking. You could see out across the water back up to the land beyond in a panorama of undulating green hills. Did it remind Bridget of North Wales, parts of the Yorkshire Moors or the Scottish Highlands? It really didn't. It was unlike anything she'd seen before.

'Well, this is the address and the woman's name is Shona Johnson. It's right here on the list,' Derek said. 'I'll get out and check she doesn't mind us being here, so we don't all get wet.'

Bridget and Gloria watched as Derek got out and walked as quickly to the front door as he could. The small amount of hair he had was immediately whipped about in the wind.

'I'm not keen on getting out, to be honest,' Gloria said. 'My hair will be ruined. I forgot to bring that hat I bought and there is no way I'd bother trying to put an umbrella up, it would be gone in an instant. Does anybody even bother to do their hair on these islands? I can't imagine the hair salons in town have much business.'

'I've got a spare hat you can borrow,' Bridget said, beginning to rummage in her bag, ignoring Gloria's shudder. 'It's a nice one.'

'I'm sure it is and thank you, but I'll take my chances. She might not even be in, hopefully.'

'I thought you were up for this list,' Bridget said.

'I am, it's just the weather, that's all. I looked at the forecast for the next few days and there's a chance of some snow too. Also, there's mention of a weather warning. You know how they name the storms? Well, this one is called Beryl, if you ever did. Sounds more like a warm breeze to me and not remotely threatening. I had an aunt called Beryl and she was a darling. They're not sure yet if the storm will reach us here or be limited to the south. We'll have to keep an eye on it.'

'We lost our greenhouse in a storm called Brian once, so you never can tell. And I don't like the sound of snow. I wouldn't want to get stuck out in a snowstorm or any storm, to be honest. This seems pretty remote.'

'It didn't take long to drive here, but walking would be a different case altogether.'

'I did see a couple of bus stops,' Bridget said.

'Yeah, but if The Beast can't manage it, I doubt a bus will.'

'Gloria, can you go back to being positive, please? It's very irritating, but less worrying.'

Gloria laughed just as Derek waved them over. It looked like Shona was in after all.

**\* \* \***

Shona welcomed them in as if it was no bother to her. Bemused, Bridget took her shoes off in the entrance hall to Shona's beautiful home, full of plants, paintings, minimalist furniture and stunning views out over the water from the huge windows in her living room.

She showed them through to her studio and then disappeared off to make a pot of tea. They were confronted with shelves of wool in the most subtle colours. Knitted garments were hanging on a wooden rail showing off what was possible to make with her wool. Bridget took a closer look at the intricate patterns and decided quite quickly that nothing there was suitable for her skill level, which was zero. Shona had pots of knitting needles and charts and books on a desk and what looked like a sweater in progress on some needles draped over the arm of a chair. There was a stove in the corner which was lit and the place was inviting and cosy.

'What a lovely place to work,' Gloria said, ruffling her hair into some sort of semblance of style after being blown to bits outside. Bridget smiled to herself, knowing full well that Gloria wished she'd borrowed the hat. 'So, what did you say to Shona? It's like she knew we were coming.'

'I just said we had a friend called Norman George and he always wanted to visit the islands and to visit her. That we were here on his behalf, ticking some things from his bucket list and that was it, she invited us in,' Derek said.

'But what are we supposed to do? Are we supposed to buy wool and knit?' Bridget said.

'Hats,' said Shona from the doorway. 'I think Norman would have wanted you to knit hats.'

She came in with a tray loaded with mugs of tea and a plate with a large rustic-looking cake.

'Did he arrange this?' Gloria asked.

'No, he didn't. A few months back he was going to join us online for Shetland Wool Week and teach an online class for those that couldn't join us in person. He's done it in years gone by and was incredibly popular. Unfortunately, as you know, he was really too ill this year. His workshop was going to be a beginners' group and they were going to knit hats. I had the kits ready to post out, but we had to scrap the idea. So very sad.'

She smiled and then began to pour the tea and dish up slices of the cake. Then she pulled a cardboard box out from underneath her desk and rummaged through the contents. There were bags inside, and Shona took them out and laid them all on her desk. She opened the drawstrings at the top of a couple and went through the contents, lifting out balls of wool with a contemplative look on her face. She kept glancing up at the three of them.

'I think this one for you, Gloria,' she said, handing over one of the bags. It was a small cloth bag printed with pictures of grazing sheep. Gloria reached inside and pulled out a ball of wool. 'The colour Champagne for you. It's my own Shetland wool, hand-dyed with madder.'

Gloria gasped in delight at the contents.

'Look at this gorgeous colour,' she said. 'What actually is madder?'

'It's a plant with evergreen leaves and tiny pale-yellow flowers, but it's the roots that are used for the dyeing,' Shona said.

'You dye it yourself?' Derek asked.

'Aye, it's our family croft here and my neighbour shears our sheep. I send the fleeces away to a fibre company to be spun and it comes back to me in skeins of natural wool that I can dye. I don't dye all of it,' she said, pulling some muted and natural-coloured wool from her shelves. 'These are all the un-dyed shades.'

'What a wonderful business you have,' Bridget said. 'Did you ever meet Norman in real life?'

'I didn't have that pleasure, unfortunately, and I wanted to come down for his funeral, but I had family commitments that prevented me, which was a shame. He was a big part of our knitting community online. Especially during the pandemic when we were only online. He was always with us for Shetland Wool Week – well, up until the last one – and he offered classes for those who wanted to learn special techniques. It's so sad that he never made it here in person. I think if he hadn't got ill when he did he would definitely have come. We had talked about it.'

Bridget drank her tea as her thoughts went back to Norman again. The thought of him never meeting those people in person that he spoke to online broke her heart. Then she thought about the Zoom calls that she and Graham had with their daughter in Germany. They felt like very real conversations. The connections she made with her two grandsons were very real indeed. They should make a plan to go, she thought in a moment of decisiveness. She couldn't keep waiting for her daughter to make the journey to see her and Graham in the UK.

'And this for you, I think,' Shona said, handing Derek his gift and getting Bridget's attention back. 'It's called North Sea, which is dyed with indigo. I think it's just the right colour for you.'

Derek smiled into his bag and Bridget hoped she would be doing the same. After the joke of their colourful knits at the funeral she was expecting something hideous, but when the bag was handed over and she looked inside, Bridget was smiling too.

'Salmon,' Bridget read from the label. It was a soft colour and very pretty. 'What did you use to dye this? Not actual salmon, surely?'

Shona laughed. 'No, it's dyed with madder again, but where

Gloria's wool is a white base, yours was dyed on a darker base so it gives that richer colour.'

'Richer than you,' Bridget quipped to Gloria, and Derek snorted into his tea.

'Always that bee in your bonnet. You're just so British,' Gloria said. 'Are there instructions? I have no idea what to do with these.'

Bridget bit back a rude retort and busied herself in the contents of the bag. There was a guide with a simple-looking picture of a hat and two sets of needles with two lengths of cord.

'Well, there are simple instructions for how many stitches to cast on and how much ribbing to knit, how much stocking stitch to do and then the decreases before the top. There are also instructions on how to make a pom-pom if you want a bobble hat, but that's not necessary.'

'Yeah, well, how about instructions on how to knit, period.'

'She means full stop. She's American,' Bridget cut in, and Shona suppressed a smile.

'That's easy enough if you're complete beginners, then. Go on YouTube and watch Norman's video on how to knit. It's a very popular one,' Shona said. 'Almost the most viewed of all of his videos. Of course, the video where he told his fans he was dying was the most viewed. But I don't really want to bring the mood down.'

Derek said that they'd taken up enough of Shona's time and what a pleasure it was to meet her and how much did they owe her for all the kits.

'Nothing, it's my absolute pleasure. I'm so glad you came on Norman's behalf. May he rest in peace. What else does he have on his list?'

'One thing is a visit to the Jamieson's of Shetland wool mill. I'm not sure we can expect them to give us a tour, though, as it's out of season. Norman might have had a connection with them, but we don't.'

'I know Louise there. She'd be delighted to show you around. Norman used a lot of their Spindrift wool in his Fair Isle designs. I'll give her a call.'

'That's really kind, thank you,' Bridget said.

'Do you think we could push our luck with your hospitality a little further and ask if we could have a photo taken with you? Perhaps against the big window with your stunning view behind us?' Gloria asked. 'We're taking Norman's ashes with us wherever we go before we scatter them. I hope that doesn't make you squeamish.'

'It makes me squeamish,' Bridget muttered.

'No, it doesn't. We're hardy folk up here, we have to be, and I don't mind at all. Are you going to put your journey up online after, for his fans? They'd love to see it. You could upload it to his YouTube channel. Or simply share some photos on Instagram. He was popular there too.'

'Yeah, we did think about that,' Gloria said, retrieving Norman's urn from her bag and arranging everyone in front of the window. 'It's what he would have wanted,' she said, and even though Bridget raised an eyebrow she lowered it again for the photo.

Derek was behind the three women, and Gloria held Norman in front with one hand and took a selfie with her other hand extended. She showed them all the image after to make sure they were happy with the result. After all, Bridget thought, they could hardly replicate this and it was number one ticked off the list. That thought made her smile.

'Shame you couldn't have looked like that in the photo,' Gloria said, but Bridget ignored her. The image was perfect with the background in view, Norman in pride of place in the middle and everyone, if not grinning, then certainly looking at the camera.

Derek turned to Shona then and Bridget watched him arrange his thoughts before he spoke.

'Norman found out that he might have family here on Shetland,' he said. 'Is that something he ever told you?'

Shona looked surprised for a moment and placed her cup down on her desk.

'He didn't, no. He never talked about family, it was always about the knitting. But how wonderful if he really did have a connection here. Although it does make it all the sadder that he never got here.'

'He did, though, didn't he?' Gloria said and held up the urn.

'How lovely to finally meet you, Norman,' Shona said.

'Can I show you this photo of Norman's mother? We wondered if it was taken here. It's a bit of a stretch, but can you tell? Do you recognise the background?' Gloria handed the photo to Shona and the woman took it and scrutinised it.

'I mean, it looks a bit like the corner of an old stone wall that she's standing next to, but I don't recognise the background. It's obviously coastal, but then we have almost one thousand seven hundred miles of coast here. Someone will know it. Can I take a shot of it and ask around?'

'Of course,' Gloria said.

Shona picked up her phone from her desk and took a photo of the picture. She swapped numbers with Gloria so they could stay in touch. All Bridget could think about was the miles of coastline – they had no chance of finding this one spot.

Then they said their goodbyes and reluctantly left Shona's cosy studio with assurances that they would send her photographs of their finished hats. The wind whipped them about again as they made their way back to The Beast, and Bridget noticed that the water behind Shona's house had completely disappeared into the fog that had descended.

# 12

## SUMBURGH

*Derek*

The first time Derek went to visit Norman after his accident at the factory, he cried. Not during the visit, but after, in the car, on the way home. He'd had to pull over at the side of the road, switch off the engine and sob for a good five minutes before making his way home with swollen eyes.

He'd never been that pally with Norman George, certainly no more pally than he had been with anyone else who worked at Taylor's factory. Norman had been an engineer and Derek worked in the warehouse. Their paths had crossed on numerous occasions and Derek had considered Norman to be one of those decent blokes. He never made crude jokes, he was usually smiling and convivial, but he didn't get in your personal space and he never made comments about Derek's weight. It was Derek's fault he'd not been more pally during those years at work; he hadn't really been pally with anyone.

He did recognise that he'd withdrawn from most aspects of life after his wife, Liz, had died. He had not only lived with crippling grief, but with a huge sense of regret for all that she would never have, children being chief among them. That was something they had both hoped for. Those tears in his car that day had obviously been for Norman, but they'd been for Liz and also for himself, for the man he'd once been and could never be again.

Now, as they drove away from Shona's knitting studio with their wool kits, he could feel his eyes getting damp again. It didn't help that Bridget was going on from the back seat of the car about how generous Shona had been and that even in death Norman was still thinking of others, helping them to make connections.

'You could think of it as bribery,' Gloria said, making Bridget gasp.

'How can you say such a thing!' she choked.

'He's sent us on a journey with his ashes, and a gift will keep us sweet on the way. Simple as that. He really is dictating from beyond the grave.'

Derek wasn't sure he agreed, but he wasn't getting involved, it really wasn't worth it.

'Which way, Derek?' Gloria asked. 'I guess we keep going south?'

'No, not unless you fancy a swim. We need to retrace our steps back up to East Voe and then head south from there.'

'Have we got time?' Bridget asked. 'It's nearly lunchtime.'

'If we don't plough on today, this list will take a lot longer,' Gloria said. 'How long do you want to be here for? Perhaps we can find somewhere to eat down there.'

Derek looked at his phone and got as much information up about Sumburgh Head as he could.

'I think we'll pass a minimarket and a petrol station. But I'm not sure if there's going to be much else down there with regards to lunch. Oh, there's a hotel actually. We might be lucky there.'

'Great, well, if not, we can buy something in the minimart on the way back, then. That will do, surely.'

They drove in silence for a while, each of them taking in the scenery, and Derek's signal dropped off for a bit, so he couldn't guide them. It didn't matter, though; there was only one road and that was the one they were on. Plus, he had his paper map as a good back-up plan.

They didn't pass another car and saw only a couple of houses and what looked like a farm.

'It's as if we have the whole island to ourselves,' Bridget said. 'I can't remember the last time we saw another car. It's really eerie.'

Derek watched as the sky darkened further and considered that they might well be getting wet. He looked Sumburgh Lighthouse up on his phone once he had a signal again and found that it wouldn't be open. They wouldn't be able to go inside and that was fine with him. He didn't fancy letting the two women know about his fear of tight spaces and heights.

They reached the brow of a hill and could see the whole of the southern tip of the island stretched out below them, a kaleidoscope of undulating land surrounded by water.

'Look at that beach,' Bridget said. 'Even in this horrible weather it looks inviting. The sand is so white, it looks almost tropical.'

'We're going to be passing the airport on this stretch of road,' Derek said, looking at his map. 'In fact, it looks very much as if we're going to drive over the runway.'

'Really? Is that safe?' Bridget said.

'I would imagine that if a plane is coming in to land they won't just let you pass. I'm sure it won't be like playing chicken with the aircraft,' Gloria said.

Further on they passed a set of lights with a small hut, but the lights weren't flashing, the barrier wasn't down and no one was in the hut, so they continued and were soon driving over the runway itself.

'How novel,' Gloria said.

'That's the Sumburgh Hotel I was talking about,' Derek said, pointing to a rather grand-looking building on the right. 'And behind it is Jarlshof. It's a prehistoric Norse settlement. I think we could stop there after the lighthouse and maybe get some lunch in the hotel. What do you think?'

'Lunch sounds good,' Bridget said, 'but let's see how the weather is, shall we? I don't fancy a Norse settlement in the howling wind and rain.'

'I'm with Bridget,' Gloria said, which was music to Derek's ears. To have these two getting on would make the whole trip so much easier.

They worked their way along the single-track road until they were at the car park. The lighthouse itself was still a way off, though.

'I'm going to drive further up,' Gloria said. 'There's no one around to tell me I can't.'

The road narrowed to little more than a track and then they parked in the empty spaces by the lighthouse.

'Take care getting out,' Derek said. 'We'll lose the doors if we're not careful.'

And he wasn't wrong. As he opened his own door, he could feel it getting tugged by the wind. He hung onto the handle until he was fully out and then closed it with a big push.

The fog that had been hanging around earlier had now lifted, but a drizzle had begun and they agreed on a very quick walk around the lighthouse. Derek pulled up a page about the history of it on his phone to make sure they all got the most from the experience. Gloria reluctantly borrowed Bridget's spare hat – a red felt thing that didn't suit her at all – and then they set off, with

Gloria planting herself between them and hooking her arms through theirs. They looked like quite the relaxed and jolly group, Derek imagined. Gloria's hip kept bumping against his upper thigh and it was a real effort to keep his concentration on his phone.

'It's all very nice,' Bridget said. 'It's beautifully painted and I like the ochre-coloured trim round all the buildings.'

'Built over two hundred years ago,' Derek read. 'There's a visitor centre, a gift shop, a marine life centre and toilets.'

'Oh, good. Toilets are going to be needed fairly soon,' Gloria said.

'The only thing is that none of it is open until April.'

'Right, in that case let's have a quick look around and get a photo of us with Norman and then get to that hotel you showed us,' Gloria said.

They all picked up the pace and followed the slope up to the main buildings, and Derek began to read again from the Sumburgh Head website.

'It was built by Robert Stevenson. It's ninety-one metres above sea level and the light flashes every thirty seconds. It can be seen for up to twenty-three nautical miles. The light is Stevenson's equiangular refractor, which has twenty-six reflectors instead of the normal twenty-one.'

Derek stopped for a moment to gauge the reaction of the women. Was he boring them, he wondered? It was hard to tell, but no one had told him to button it yet so he took a chance and ploughed on.

'"The light was fully automated in 1991 and ownership of the lighthouse buildings passed into private hands. In 1994 the area was designated as an RSPB nature reserve and the local office was relocated to Sumburgh Head in 1996. In 2002 Shetland Amenity Trust purchased the lighthouse buildings and began offering an accommodation service as part of Shetland Light-house Holidays." So, these buildings would have housed the keepers and their families and now they house holidaymakers.'

'Not sure I'd want to holiday here,' Gloria said.

'I think it would be lovely in the summer,' said Bridget with a little edge to her voice.

They walked up and around the lighthouse itself and Derek was quietly delighted that they couldn't go inside, but they did walk up the steps of the old and very large foghorn and that was where Gloria suggested taking a photo. They posed with Norman in front and the lighthouse behind them and then they turned and took another with the sea in a panoramic shot. They leaned on the rail and looked down to the waves crashing against the rocks. Derek noticed little flashes of vivid blue water around where the waves crested. It almost looked inviting if it hadn't been for the icy pinpricks of rain on his face reminding him how cold it would be.

'Thanks for the potted history, Derek, but I think I've had enough now and would be delighted to get a hot coffee in my hands and the chance to use the bathroom,' Gloria said.

'I second that,' Bridget chipped in.

The mention of the bathroom made Derek's own bladder twitch and he agreed they should head back.

\* \* \*

The hotel was a welcome sight after the cold walk around outside. It was a large and austere-looking building and had the whiff of a castle about it. The airport was a mere stone's throw away and oddly sat right next to the white sands of a beach in a perfect arc. The prehistoric site of Jarlshof was right beside it and Derek was determined to go to see it once they'd had lunch. If the ladies didn't want to go with him, then he'd take Norman and do it alone.

After using the bathroom, they settled at a table in one of the bay windows with a view back up to the lighthouse. There was very little light now as dark clouds had covered the sky and the rain had become heavier. It was cosy being inside and watching the weather worsening through the glass. Derek and Bridget chose sandwiches and soup, while Gloria opted for a jacket potato. They'd had a cooked breakfast that morning, but that didn't stop them from tucking into their lunch. Derek wondered if the walking they'd done might be enough to work it off, but he knew it couldn't really be true. After the years he'd spent overeating and then the effort it had taken to change his habits and lose the weight, he knew a stroll around the lighthouse wasn't going to be enough to work off the two sausages, black pudding, mushrooms, two eggs and the pot of baked beans he'd had that morning. He left a crust of his sandwich and a couple of spoonfuls of his soup in a half-baked gesture of self-control.

Just then his phone pinged with a message and Derek, expecting more information from Charlotte, was surprised when no one else's phone vibrated; it was just him. He slipped his phone out of his pocket and found a notification from the Mature Companions app. A woman called Penny with startlingly blue eyes wanted to meet up with him. She suggested lunch in a pub near where she lived in Devon, reminding him he must change the range in his settings. She said she didn't like timewasters and demanded a swift response, preferably within the hour but, without fail, by the end of the day. Derek had an image of being bullied by this woman that looked a little like his old school librarian and deleted the message. There, he thought, have a swift response within a minute.

'I'm going to the Norse site,' he said. 'Anyone coming with me?'

Both women looked out of the window and shook their heads.

'I'm going to have a look at this knitting kit,' Bridget said. 'In the dry.'

'And I want to send Charlotte some photos and see if she can upload them to Norman's Instagram account. I think we should get the ball rolling on his final journey. Judging by all the positive messages he got, I think his fans would appreciate seeing us giving him a good send-off.'

Derek put his coat on and after pushing his hat low on his head he lifted his hood up and over the top, pulling the drawstrings to tighten it around his face.

'You're a better man than I, Gunga Din,' Bridget said.

'Just a quick walk around a tourist site,' he said. 'Hand him over, Gloria.'

'Take the bag,' she said and passed it over to Derek. 'I don't really want Norman to get wet.'

Derek lifted the strap of the pink rucksack onto his shoulder and turned to go.

'Very fetching,' Gloria said, following up with a wolf whistle.

Derek was pleased with the cold blast of air that hit the small part of his face that was exposed as he opened the door to leave the hotel – it cooled down the heat that had risen to his cheeks.

# 13

## FOLLOWING

*Gloria*

Gloria had almost forgotten Bridget was in the back seat, she was so wrapped up in thoughts about Derek's strong arm opening her car door for her when he returned. To be fair, he was probably worried about her losing the door more than being chivalrous. Derek was a very practical man. And then Bridget made herself known from behind Gloria's head by bleating on about a motorbike.

'I think we're being followed,' she said.

Gloria glanced in her rearview mirror and caught sight of a black motorbike a little way back down the road.

'Don't be ridiculous,' she said. 'There's only one road, of course we're being followed.'

Gloria glanced over at Derek, who was looking in the side mirror, and then he looked over his shoulder.

'What makes you think it's following us?' he asked.

'Because I saw it going the other way when we left the restaurant and it must have turned around because it's following us now.'

'Bonkers,' Gloria said.

'I don't appreciate that, actually,' said Bridget. 'I know I can be a little forgetful, but I'm not imagining what I saw. I mean, what if it's because of those messages Norman was getting from The Knitting Warrior, or perhaps it's a disgruntled family member who doesn't want the past being raked up?'

'Why would it be?' Derek asked gently, and Gloria sighed.

'I've been thinking about it. We believe Norman's mother was here when she fell pregnant with him in her early twenties, judging by that dated photograph, and now we find out that Norman was getting weird comments or messages or whatever they were.'

'Please don't say *fell* pregnant,' Gloria interrupted. 'You can't fall pregnant, you are impregnated. For millennia women have been accused of getting themselves pregnant and falling pregnant. As if it was something they could do all by themselves. Ridiculous! And for those who desperately want to be pregnant, the thought that it could happen with the merest little stumble is gaslighting at the worst.'

She gripped the steering wheel tighter and kept her eyes firmly on the road ahead.

'Well, of course I hear what you're saying, but perhaps we could keep the feminist rant for when we're not being followed by a madman,' Bridget said.

Derek looked out of the side window, seemingly desperate not to be involved in this particular altercation. Gloria recognised that there was probably nothing he would dare to bring to this topic of conversation. She felt that deep-buried unhappiness resurface and then, as quickly, it subsided. She'd always found it difficult to hear women talk about having children as if it was as easy as breathing. Worse were those that complained about motherhood as if they weren't the luckiest people on the planet. When it was clear she was not going to ever be pregnant, she talked to Tim about adopting, but he wouldn't consider it, which was rich bearing in mind it was his fault they would never have a child between them. He said he couldn't contemplate raising someone else's child. He completely missed the point that his son from his first marriage stayed with them at the weekends and that was exactly what he expected Gloria to do while he played golf. The trouble was that Tim's son didn't really like Gloria, no matter how much she had tried. He'd been programmed by his mother to hate Gloria as much as *she* did. Gloria didn't have a hope. Tim told her that having a stepson was still a blessing, and she told herself the same even though it wasn't true. She hardly ever saw him now.

'A madman? Are you sure you haven't been hitting the whisky when we're not looking?' Gloria asked Bridget, and Derek kept his post at the side window.

'We all heard what Charlotte said. Those messages got quite demanding at the end,' Bridget said.

'A fan, that's all. Someone who greatly admired Norman and his contribution to the knitting industry. Nothing more than that,' said Gloria. 'We should concentrate our efforts on finding his family. So, we know that Ida was newly pregnant, judging by the dates on the back of the photograph. So, if we can prove the photo was taken here, it's likely the father was here too. Why didn't she stay and marry him? Why did she tell Norman his dad was a fling she had in London? You wouldn't ask those questions of young women now as you'd like to think they have more choices, but this would have been in the early fifties. A different time altogether.'

'I know Norman was confused at the end, but the messages

speak for themselves. I went on YouTube and read them. I worked out how to do it,' Bridget said.

Gloria glanced in the rearview mirror to see Bridget reading from her phone.

'"We have a connection, Norman. I want to find you and heal you. I can make it all better if you just tell me where you are. I'm about as far north as you can get, but I don't mind coming down south for you..."'

'You see? It's not just me being bonkers,' Bridget said. 'I really do think he is or was a bit of a nutter.'

There was silence in the car for a moment and it was broken by the sharp trill of Gloria's ringtone. She leaned forward and pressed to take the call. The sound of sobbing filled the car.

'Gloria, when are you back? I can't live without you.'

'Oh, for God's sake. You're on speaker, Paul. I'm with others in the car.'

Gloria jabbed at her phone and Paul was immediately cut off.

'Just an old friend,' she said to an open-mouthed Derek while Bridget stifled a snigger from the back seat.

'Nothing like my friends,' Bridget said.

'I have a varied friend group actually; you should try it, Bridget,' Gloria said, but it wasn't with much conviction.

The dark cloud bank that had been following them veered off to the east and there was a short time where the wind dropped a little and the light was brighter as the sun shone through, although it was so low now it had almost set.

'Have we got time to fit in one other thing on Norman's list before we head back to the hotel?' Gloria asked, and Derek turned his attention back into the car.

'Unfortunately, the Shetland Croft House Museum is closed until May. It's an original building from the 1880s.'

'Shame,' Gloria said, although her voice betrayed her delight at not having to visit. 'Was that on the list?'

'No, but I just thought it might be fun,' Derek said to a stony silence.

'We didn't ask you how the Norse settlement was,' Bridget said, and Gloria suppressed a sigh. She prepared herself for a long history lesson.

'Actually, it was good to be somewhere that others had been so many years before. I mean, fragments can be seen of the earliest dwellings at Jarlshof, dating from around 2700 BC. That's really something isn't it? There's a Bronze Age settlement, an Iron Age village and so much history going through until the coming of the Vikings from Norway in the 800s, and then the 1500s with the Old House of Sumburgh that still dominates the site today.'

Gloria smiled at him. His enthusiasm was charming and maybe if she chose to be interested she might actually learn something.

'It sounds pretty amazing,' she said.

'Well, in truth, I didn't stay long as it was so bloody wet, but I did get a photo with Norman for the album. I'll share it in the chat and Charlotte can add it to the pot.'

'So, going back to this list,' Bridget said.

'Oh, right, yeah. We could stop at St Ninian's beach. That's on Norman's list. The sun is out-ish, for now, but won't be for long. Perhaps a quick stop while it isn't raining?'

They all agreed and Gloria retraced their steps back up the main road until they reached a sign directing them to turn off to Scousburgh, Spiggie Loch and then St Ninian's. She took the occasional glance in her review mirror, but there was no sign of the motorbike now. Bridget was losing her mind. But it was hardly surprising with her father's dementia diagnosis. She remembered Bridget confiding in her many years ago during a lunch break how difficult her life was, trying to work, run a home, look after her teenage daughter and care for her father in his ailing health. Gloria had given her some time off to work it out, but Bridget hadn't stayed away long. She enjoyed her job and wanted to juggle her responsibilities. Gloria always admired her for that.

The road was narrow and had passing places, but they didn't see another vehicle. The land was grassy, rocky and barren and stretched out around them, treeless and sparse. They were never far away from the water. As the road dipped and rose, Gloria kept catching glimpses of it. They did pass some properties, but they seemed to be randomly dotted about. She tried to imagine herself living somewhere as remote as this, but she couldn't. Gloria enjoyed city-centre visits. Lunch with friends, shopping in large department stores, art galleries and theatre trips. She couldn't live somewhere like this. There would be too much time to think and dwell, something she didn't like to do. An image of Ida here for a summer visit, getting knocked up and realising the reality of staying here and having a child flicked through Gloria's head. She had only met Ida a couple of times, but she had been a woman full of life. Norman told Gloria she'd been a dancer and an actress in a few small stage shows in her younger years. She'd been busy, energetic, funny and accomplished. But had that come at the price of denying Norman a home with his father?

\* \* \*

They parked up next to the beach and pulled on their coats, hats and gloves.

'And what is the significance of coming to this particular beach on a day of such awful weather?' Bridget asked. 'We won't be setting up deckchairs, will we? Do you fancy building a sand-castle, Gloria?'

'It's a tombolo beach,' Derek said as he tied his scarf around his neck. 'It means it's a natural sand causeway with sea on either side. The waves are coming in from opposing directions. I think they're quite unusual; I've never seen one. And Norman wanted to visit.'

They left the comfort of The Beast – which Gloria had decided was more of a help than a hindrance now, because they at least weren't all on top of each other – and headed down onto the sand.

'Imagine this in the sunshine,' she said, which earned a harrumph from Bridget.

'Yes, well, we can only imagine, can't we,' she said.

It was just as Derek had described; a strip of sand led them to a little island and it was buffeted from either side by the waves.

'We should take a photo of us with Norman on the island. We can get a shot of us with the beach behind us. Charlotte has already uploaded the photos I sent her to Instagram – I checked – and they're getting lots of likes and comments,' Gloria said.

'Does the beach get covered at high tide?' Bridget asked. 'I don't want to get stuck over there.'

'It says here that it doesn't, usually,' Derek read from his phone. 'Only in very bad weather in the winter. You wouldn't ever get stranded, but you might get wet feet. I've checked the tide times and it's low at the minute, so we'll be fine, but it'll be getting dark soon, so we should be quick regardless of the tides.'

They set off across the sand and reached the island in no time. Once they had walked across the grass away from the beach, they had reached a bit of height and Derek took photos of the rock formations in the sea below.

'Here is a perfect place for a selfie,' Gloria said, and she pulled Norman out of her bag.

They all posed with the beach behind them and Gloria handed Norman to Derek so she could take the shot. It was only as they began to walk back and Gloria checked her photos to make sure the shot was clear that she noticed that she could just see The Beast in the car park and next to it was a black motorbike with someone standing with their hands on their hips. It was impossible to see their face from this distance, even when Gloria enlarged the image. The person was wearing black leathers and an orange crash helmet and seemed very much as if they were looking straight across at the three of them on St Ninian's Isle. Gloria glanced over to Bridget, who was hanging onto Derek's arm as they navigated the bumpy ground back down to the beach. It had to be a coincidence, she thought. The sun was disappearing fast now and they all picked up their pace to get back to the car park before they lost the light completely. By the time they were back beside The Beast they were the only vehicle in the car park. The motorbike had vanished.

## 14

### LEARNING TO KNIT

*Bridget*

It was dark by the time they got back to the hotel and Bridget had an overwhelming ache to get under the covers of her bed, even though it was actually only four o'clock. She left the other two in the bar, saying she needed to freshen up, but she actually stood in front of the mirror above her dressing table for a good ten minutes scrutinising her face.

Gloria was attractive, there was no denying it. She had high cheekbones and only one chin. Yes, she had a few lines radiating from her eyes and her jawline didn't have the sharp edge it used to, but she looked good for a woman in her seventies. Actually, she'd look good for a woman in her sixties.

Bridget turned her mouth up into a smile and moved her face from side to side to see if she could catch a good angle. The real truth about Gloria, it pained Bridget to admit, was that she seemed to be happy and it showed through in her expression. Bridget spent too much time in a bit of a sulk, she realised this, but found it hard to break out of it. She ran a brush through her hair, swept a pale pink lipstick across her mouth and smiled broadly at her reflection, then she dialled it down a bit when she could see she looked manic.

'Gin and tonic?' Gloria called out as Bridget stepped into the bar.

Derek had his phone propped up against the side of a pint and was watching something on the screen. Bridget opened her mouth to say that she'd like a lemonade but changed her mind at the last minute. She couldn't keep saying no to everything and wanted to prove to Gloria that she could relax too.

'Yes, please, Gloria. That will be lovely.'

She pulled out the dialled-down smile and ignored Gloria's look of surprise.

'Derek's got Norman's "How to Knit" episode up on YouTube. We thought we could settle in tonight and have a bit of a play with the wool, raise a glass to Norman,' Gloria said, walking over with their drinks.

'Okay,' Bridget said, taking the glass. 'All I really managed earlier was to read through the pattern. Once I got to the bit where it said to cast on the stitches, I realised I didn't really know how to.'

'Don't worry about that, Norman has it covered in great detail,' Derek said.

Bridget's first thought was that her drink might be a double as the freezing liquid hit the back of her throat and made her cough, but she kept up the smile and thanked Gloria. Gloria wasn't really listening though, because Bridget could see her attention was momentarily diverted by a man in a black leather jacket and an orange hat approaching the bar.

'Friend of yours, Gloria?' Bridget asked. She wondered if it might be the chap from the phone earlier. Paul? Maybe he'd followed Gloria to Shetland. He clearly couldn't live without her.

Could Graham live without Bridget? She thought, increasingly, that he probably could and made a mental note to phone him. She hadn't spoken to him today as there had been so much else going on. She'd give him a quick call after dinner, before she went to bed, remind him she was still here.

'No, I thought for a minute... no, I don't know him,' Gloria said, turning back to the table as the man joined a group in the far corner of the bar. 'Let's see if we can learn this knitting lark, shall we?'

Derek turned his phone around so they could all watch the video.

'He was good, wasn't he?' Derek said. 'So clear in his instruction and engaging and funny. No wonder his videos were popular.'

'I miss him,' Gloria said. 'He was the least complicated man in my life.'

Bridget noted that Gloria's phone was silent and face down on the table, but it had vibrated a couple of times with incoming phone calls.

'That chap that phoned earlier,' Bridget started. 'When he said he couldn't live without you, he didn't mean...' She trailed off, not quite sure if she could say what she was really thinking, but she needn't have worried because Gloria picked up on it straight away.

'No,' she said quickly. 'No, nothing like that. He just doesn't like his wife very much.'

Bridget was surprised at the sharp intake of breath from Derek beside her.

'Oh,' was all Bridget could manage herself. Somehow she wasn't surprised, though. Didn't Gloria always take what she wanted? After all, if she'd been thinking about her staff instead of herself on the day Norman had his accident, it likely wouldn't have happened. Or he certainly would have been found more quickly. He'd have been saved unnecessary suffering. But then, if Bridget had done the things she was supposed to have done, if she hadn't been making all those personal calls to her mother begging her to come and help look after her father... She took a large gulp of her drink. It was in the past. Norman had never held any of them responsible. They had, but he hadn't.

Bridget excused herself to go and get her own knitting kit and by the time she was back, Derek had some stitches on his needles and Gloria had bought Bridget another drink, even though she was only halfway through the first. Sod it, she thought. She would relax and enjoy herself this evening. Everything else was tomorrow's problem.

They ate a light meal in the bar and had several more drinks between them. They all got some stitches on their needles with Norman's help.

'You know, I didn't realise Paul was married when I first met him. It came to light a while later. I wouldn't have gone after a married man,' Gloria confided after her third glass of wine.

'And after you did realise?' Bridget asked. 'Did you immediately stop seeing him?'

She felt emboldened by the gin, although she needed to concentrate on her hat – well, her two wonky rows; it was a long way from a hat and she was sure she'd dropped a couple of stitches, but every time she tried to count them she forgot where the row started.

'Honestly, no, I didn't, not quite. I'm not married and I liked the fact that he wasn't really available to me. I didn't want any commitment.'

'His poor wife,' Bridget said.

'Yes, well, I don't know her and I'm not seeing him any more anyway.'

'Hasn't got the message, has he?' Bridget looked up from her knitting and stared at Gloria, but she refused to catch Bridget's eye.

'Do you see much of your stepson at all?' Derek asked. 'I've forgotten his name, sorry.'

'It's Timothy junior, or Tim the third really, which he's always hated. I really don't know why Tim and Brenda did that to him. Actually, quite cruel to turn your child into some sort of accessory. He picked out the middle few letters of his name and calls himself Moth, which isn't a vast improvement, but it's on his terms at least. He lives in Manchester with his wife and their two girls. I mean, I don't see him; Brenda wouldn't like it and that's fair.'

'You have odd, twisted morals,' Bridget said. 'In one breath you sound like the most grounded and reasonable person, but then you have an affair with a man who belongs to someone else. If you'd chosen to have your own children, I doubt you'd behave that way. There's something about kids that brings you to a better place.'

There was a loaded silence for a moment and Bridget's words caught up with her. Her head was beginning to feel a bit fuzzy and she'd definitely had too much to drink now.

'Firstly, Bridget, you are very judgemental. You don't really know me and how I operate my life and whether my childlessness is through choice or for other reasons. Making sweeping statements is unkind. Judgement without knowledge is a dangerous thing. Please don't be one of those smug parents who think that just because they had a child they know everything. I'm going to show this photo of Ida around and see if anyone here recognises the background.'

Bridget went to say something, anything to justify her words, but nothing came and she just sat mutely in her seat. She watched as Gloria walked across to the table opposite, took the photo from her pocket and shared it with the group.

'I think it's best if I go to bed,' she said to Derek, whose knitting seemed to be suspended in the air in front of him, his needles poised mid-stitch, a look of shock stuck on his face. He lowered his project to the table and picked up his pint.

'Do you not remember, Bridget?'

'Remember what?' Bridget asked as a creeping sense of dread began to crawl over her. This happened a lot. It could just be that she'd forgotten to close the fridge, or it could be so much more, but the dread felt exactly the same.

'About Gloria's husband and what he did, what you told me at the factory.'

Derek's voice was low, barely more than a murmur and Bridget stood up and began to gather her things. She didn't remember and she didn't want to. Instinctively, she knew she wouldn't come out of it looking good.

'I don't want to rake up the past,' she said. 'I'm going to go to bed.'

'Maybe that is best,' Derek said gently.

Bridget walked up to her room, sat on the side of her bed and closed her eyes. Then tears started to come and she wiped them away with the back of her hand.

'No point feeling sorry for yourself,' she said, but what she really wanted was a big hug from Graham. He would tell her everything was going to be okay and not to worry about a thing. She realised Gloria didn't have that herself. If her relationships were all rather fleeting she probably didn't reach that level of intimacy. Who told Gloria that everything was going to be okay? Maybe she told herself or perhaps she was intimate with her friends. That was something Bridget hadn't ever had – a close best friend. She held herself back somehow. She didn't want to be judged and to be found wanting so it was better to have acquaintances and not to get too close. She thought about how she judged Gloria. It was so easy to pick up on others' worst traits because it stopped you looking at your own.

She stood up and went to the bathroom. Enough of the self-analysing. She ran herself a bath and squirted some shampoo into the hot stream of water in lieu of bubble bath. After drinking a mug full of cold water from the sink she sank down into the water, letting it wrap its warmth around her body. Bridget thought she'd be home in a few days, but that wasn't looking like the case now. They had a family member to find before they could scatter Norman and she didn't think that was going to be easy. Then she remembered the motorbike and how dismissive both Gloria and Derek had been and felt a little less bad for her comments in the bar.

* * *

'Hello, Graham,' she said later when she was dry and in her pyjamas. She was lying on her bed with her phone next to her on speaker. She was drying her hair with a towel where it had got wet when she'd fallen asleep in the bath. She hadn't intended to wash it as she couldn't be bothered to blow-dry it, but she'd have to do something with it now.

'Sweetheart, lovely to hear from you. How's it all going?'

'Not great, Graham. The weather is appalling, I'm knitting a hat that has more holes than stitches, I'm convinced we're being followed and I've been unforgivably rude to Gloria. Oh, and I think I'm a bit drunk.'

'Goodness, that sounds like a lot. Not a boring holiday, then?'

'It's not a holiday, Graham, it's more like a pilgrimage, although we've yet to find any evidence of Norman's family.'

She sighed and picked the phone up, putting it to her ear. Bridget didn't like using it on speaker, it felt so impersonal and the urge to shout into the phone was intense. She filled Graham in on Norman's family connection and how it was likely she'd be a few more days on the islands fulfilling his bucket list too.

'It sounds like an exciting challenge,' Graham said, and Bridget didn't bother to respond as she knew she'd be negative. 'What makes you think you're being followed, anyway?'

'Just a sixth sense, and someone on a motorbike that saw us and turned around. And Norman's assistant, can't remember her name—'

'Charlotte,' Graham said.

'Yes, that's it. She told us he was getting creepy messages and then I felt the bike was following behind us, but neither of the other two agree.'

'Well then,' he soothed. 'It's most likely nothing.'

'Because the other two disagree, it's most likely nothing? As ever, thanks for the vote of confidence.'

'Don't be like that, Bridge. Honestly, how likely is it that someone would be following you three and an urn of Norman's ashes across Shetland?'

Bridget didn't really have anything to say to that, so he continued.

'Tell me something good about what you've been up to.'

Bridget dropped the towel onto the bed beside her and began to run her fingers through her hair, wishing she'd brought her hot brush.

'The food is nice,' she said.

'Neeps and tatties?' he said. 'Have you had haggis? Wonderful comfort food.'

'I want to come home, Graham,' she said suddenly, surprising herself. 'I could fly, you could book me a ticket. I'm not needed here. Gloria and Derek seem tight, they can do without me being a sulky cow and saying unkind things.'

'Hey, I'm sure whatever you said to Gloria will glance off her hard shell. She's not going to worry about it,' he said, but Bridget wasn't sure about that. She'd seen the look on Gloria's face. Not when she'd said about her with a married man, but when she'd talked about her not having children. Bridget didn't remember if it was a choice Gloria made or whether it was forced upon her. But there was something niggling the back of her mind, a memory from the distant past that was just out of her reach. Derek was right, she did know something, once. As the effects of the alcohol began to ebb away she felt an overwhelming guilt. 'Just tell her you're sorry. I'm sure it will settle down when everyone's had a good night's sleep.'

Graham was giving her soundbites of good advice, Bridget recognised that, but he wasn't here, he didn't know what had been said. She was going to have to get on with it. Woman up, apologise to Gloria and sort out the sulk. Maybe Gloria would apologise to her for her own little digs, she wasn't perfect herself, although Bridget knew her own comments had come from a place of spite and she guessed that Gloria's had not.

'I won't be coming home, Graham, not yet. I said I'd do this for Norman and I will.'

They said their goodbyes and not long after Bridget hung up she fell fast asleep on top of the covers.

## 15

## HEADING WEST

### Derek

Derek woke up thinking he was back on board the NorthLink ferry. The room seemed to sway as he made his way to the bathroom. He ran the cold tap and splashed water on his face until he felt marginally better. He had to stop Gloria talking him into drinking too much. No good could come from it, although he did remember a very pleasant evening with some good conversation between Gloria and Bridget before it had taken an unexpected turn for the worse. How could the two of them be smiling and cordial one minute and then all handbags at dawn the next? He was at a loss and now thinking that the throb in his temples really wasn't worth it.

They were planning to get to Sandness this morning after breakfast. They could tick a couple more things from Norman's list and continue to inch their way up to where they were going to scatter his ashes, although that wouldn't be happening today of course.

The two women were in the dining room, both with a full

Scottish breakfast in front of them, although Bridget was only picking at hers. Gloria was getting stuck in as she usually did with a great gusto that Derek found so appealing. They were not talking and he wasn't surprised. Bridget's comments had been quite spiteful, he felt, not that he'd intervened. Once Gloria had asked everyone in the bar if they knew the location in the photo and returned to their table, Bridget had gone to bed and Gloria didn't mention the altercation. Derek hadn't wanted to rake up the past, the same as Bridget. Too much miscommunication between himself and Gloria had occurred in years gone by. He'd much rather they could continue now as friends. He was surprised that Bridget couldn't remember what had happened back then. It was probably for the best, though. A trip down memory lane for Norman was one thing – that was what they were here for after all – but for themselves? No, that was best left in the cul-de-sac of their past.

No one had recognised the backdrop to Ida's pose in the photo Gloria shared around the bar, which was hardly surprising as it could have been any coastal scene next to any stone building. There were no distinguishing markers, no handy signposts, the background wasn't in focus and he had begun to wonder if they were on a fool's errand.

'No matter,' he'd said to Gloria. 'We're here for one reason and that's to scatter his ashes. We can be in control of that at least.'

And then Gloria had admitted to seeing the black motorbike and that she now wasn't convinced they *weren't* being followed the previous day. She didn't go so far as to admit Bridget may have been right. When she'd shown him the photo they'd taken on St Ninian's Isle with the ominous figure standing in the car park in the background, he'd begun to wonder himself.

'So, Bridget may have been on to something?' he'd said and Gloria had sighed.

'Well, I won't be telling her, that's for sure. She needs some time to stew in her own juices.'

And Derek had suddenly wanted to say something then, to lay it all out on the table. To finally be clear about what he thought he'd known back then and what he now knew to be untrue. Maybe the cul-de-sac wasn't the best place to park their memories. But it would all come out wrong. He'd make a fool of himself. No matter how many times he tried to arrange the words in his head, he knew that as soon as they were on his lips, he'd make a hash of it. So they'd chatted about nothing and drank.

Now, at the breakfast table, it was clear that Bridget *was* stewing in her own juices as she picked at the food on her plate, looking contrite. Gloria was not going to make it easy for her. He approached the round table tentatively and slipped onto the chair between them.

'Good morning, ladies,' he said, and they both looked up and smiled. Perhaps it would be okay after all.

A waitress came and offered him coffee, then he took a plate and chose a couple of hot items for his breakfast. He would always be careful with what he ate. The last thing he wanted to do was to go back to being that unhappy, lumpy man from before. He wasn't exactly full of the joys of spring now, but at least he was no longer carrying all that extra weight around with him – not on his body anyway. He liked to think he had a healthier relationship with food now; he certainly had a healthier relationship with exercise. It was walking every day that had kick-started his weight loss. Norman had set him up with a group of local people who walked dogs for owners who couldn't, for various reasons, walk them themselves. The irony wasn't lost on Derek, but that was Norman, always there to help others.

He picked up two sausages and put one back, decided on toast and changed his mind. No one needed a side order of bread with a meal.

'So, we have a plan to head to Sandness today. That's to the west and we can tick off a couple more things from Norman's list en route,' he said.

'I've been checking his Instagram and there are so many well-wishers. Loads of messages. Some are from local people who say they'll look out for us. Not sure how I feel about that,' Gloria said.

'Motorbike,' Bridget said so quietly that Derek almost didn't hear her.

'I was thinking that we might post the photo of Ida to see what it will unearth. What do you both think?' Gloria said, and it was if she was offering a lifeline to Bridget.

'I don't think it's a bad idea,' Bridget said, gently. 'But do you think it might upset some people? It's one thing for us to be making quiet enquiries, but a whole other to invite the world to investigate.'

'You do of course have a point,' Gloria said, and Derek thought it quite gracious. 'I think we really need to ask ourselves what is our objective? Us three piddling around these islands is unlikely to yield answers, but a photo online could well do the job for us.'

'Or could invite a whole load of trouble,' Bridget said. 'But I suppose that Shona is already asking around. What do you think, Derek? To post or not to post, that is the question.'

'I think we should message Charlotte and ask her,' he said.

\* \* \*

An hour later they were all in the car ready to leave. Derek had his phone fully charged up and primed for map reading and to offer interesting information. He had Norman's list and was quietly adding his own wishes to it. It would be very unlikely he'd be coming back here, so it couldn't hurt to see what the islands had to offer. He was sure the others wouldn't mind. Bridget seemed happy to let him take the lead and Gloria was busy driving and grateful for his navigational skills. He chose not to ask them.

It was a crisp and clear morning with no forecast for rain over the next couple of hours. They did have to scrape some ice from the windscreen of The Beast, but for now, the two women were not at each other's throats. Derek was beginning to feel quite good about the day ahead.

Then, as they pulled out of the parking space on the harbour road, he noticed a motorbike parked up not far from them, the rider dressed in black leathers with a dark orange helmet. It was definitely the same rider from Gloria's grainy photo she'd taken at St Ninian's beach. Bridget was looking out to sea, but Gloria saw it. She locked eyes with Derek and then began to drive them out of Lerwick with most of her attention on her rearview mirror.

They followed the road north, uphill out of the town, past where they'd disembarked the ferry only two days ago and through the businesses and industrial buildings until they were onto the country roads of undulating hills peppered with bodies of water.

'I'm not gonna lie,' Gloria said. 'I miss trees. I couldn't live here. It's too flat, too bleak.'

'I like the peace,' Bridget said.

'Yeah, until you open your car door and have it ripped out of your hand in the howling wind.'

Derek suppressed a sigh – they were off again.

'Do I turn off here?' Gloria asked as they came to a wide bend in the road with a left turn.

'No,' Derek said, checking the map. 'Keep going round to the right. You see the sign? Twenty-four miles to Sandness. And that water down there is Burn of Dale.'

'Does it feed into a loch?' Bridget asked from the back seat. She didn't usually ask questions and it pleased him she was taking an interest.

'No, it looks like it feeds into the sea,' he said.

Derek found a website with a detailed map of all the lochs and burns of the Shetland Islands. It had him quite enraptured for a good while.

'My mistake,' he said. 'It feeds into Dales Voe.'

'What's a voe?' asked Gloria.

'In the Shetland dialect it's a sea inlet, so I suppose it eventually ends up as the North Sea.'

'That's fascinating,' said Gloria, but Derek didn't think she sounded all that fascinated. Bridget said nothing.

'Tingwall Airport to your right,' he said after a while of silence.

He noticed Gloria had stopped bothering to look in her rearview mirror and he hadn't noticed the bike for a while from his glances in his side mirror. Small place, he supposed, and they were bound to bump into the same people doing the same touristy things, although this wasn't tourist season, he had to admit.

'Every time we get to the brow of a hill and then drive down the other side, I feel like a child on holiday seeing the sea for the first time,' Bridget said.

'I know what you mean,' Gloria agreed. 'We used to take Moth down to Cornwall quite a bit as he loved to surf. He was always sitting forward eagerly waiting for the first glimpse of the ocean.'

'It's every hill here,' Bridget said. 'It still feels exciting, though.'

'That's the loch of Tingwall,' Derek said, wondering if he was spoiling the excitement. He decided to stop the commentary for a bit.

They passed colourful holiday chalets and remote homesteads. They skirted lochs and then just as quickly disappeared into the hills. As many abandoned buildings as newly built homesteads appeared in their eyeline and disappeared out of it.

Then, without any warning, Gloria skidded to a halt at the side of the road next to a building and then pulled into the car park which sat on the edge of the water.

'I saw a sign for Shetland Jewellery,' she said. 'Sorry, but I couldn't resist a quick look.'

Derek watched as she jumped out of the car and he didn't have time to remind her to be careful of the door, but in truth it was an unusually still and calm morning. Almost too calm, he thought as he opened up his weather app.

Bridget opened her door, but she didn't walk towards the shop, she headed down to the water and stood with her arms folded across her chest, looking out over the loch.

The weather wasn't going to last. Derek could see that the wind was going to pick up by lunchtime, and there was a chance of a flurry of snow. He got out and went to find Gloria. It was fine to go shopping in bad weather, but sightseeing across the western part of Shetland was best done in the dry.

'It's not open,' Gloria said when he got to the door. 'It's actually a workshop and they only open to visitors between May and September. They have a shop in Lerwick, the sign says. Maybe I'll pop by there later.'

Bridget called them both over to where she was still standing by the water.

'I've seen otters,' she said excitedly. 'They were playing in the shallows. Look down there.'

Derek followed to where she was pointing and he could see two animals tumbling together.

'And who said we wouldn't see any wildlife while we were here, because it was the wrong time of year?' Gloria asked, a small smile playing on her lips. 'I've read that we might see seals in the sea if we're lucky.'

They all watched until the otters swam away and then they got back in the car.

'I've brought my knitting,' Bridget said, 'but I can't keep my eyes off the landscape.'

'It is stunning, isn't it?' Derek said as he got the directions back up on his phone. 'Oh, we've had a reply from Charlotte about Ida's photo. She thought it was a great idea and has already posted it on Instagram,' he said, and Bridget squeaked from the back seat.

'I thought we were going to think about it,' she said.

'I thought we were just going to get on with it, otherwise we'll have finished Norman's bucket list and scattered him before we find any answers. It'll be too late then. That's what we said, didn't we?' Gloria said.

'No,' both Derek and Bridget said at the same time.

'Well, not really,' Derek corrected himself, 'but it's done now; let's just see what happens.'

Just as Gloria was about to pull out of the car park, the sound of a motorbike could be heard and then it roared past them. All three looked up and Derek just made out that the colour of the bike was blue and the rider had a matching helmet. Not their man. Bridget must have thought the same, because she leaned her arm on the handle of the door and went back to looking out of the window.

Gloria followed the road to the end before a sharp left bend took them back up the other side of the loch. And the hill was quite steep, so that by the time the road was levelling out they could see out over the vista below. Derek read from his phone that they had reached the Scord of Weisdale Viewpoint, but didn't bother to say. He felt as if he needed to limit what he told them both for fear of being tedious. It was as if he was on a knife edge with Gloria and all he wanted to do was impress her. Perhaps he should get married and call himself Paul. Gloria might take notice of him, but then he remembered that Paul had been dumped.

'I feel as if we are weaving back and forth,' Gloria said.

'We are,' said Derek. 'It's the only way to navigate the fractured lands and to get around the water.'

'And it means if you miss something the first time, you're very likely to have another chance to see it,' Bridget said, and Gloria laughed.

Derek was prepared for a sharp retort from Bridget but she didn't give one. Instead, she said something really quite nice, to his surprise.

'Thanks for stopping, Gloria,' she said. 'I've never seen an otter in the wild. It was a great opportunity. I hope you do get to see some seals.'

And then no one had much to say after that for a while.

As they travelled further west, the roads narrowed. There were passing places in case of oncoming traffic, but they hadn't seen another vehicle since the motorbike. The car wheels clattered over cattle grids and Gloria slowed right down.

'What is it we're doing when we get there?' Bridget asked.

'We're popping into the wool mill,' Derek said.

They'd talked about it over breakfast. They'd had a message from Shona to say that Louise would be expecting them. Shona also asked if they would join her this afternoon for a get-together. A few local knitters were meeting and wanted to have the afternoon with them and Norman. Makkin and yakkin, she'd called it – a Shetland knit and natter. Bridget seemed to have forgotten already. Derek was going to remind her to look at her phone occasionally. They could all read the messages in the group chat, but it seemed that Bridget didn't bother.

'The wool mill,' she repeated. 'Oh, yes, the wool mill. I'm looking forward to that.'

He chanced a glance at Gloria, but she had her eyes firmly on the road.

'Once we've been in the mill, there's a coastal walk and we can get a photo with Norman in the most westerly point of the mainland. We've been down to the most southerly point and we'll end up at the most northerly, so it makes sense.'

'What about the easternmost point?' Bridget asked.

'That's the tricky one,' Derek said. 'That's Bound Skerry, which is an island thirteen miles from the mainland. There aren't any ferries running, but I did think we could travel to Lunning and get a photo of it in the background.'

'Thirteen miles?' Gloria said. 'I imagine it would have to be a very clear day for that.'

'Aren't we just adding things to this list that we don't need to, or did Norman ask for this specifically?' Bridget said.

There was silence for a moment while Derek thought how best to answer. In truth the list wasn't that extensive and Norman's wishes were mostly related to people and places in his knitting world. But Derek was here right now, he felt as if he was on holiday and it was the most interesting thing he'd done in a long time. He wasn't ready to go home yet. Would it hurt to string it all out for a bit longer? If he could just keep the women in order. He nearly laughed out loud at that thought. Neither would be impressed if they could hear what was going through his mind and the idea that he had any control over the situation was laughable.

'Let's see how things pan out,' he said.

They drove into Sandness, which was little more than a church and a small school with a few homesteads. It was here that Derek pinpointed what it was he was beginning to love about Shetland. It was the big sky. Because there weren't any trees and the land was fairly flat here, the sky was completely uninterrupted for a full 360 degrees. It seemed to fill his heart in a way that he couldn't quite understand. He kept his revelation to himself and they drove on until they got to the mill and Gloria parked up outside. It wasn't like the many-windowed, huge brick mills Derek knew in the north of England; Jamieson's was a modern, flat-roofed, sprawling building.

'I feel like we're on a school trip,' Gloria said as they pushed the door open.

Derek knew very little about wool and how it got from the sheep grazing in the fields outside to a ball attached to his knitting needles, but after half an hour with Louise explaining the process, he felt like an expert. The mill ran at full speed all year round and was usually only open to visitors during Shetland Wool Week and for organised knitting tour groups, so Shona had worked her magic to get them through the door.

Gloria held Norman's urn as Louise told them about the buying in of the fleeces from the local crofters, the washing process through huge machines, the dyeing and then the carding and tearing before the spinning and plying and then the skeining and packaging. Derek began to feel a bit choked thinking about how much Norman would have loved this. Gloria put a hand on his arm.

'Are you okay?' she asked him, and he embarrassed himself by sniffing.

'Just thinking about Norman missing this,' he said.

'Norman did a tour with me,' Louise said.

'What? How?' asked Gloria.

'I did a live tour online and Norman was in the group. It was last year.'

'That makes me so happy,' Bridget said. 'It's not quite the same as being here, but he didn't miss out completely.'

'I think this is a lovely thing you're doing for him,' Louise said.

'We owe him,' said Gloria, and Derek couldn't help but sniff again.

# 16

## SUNDAY TEA

*Gloria*

They left the mill after posing for a photo with Louise and with an intention to visit the Jamieson's of Shetland shop in Lerwick to see Lynn, at Louise's suggestion, and their range of three hundred colours of wool.

'Haven't made all that much progress with my salmon colour yet,' Bridget said. 'Not sure I need to be buying any more.'

'It will be nice to see it, even if we don't buy any,' Derek said. 'I feel so inspired after listening to Louise.'

'You'll have time to catch up with your knitting at the lunch this afternoon,' Gloria said.

'I don't think I can show myself up in front of proper knitters,' said Bridget.

'They'll probably be happy to help you with it,' said Derek.

'But I'd feel like a fool.'

'Well, I don't care,' said Gloria. 'I want to get some done and it will be the perfect place to do it.'

She drove away from the mill and kept going until she ran out of road and then stopped the car. There was a tourist sign with a map of the headland and another telling them they were on their way to Huxter Ancient Water Mills.

'Is this on his list?' Bridget asked.

'Looks like it is now,' Gloria said.

They set off along the coastal path until they could see the drystone walls of the water mills. There was a set of three with the one closest to the sea in the best condition, with a thatched roof covered in what looked to Gloria like fishing net. The ground was uneven and not the easiest to navigate, but they made it down to the stream and looked inside to see the horizontal paddles. Derek had been reading to them about the ancient water mills and Gloria didn't want to say it, but she wasn't that interested.

'Well, they're super cute,' she said and then got Norman out of her bag and asked them all to pose for a photo because she was keen to find a bathroom sooner rather than later. It was the running water; it really didn't help.

They posed with Norman in front and a view of the islands of Papa Stour behind them, then they set off back to the car, content that another of Norman's wishes had been fulfilled.

Gloria's phone hadn't stopped buzzing in her pocket for the last hour. She wasn't sure how many other ways she could tell Paul to get lost. She was mostly just annoyed at herself for letting it go on so long. When he told her he was married she was shocked. She wasn't into dating married men, but by that point he'd got under her skin, made her feel wonderful, desirable, and he made little to no demands on her. She thought that if she didn't think about a wife, if he didn't talk about her or his other life, it didn't exist. What a fool she was.

She saw them together once and it was that that had sealed their fate. She was driving through town, not intending to be anywhere near Paul's house, but she had to get to a friend's for lunch and it was the most direct route. There they were, walking up the high street looking like the epitome of the older married couple. They were holding hands, for goodness' sake. Gloria had put her foot down until she'd cleared the town centre and then pulled into a side street, opened her car door and tried to get out, but she realised her legs weren't working properly. She sat for ten minutes breathing deeply and wondered if she might be sick. In the end, a man who was walking his dog asked her if she was okay and she'd smiled, nodded and then closed her door and drove away. The next time she'd seen Paul had been the night before Norman's funeral when she'd felt so low she hadn't been able to say no. It wasn't just sex she wanted. She'd hoped that Paul would wrap his arms around her and tell her everything would be okay. She'd meant to say that was it then, but she hadn't. She'd chosen to wait until she was in a car on the way to Shetland, just as he was leaving his wife.

She pulled her phone out and checked the screen as they left the water mill. Yes, there were five missed calls and two messages from him, but there was also a message from Charlotte. It had come through on their group chat, but neither of the other two had read it. Derek was always busy with his history of the islands and Bridget never looked at her phone.

> Hey, you three! Well, I posted the photo of Ida on Norman's profile and we've had several positive suggestions, although different locations. Go on Insta and have a look for yourselves. You'll see that someone thinks they might be a family member. Douglas Makay is his name. He doesn't have much of a profile. Just says he's from Shetland and there's a pic of him with his dog. Not very encouraging. I've sent him a message and waiting to hear back.

Hope you're all okay and I'll get back to you if I
hear anything.

Gloria opened her Instagram app and looked at the messages. There were loads. Norman's popularity hadn't waned since his death; quite the opposite.

'Look at this,' she said, turning to the others. 'We've had a bunch of suggestions about the location of the photo. I knew it was a good idea. There's someone who thinks they might be family too. Charlotte's going to get back to us when she's heard back from them. I think we're closing in.'

'Where are the locations?' Derek asked.

'One in Yell, wherever that is, and all the others are a castle in Unst. I think we should go with the majority. Isn't that the northernmost island where the lighthouse is? Norman's ashes lighthouse, I mean. So, it means a couple of ferries doesn't it?'

'Yell is the next island north and then you're right, Unst is where Norman wants us to scatter him,' Derek said, and Gloria saw he looked animated. He was enjoying himself.

'Tomorrow then?' Gloria said. 'We won't have time after the lunch; it'll be too dark.'

'How long will it take?' Bridget asked.

'It should only take about an hour to get up there but depends how much driving around to find the locations we'll have to do,' he said. 'I wondered. We don't go too far past Brae and there's the UK's most northerly fish and chip shop there – Frankie's. It's supposed to be good. What do you both say we divert and stop there on the way back for dinner? It's another box ticked.'

'Fine with me,' Gloria said, and even Bridget perked up a bit.

'What about the weather?' Bridget asked. 'Will the ferry be running if it turns bad?'

'We can check before we leave. Apparently the website says

there's no need to book. Especially at this time of year, there won't be many, if any, tourists and it'll mostly just be used by the locals.'

'You're starting to sound like a local yourself, Derek, with all this information,' Gloria said. 'And don't forget, we are tourists.'

She posted the latest photos to Charlotte and then they headed down to Sandwick.

* * *

The community hall was just outside the centre of the village and there was a pleasant vibe inside. Several tables were laid for lunch and a group of people were serving bowls of soup with bread, and there were dishes filled with dessert lined up for afters.

'This isn't for us, surely,' Bridget said.

'No, it's one of our Sunday teas.'

Gloria spun round to find Shona behind her.

'Shona, lovely to see you again,' she said. 'You do this a lot, then?'

'Aye, there are many places around the islands you can get your Sunday tea. They're a tradition in the local community. So many places are remote and it's a warm and welcoming atmosphere to bring folk together. A few of our local knitters were keen to meet you three when they heard you were here with Norman. Your tea is on us. Go and pick up what you want and come and join us.'

Gloria could sense Derek tensing up beside her, and when she turned she could see his lip was trembling.

'That's really good of you,' she said and steered Derek over to the food.

Gloria and Derek took some soup and bread while Bridget went to get a tray.

'Are you okay?' she asked him again, and he nodded.

'I am, but every time someone shows Norman some love I feel so sad for him.'

'I get it, but remember what Louise said earlier about how he'd already had a tour of the mill and how Shona told us about his involvement with Shetland Wool Week. You know what I think. While we three have been agonising over Norman's accident and our part in it, he'd just been getting on with the business of living.'

Derek looked at her, surprised. It was the first time any one of them had openly acknowledged this.

'It's the biggest elephant in the room, Derek, and at some point we're really going to have to talk about it, don't you think?'

He didn't respond, though, because Bridget bustled back with a tray.

There were eight knitters at Shona's table. Some had already eaten and were hard at work with their needles. Gloria was amazed at how fast their fingers were moving and she said so to the woman sitting next to her, who introduced herself as Janette.

'Not as fast as our very own Shetlander, Hazel Tindall,' she said. 'She has the title of the World's Fastest Knitter.'

'Goodness,' Bridget said from across the table as she finished her soup. 'Is she here today?'

'Yes, she's right there.'

Janette pointed to a woman at the other end of the table who was wearing a belt around her waist which had a knitting needle sticking out of it. Her fingers were moving at such a speed, it was a blur to Gloria. These women were serious knitters.

'I think I'm completely out of my depth,' Gloria said.

'If you ever get the opportunity to do one of her classes then do, she's amazing at showing you how to put colour combinations together in her Fair Isle knitting.'

Bridget put the spoon in her empty bowl and reached into her bag for her own knitting and Gloria was surprised and pleased when she handed it across the table to Janette.

'I only learned to knit yesterday and this is what I've achieved so far,' she said. 'The ribbing is wonky and I'm sure I've dropped stitches along the way. My knit and purl don't seem to match up.'

'I think you should be immensely proud of yourself for bothering to pick up the needles in the first place and have a go, and then to keep at it.'

'I'm doing it for Norman,' Bridget said.

There was a ripple of agreement around the table and the knitters talked about their own personal interactions with Norman and how much he had been part of their community even though it had been online.

'See, I told you,' Gloria leaned in and whispered to Derek.

'And Norman's advice was that it's always better to spret back,' Janette said, handing Bridget back her unfinished hat. 'It's painful, but it's better in the long run.'

'Spret back?' Gloria said. 'What on earth is that? Throw it in the trash?'

'No.' Shona laughed. 'It just means to unravel it to where you think you've gone wrong.'

'If you do that, Bridget, I'll help you get your stitches back on the needles,' Janette said.

'I'm going to sit with Hazel Tindall,' Derek said. 'I'd like to ask her about the belt she uses.'

They spent a relaxing couple of hours with the women and Gloria surprised herself with how much she enjoyed sitting, knitting and nattering, or makkin and yakkin as the women called it. Then, just before they were about to leave, Gloria insisted they all pose for a photo with Norman. They all lined up with Derek in the back and Gloria in front of him holding the urn. Later, when she had time to look properly at the photo, she would see that Derek wasn't looking at the camera, he was looking down at her. But right then she sent it to Charlotte to update their progress and they thanked the knitters for their stories and their hospitality and began to gather their things.

It was only as they were driving back to the hotel that Gloria thought of something.

'We should have asked them if they'd heard of The Knitting Warrior,' she said. 'I'll message Shona and see if she knows who they are.'

Her eyes went to her rearview mirror as she approached a junction and there, a few metres back down the road, was a motorbike.

'For goodness' sake,' she said, and both Derek and Bridget turned round to see what had caught her attention. 'This is ridiculous.'

She slammed on her brakes and stopped in the middle of the road.

'What are you doing?' Bridget said.

'I want to know why we're being followed. I want to give them the opportunity to stop and tell us.'

But the bike wasn't bothered by The Beast and the rider skipped around them and was gone.

## 17

### BACK IN TIME FOR FRANKIE'S?

*Bridget*

They set off quite late the next morning because Gloria overslept. Bridget didn't mind because she wanted a leisurely breakfast after complaining they were doing everything at one hundred miles an hour, and Derek popped along to the wool shop. He came back with a kit to make a cowl and the colours he'd chosen made Bridget think it wasn't going to be for himself. They looked too feminine for Derek.

'I was so inspired by Hazel, yesterday,' he said. 'Did you see her cutting down the front of her work to open it up for a cardigan? She just took the scissors to it, but I think I was the only one who winced. Steeking, she called it. The speed of her needles when she was knitting was impressive. What an interesting woman.'

'As interesting as Gloria?' Bridget asked with a small smile and was convinced that Derek blushed.

'Just different,' he said, busying himself with his purchases. 'I bought a knitting belt too.'

'Do you know how to use it?'

'No, but Hazel showed me a little bit and I'm going to get her instructional video from her website. If you want me, I'll be knitting,' he said and laughed.

They were just climbing into the car a while later as the first drops of rain began to fall. Gloria set her windscreen wipers to a steady rhythm and pulled away from the hotel with her eyes peeled. Even from the back seat, Bridget could tell she was on high alert.

Bridget looked behind her, but there were only a couple of other cars on this stretch of road out of Lerwick.

'I feel really uneasy,' she said. 'I just can't understand why we'd be followed. Three pensioners hardly pose a threat to anyone.'

She began to yawn. Another night where she'd found it difficult to sleep. She nearly phoned Graham at three to hear some comforting words but felt it would be a little bit too mean to wake him up. When she phoned him after breakfast he didn't answer at all and then she began to worry he'd had an accident or something. He sent her a message to say he was in the supermarket and he'd phone her back later and Bridget relaxed a little.

'I really don't know, Bridget,' Derek said. 'But I'm choosing to assume it's someone who's interested in our journey and even though it's a bit odd, it's no more than that.'

'It's completely weird and creepy if you ask me,' Gloria said. 'Perhaps I'll run him off the road next time I see him.'

Derek's attention was firmly on the screen of his phone, but he did smile. Bridget didn't think a car accident was remotely amusing, but she was grateful for Derek's presence in the passenger seat. He was merrily reading up about whatever history he could relay to them both later. He was capable and strong. He was keeping them on the right track. Bridget doubted *she'd* be any good at navigating. Despite the late start, her eyes were feeling heavy again. In fact she might have just dropped off for a bit, because all was quiet and settled one minute, and the next she could hear Derek's voice from the front.

'Hang on a minute, Gloria. Where are we?'

Bridget looked out of her window and could see the jewellery place they'd passed the day before, where she'd seen the otters in the water.

'I think I've taken a wrong turn,' Gloria said. 'This is the route from yesterday, isn't it? Clearly I wasn't concentrating. Shall I turn around?'

'Carry on a bit further and then take the turning off to the right, just up ahead, towards Aith,' Derek said. 'We may as well go up and rejoin the A470 at Voe, then we'll be on track to get to the fish and chip shop in Brae. It's hardly worth turning around now, anyway, and we'll see a stretch of Shetland we wouldn't have otherwise.'

She took the turning and they travelled uphill for a while. Bridget noticed a sign for a place called Twatt and was going to make a joke but couldn't form the words correctly in her head. She had a feeling it might fall flat and she'd be left looking silly.

Once they had passed Aith the road narrowed considerably.

'The locals call this stretch of road The Alps,' Derek said.

It was narrow, winding and hilly in places with no pavement and the tarmac dropped away either side into the grass. Bridget thought she wouldn't fancy driving on this road and had a moment of admiration for Gloria.

'Have you noticed how good all the roads are here? Round my way they're potholed everywhere,' Gloria said.

'Same as round my way,' said Derek. 'I guess we get more traffic, lorries and the like.'

'My way too, although I don't drive that much any more. Graham's the driver in our household.'

'You wouldn't have thought it, though,' Gloria said. 'These remote islands with their wild weather and super smooth roads.' She flicked the lever to make the wipers speed up as the rain increased in volume. 'Anyway, what do you think we'll hear from this mystery family member?'

'Absolutely no idea. I expect it's a wild goose chase. A seventy-year-old photo and someone says, *I recognise that lady.* I'd be very surprised,' Derek said, and Gloria laughed.

'You could easily be the new least complicated man in my life,' she said.

Bridget suddenly felt like a gooseberry in the back of the car. She could see the side of Derek's face and his cheek wasn't a dissimilar colour to her salmon wool.

'What's that?' she suddenly said at what looked like a huge fridge on the side of the road.

'It looks like a cake fridge with an honesty box,' Derek said, and Gloria pulled in. 'They have them all over the Shetland Islands apparently. I've been reading about them.'

It wasn't just the fridge, there was a small café too, although Bridget saw from the sign it was closed. She got out in the rain to investigate and Gloria followed her, their coats pulled up over their hair. It wasn't just cake, there were jams and chutneys, honey and biscuits. One section wasn't a fridge at all and had knitted hats and greetings cards, handmade jewellery. Everything had a price on it and there was a locked box with a slot in the top.

'I'm amazed,' Gloria said. 'The trust is incredible.'

'These chocolate brownies look delicious,' Bridget said, lifting out a box of four.

'I'm tempted to buy that hat to save me from knitting one,' Gloria said.

They shared a smile and then pushed enough money in the slot before dashing back to the car.

'Impressive,' Derek said.

'All you get near me is a few eggs occasionally and some manky-looking cooking-apple windfalls in the autumn,' Gloria said. 'Right, come on, let's get to this fish and chip place; I really need a wee now.'

They began steadily driving uphill and then reached a bit of a plateau at the top. Bridget could see another body of water ahead of them down the other side of the hill.

'This is big sky country,' Derek said with admiration in his voice.

'I think that phrase is usually attributed to Montana,' Gloria said.

'Look around you, Gloria. A three-hundred-and-sixty-degree view of the sky, and you can't deny it,' Derek said looking straight at her and not at the view at all.

'I wouldn't dream of it,' Gloria said, and for once she didn't sound condescending.

Bridget noted there was admiration in Gloria's voice and she wasn't looking at the view. She was looking right at Derek.

Brae was another beautiful place on the water with houses that had a Scandinavian feel. Frankie's café was so clean and the menu so inviting that Bridget wished she'd skipped breakfast and that they were here for lunch. They all popped in to use the loo and booked a table for dinner for when they were on their way back. The woman that took the booking reminded them that the last orders were taken at six and they promised they'd be back in plenty of time.

Then they were off again up to Toft, where the ferry terminal was. Gloria got in the lane that had the words *un-booked* painted on the tarmac and they sat and watched as the ferry sailed in and some very ominous-looking black clouds seemed to roll in with it. The rear windscreen wiper wasn't working and, because of that, when Bridget glanced over her shoulder to see how many other vehicles were using the ferry, she didn't notice the motorbike roll in next to the van that sat behind them. The rider's helmet was orange.

Bridget had nearly fallen asleep on the journey up to Toft. Just as she had relaxed into her seat, though, as her eyes had grown heavy again and she shifted her position to get more comfortable, her knitting needles had poked through her bag and jabbed in her hip. After that she had just kept her eyes closed in the hope she'd drop off again, but sleep eluded her and instead her thoughts went back to the person on the motorbike. She was annoyed that neither Gloria nor even Derek had taken her seriously when she'd first mentioned it and then, when it was clear she was right, she'd not had even a hint of an apology. It was as if they were treating her like a child that had a tall tale not to be believed. Yes, she had memory issues, but she wasn't stupid.

Sitting there now in the queue for the ferry, she was beginning to feel a bit sullen, a bit like a child, actually. She pulled her knitting out of the bag and tried again to work the hat's ribbing in the round now that Janette had got her stitches back on the needles. It wasn't going very well and she was ripping it back as much as she was knitting. Then she remembered the word the women had used at the Sunday tea. Spretting it back, that's what she was doing.

The ferry arrived and cars began to roll off, then they were waved forward and they drove into what looked like the mouth of a blue shark. It was the front of the boat that had opened up like jaws and it even had a serrated edge, like teeth.

'How do we pay?' Gloria asked. 'I hope this isn't going to be like one of those parking lots where you have to have already done it online or have an app.'

'It isn't,' Derek said. 'I'm looking at it online and it says that someone will come around to take the money.'

'Like the good old days,' said Gloria.

They sat in the car and waited on the car deck. The ferry wasn't anything as big as the one that came from Aberdeen and they hadn't left Toft at that point, but Bridget could already feel the swell beneath them and her night of vomiting came flooding back to her. Derek turned around in his seat and offered her a warm smile.

'Thirty minutes tops,' he said. 'We'll be in Yell in no time.'

Gloria actually used her card when the chap came round to take payment and Bridget very nearly made a comment about that not being very *good old days,* but she chose to keep her thoughts to herself. He told them to check the ferry times for coming back because the Met Office had issued an amber weather warning, so they might stop running after a certain time. Gloria seemed unfazed, but Bridget's worry sensors pricked up. Storm Beryl was coming.

'We need to be able to get back later. We don't want to be stuck on the island with nowhere to sleep.'

'The last one is eleven-thirty tonight,' said Derek. 'We'll be long back before that.'

'If the weather holds,' Bridget said.

'I'll keep a close eye,' he said, although it wasn't lost on her that he'd not been keeping that close an eye up until now.

They left the car and decided to stretch their legs and find somewhere to sit upstairs.

'I'm so impressed with all the ferries up here,' Gloria said. 'So comfortable, so clean and actually quite plush.'

They found plenty of seats available as it was so out of season, they were almost the only people on board, and they watched the view from the huge window as they made their way across the water.

'This body of water is called the Yell Sound,' Derek informed them.

Bridget wasn't listening, though, because she'd just noticed a man in black leathers with an orange helmet on his head. She almost jumped at the sight of him.

Derek stood up. His stance was defensive and also protective, Bridget noticed. She moved into the seat next to Gloria and felt her heartrate increase. Did he have a gun, a knife, a weapon of any kind? Bridget felt her hand clutched all of a sudden by Gloria's. She didn't have time to wonder if Gloria was fearful or just being kind to her, as he was almost upon them. Then, just as he was a couple of metres from them and just as Bridget imagined him reaching into a non-existent pocket to pull out an equally non-existent gun, he veered away and headed down towards the toilets as if he'd never intended to approach them at all.

Gloria snatched her hand back and began to laugh.

'Well, that was intense,' she said. 'Think I need a drink.'

'Shall I go and find him, have it out with him?' Derek said.

'I think not,' said Gloria.

'You're the one who stopped in the middle of the road yesterday to square up to him,' Bridget said.

'Yes, but on reflection I think maybe we should keep our distance.'

'Why the change of mind?'

'Sensible sanity,' Gloria said. 'And I wouldn't want you taking a punch on the chin, Derek.'

They sat quite tense and waited for the man to come back past them, but he never reappeared. Almost as if he was a figment of their imagination, but they couldn't possibly have *all* made him up.

'I could still track him down,' Derek said. 'We can't actually lose him on a ferry. He'll be easy to find on the car deck.'

'No, I think we stay away and hopefully he'll go away,' Bridget said. 'Gloria's right, we should keep our distance.'

The wind was picking up and the water was getting choppier. By the time they docked in Ulsta, Bridget was keen to get back in The Beast and get off the ferry. The motorbike was right at the front of the queue of parked vehicles now and had obviously moved, but they got in and shut their doors. The man in the orange helmet didn't look back at them and as soon as the vehicles began to move he was gone. The sky was almost black now and Gloria said she had to hang onto the steering wheel to stop the car getting tugged away from her as they made their way onto Yell.

'I think we should just wait for the next ferry back and not be messing around like this,' Bridget said. 'We can do it tomorrow. I doubt the view will change overnight.'

'But we might not find it easily; we might well be coming back tomorrow anyway. We're still waiting for a message back from Charlotte with a lead on the family member, don't forget,' said Derek.

'But the weather!' Bridget said.

'This is Shetland,' Gloria said. 'They often have bad weather. They wouldn't run the ferries if it was unsafe and it's such a short hop across the water that if it's a bit rough then we can handle it. Anyway, Storm Beryl? Like I said to you before, Bridget, it sounds like a mild breeze to me. What do you say, Derek?'

Bridget turned her attention to Derek at the same time that Gloria did and he looked uncomfortable for a moment.

'Yes, Derek,' Bridget said. 'What do you think we should do?'

Bridget could hear the slightly scathing tone in her voice. She already knew what Derek thought. He'd be going with whatever Gloria suggested. They were back to being a team again, just as they had been in the factory, but neither of them seemed to realise it. Derek always used to stick up for Gloria if another worker was disrespecting the boss and Gloria seemed oblivious to the special attention Derek would get from her. It might be the offer of an hour off if he needed to do something, leaving his favourite brand of teabag (Yorkshire Tea, obviously) in the staff kitchen or just simply singing his praises when he worked harder than a colleague. Bridget had forgotten all of this, but it was coming back to her now she was with the two of them.

'I do think as we've made it this far that we should keep going. As you've said a few times, Bridget, you'd like to get home sooner rather than later. The quicker we solve the family mystery and get Norman's ashes to the top the better, surely,' Derek said.

That, Bridget thought, was a low blow, but she just took a breath and said nothing, like the child in the back of the car that she was.

'It's less than a thirty-minute drive across Yell to Gutcher, where we can get on the ferry to Unst. That's only ten minutes on the water. So, we can be up on the northernmost island within an hour. Let's go for it!' Derek continued.

Gloria looked at Derek with a broad smile. If she had been testing him, he'd passed with flying colours. Bridget sank back in her seat and tried very hard not to sulk again.

'Well,' she said. 'When it all goes wrong later, don't be blaming me.'

The A road that took them across the island hugged the coast-line for a while and the sea was always in their sight down to the left. Apart from a couple of properties, there didn't seem to be anything else other than some grazing sheep, contained by cattle grids. It felt as if they were the only people on the island. However stunning the scenery was, it was as if there was a whole lot of nothingness. Whenever Bridget did spot a house she was reminded that Gloria might be right about the ferries. For these people they would be a lifeline.

Eventually they moved away from the sea and inland. They passed a series of small lochs and there were plenty of sheep, but still no trees, although Bridget had got used to this now. She saw a couple of bus stops but had yet to see an actual bus.

'Oh, a B&B,' Gloria said as they passed an attractive stone house on the side of the road. 'There is life here after all.'

There was a sign hanging on the wall with *Vacancies* written on it and it gave Bridget immense relief that they wouldn't be stranded in the middle of nowhere after all. If there was accommodation here, there could easily be more on the next island, bearing in mind that they would cater for tourists and at this time of year, they could have the pick of the lot. She settled a bit more after that and turned her thoughts to hopefully finding the location in the photograph. She did have her doubts about it, though. How likely was it that the place mentioned would be easy to find and that they'd just stroll up and there it would be – the exact place where Ida had stood? And then there was the other thought that had dipped in and out of her mind over the last couple of hours – then what? They could take a selfie with Norman in the spot his mother stood, but that was about it. She opened her mouth to voice this thought, as was her habit of sharing so she wouldn't have to remember, but she closed it again. They already thought she was a Moaning Minnie, they didn't need reminding of her negativity. Instead, she took a breath and chose to say something she didn't feel at all.

'I've got a good feeling about this, actually.'

Derek glanced back at her and turned his confused expression to a smile and Gloria looked quizzically at her in the mirror.

'Me too, Bridget,' she said. 'Me too.'

And then Bridget remembered the bike and the odd man with that orange helmet on the ferry, but that she was silent on also. They all knew if he was on the ferry, he'd be on the island. There was no need to state the obvious. She'd look out for him at the next ferry terminal. Perhaps this time she'd play the hero like Derek had. She'd been impressed how he'd stood up to protect her and Gloria. Derek didn't know if the man had a weapon, but that didn't stop him. She glanced over her shoulder and out of the back window, but she couldn't see anything as the rain had intensified. She was about to take out her knitting and unpick the last mess she'd made when Derek announced they were driving into Gutcher. He'd been correct in his timings. With a long empty road and no traffic at all, it had only taken twenty-five minutes.

'Make sure you get in lane two,' Derek told Gloria. 'We don't want to end up at Fetlar.'

'Is that a bad place?' Gloria asked.

'No, just the wrong place.'

Bridget was pleased to see that there was already a ferry there and waiting. Hopefully going to Unst. There was only one other vehicle and it was a motorhome that looked rather top heavy to Bridget. She thought she could see it moving in the wind. The white crests on the water made her feel queasy again, before they'd even boarded.

There was a sign up with information flashed up in lights. It gave the last crossing back here at eight this evening, not the eleven something that Derek had suggested.

'See that?' she asked the others. 'We need to be mindful of the time.'

'We do,' Derek said. 'You're quite right.'

'It's only one o'clock,' Gloria said. 'We've got hours yet. Anyway, we need to be back at Frankie's for six. I want my most northerly fish and chips.'

'Did you say it was only ten minutes, the crossing?' Bridget asked Derek.

'Yes, that's it. Don't even need to get out of the car for this one. Be there before you know it.'

He was a kind man, Bridget thought. A strong man. A good man. Too good for Gloria, that was for sure.

# 18

## MUNESS CASTLE

*Derek*

Derek had his mind firmly on the biker. He was annoyed with himself for not approaching him when he had the opportunity. He felt like a wimp standing there on the ferry with every fibre in his body hoping there wouldn't be a confrontation. He wasn't a man who did altercations. The last time anything close to a situation had occurred he'd been in the car park in Asda supermarket – the big one out of town. A man in a big four-by-four had cut in front of him and pinched the space Derek already had his indicator on for. Derek had been annoyed. It was clear it was his space, but the bloke just parked up, got out and gave a vulgar hand gesture at Derek before striding into the store. Derek had simply found another space further from the front doors and parked there. Once in the store with his basket – he only actually needed some bacon and a pint of milk – he hadn't wanted to bump into the man who'd taken his space. Derek kept his head down and gathered the things he'd needed before heading to the checkout. But there he was, the man from the car park, standing in the aisle pondering over which washing powder to buy, of all things.

'Something you wanna say, mate?'

He was a big bloke, a tough guy with – and Derek usually prided himself on not being judgemental over people's appearance – a tattoo of a snake coiled down his muscled forearm. It was menacing. Well, the bloke was menacing, but the tattoo gave Derek pause for thought. His thought was basically *Keep your trap shut and get to the till as quickly as possible. Do not engage with this man, otherwise he's likely to rip your head off.* Derek was a pensioner and absolutely could not hold his own in a fight. He'd never tested that theory, to be fair, but he was pretty sure he was right.

'No problem,' he'd said. 'Good morning to you.'

Afterwards, as he was driving home, pretending he hadn't been in any sort of situation at all, he felt a sudden and overwhelming sadness at how pathetic he was. He might have lost the weight he'd been carrying around for most of his life, but he hadn't lost that little schoolboy feeling of being bullied and wanting to run away.

Gloria drove onto the ferry and showed her ticket when the chap came round. He reiterated the information about the ferry times.

'Storm Beryl doesn't sound too troublesome,' Gloria said, laughing.

'Don't be so sure; it can get treacherous up here. Don't get caught out,' the ticket man said.

Derek could hear Bridget making a quiet but triumphant noise from the back seat, but Gloria ignored her. They sailed away from Gutcher towards Belmont on Unst and even Derek had to admit that the sky was looking just as threatening as the tattooed man in Asda.

Derek hadn't seen the motorbike on the second ferry, so he

felt more comfortable. If he wasn't on the ferry he couldn't be on the island, it was as simple as that.

'Right, which way?' Gloria asked.

'Straight on,' Derek said.

'Gloria, there is only one road,' Bridget chipped in from the back.

'All right, thank you.'

'There seem to be so few roads on these islands, I would imagine it would be difficult to get lost,' Derek said.

'Don't tempt fate,' said Bridget.

'I managed to get lost earlier,' said Gloria.

'A diversion, that was all,' Derek said.

They followed the road north and the scenery was very much like it had been on Yell. Perhaps a little rockier. After thinking he was looking at a sheep for a few minutes, Derek actually found out it was another one of the white rocks that seemed to litter the grass.

'Turn right here,' he told Gloria when he saw the sign for Uyeasound.

The road was narrower with cattle grids and drystone walls that lined the lane. Not the warm-toned York stone that he knew so well in Yorkshire, but here they used the white rocks that had a chalky appearance. Some were odd shaped and rough; thrown up from the earth, perhaps, rather than smoothed by the sea. They still managed to look coastal, though.

'Take this turning for Muness,' he said, and Gloria steered them onto an even narrower lane. They skirted the water for a bit and then it was flat land and sheep again, cattle grids and only the occasional house. Gloria mused about there being any at all, reminding the other two that this was the last place she'd want to live. In truth, as the wind began to pick up even more and the rain continued, even Derek thought it would take some mettle to survive out here. Yes, you had a car, but you were very much at the mercy of the ferries running in order to get back to civilisation. Then he remembered the honesty fridges dotted around the islands. The people of Shetland were obviously resourceful. And it wasn't just that: could you be a loner up here? He doubted you could be anonymous; the only place you could do that would be in a city. There was a close-knit community spirit, that's what Shona had said. Derek lived in a perfectly nice road with perfectly nice neighbours within a walkable distance to the town centre. How many of his neighbours had he bothered to engage with? Hardly any. He had a sudden wish to move somewhere like this and start again, to become part of a close-knit community spirit. Could Derek start again at seventy-five? He couldn't help but glance at Gloria as he thought this.

'We're very much off the beaten track here, that's for sure,' he said, 'but there are villages on this island too. Not everything is so remote. We passed a bus stop back there.'

'Yes, but as Bridget said before, we've yet to see an actual bus. Oh, is that the castle? Yes, it must be. We're here and it's not taken long at all. We can check it out, go and find somewhere for lunch and be on the ferry home in no time. Oh, ye of little faith, Bridget. It's all working out brilliantly.'

Gloria pulled over by the small and very well-preserved castle and Derek opened the screenshot of the history of the castle he'd taken earlier because, as he suspected, there was no signal here at all.

'"Muness Castle is the most northerly fortification in the British Isles",' he began. '"Built in 1598 by Laurence Bruce of Cultmalindie, half-brother to Robert Stewart, 1st Earl of Orkney. Bruce gave it to his son, Andrew, in 1617. It was burnt by foreign privateers in 1627 and may never have been fully repaired. It was abandoned by the end of the century and sold out of the family in 1718."'

'Well, that is absolutely fascinating, Derek,' Gloria said. 'But the big question is, is it the location in the photo?'

'The only way to be sure is to get out and look,' Bridget said. 'Does it need all of us?'

'Yes, it does,' Gloria said, reaching into her bag for Norman. 'Come on, Norman, let's go and see if your mother was here.'

'Just so you know, there's no roof on that castle,' Derek said as Gloria went to open her door. She stopped and pulled the zip up on her coat. 'And please mind your door. That wind is getting ferocious.'

When Derek opened his own door he thought it was going to be ripped out of his hand and he needed his other to steady it. He glanced back at Bridget, who looked apprehensive.

'Are you staying here?'

'No,' she said. 'I'd better come too or I'll never hear the end of it.'

'I'll get your door,' he said and slammed his own shut.

They battled against the wind to get to the castle and once inside they were able to walk around the crumbling interior. Derek reflected on the lives of the people that had lived there all those centuries ago, although reflection wasn't that easy with the rain coming down from above and the wind howling through every open window.

'The photo wasn't taken inside,' Gloria shouted into the wind. 'We need to get outside.'

'I feel like we already are,' Bridget said.

'Now, logically it must have been taken on this side of the castle,' Gloria said. She'd taken the photo from her pocket and was examining it by holding it up and checking for a match. 'You can see the headland in the background. Over there.'

'You're going to lose that if you're not careful,' Bridget shouted. 'It will blow away.'

'You take Norman, then,' Gloria said and thrust the urn at Bridget, who looked as if she really didn't want to take it. She did, though, just before Derek was going to come to her rescue.

Gloria pointed over her shoulder down to the sea. Derek followed the line to the headland and then looked again at the photo. The houses that were there now were not present in the photograph and must have been built later, but the coastline was unchanged. He made his fingers and thumbs into a square like an artist does to find a composition and he moved them to the edge of the castle and to where Gloria was standing in the same pose as Ida had, all those years ago.

'That's it!' he said. 'I think we've got it.'

'We'd better get a photo with Norman,' Gloria said. 'I want to get the photo to Charlotte as soon as I've got a signal, and she can share it. There are so many positive messages. It's lovely to see.'

Bridget stood in front of the other two as she'd been given charge of Norman and it was Derek's long arm that stretched forward with Gloria's phone to take the photo.

'Can I take a picture of you standing there, Gloria? It would be fun to compare the original with this one now.'

Bridget moved away to the shelter of the other side of the wall and Derek felt bad for a moment that he was basically asking her to get out of the picture. But Gloria seemed to be game and she posed again as she had before.

He lifted his phone to take the photo, one that they could compare with Ida's and one that he already knew he'd spend a lot of time looking at. Derek thought she looked quite majestic standing on the headland with the wind whipping up around her, her hair flying about her face.

They didn't hang around after that. Once he'd taken a couple and Gloria was happy with them, they made their way back to the car at speed, jumped in and all slammed their doors simultaneously.

'I'm beginning to see why Ida did a flit,' Gloria said.

'What do you mean?' Bridget asked, but Derek knew what she was going to say.

'I mean, imagine you're twenty, knocked up, and find yourself here. Maybe she thought she'd never be able to have nice hair again.'

Gloria laughed, but Bridget didn't.

'You don't have to be so flippant all the time,' Bridget said. 'I'm sure there was a deeper level of thought about her predicament than her hair. Not everyone is so obsessed with their appearance.'

'Be honest, Bridget. Most twenty-year-olds are.'

# 19

## HONESTY CAFÉ

### *Gloria*

'Now what?' Bridget said.

'Now we go and find somewhere nice for lunch. Somewhere nice and dry,' said Gloria.

'I didn't mean *what now* as in, *where are we going for lunch*,' Bridget said. 'I meant, now we know where the photo was taken, what now? It really doesn't feel like such a big deal.'

'We weren't sure if she was ever in Shetland for certain, other than her confused and dying words to Norman. Now we do know she was here. We have a photo of Ida dated July 1951, when we know she would have been pregnant with Norman, and she's in Unst. Somewhere she never ever told Norman she'd been. Derek, help me out here. Bridget isn't getting it.'

'I do get it, actually,' she said, indignantly, 'but what do we do with that information? Hang around in the hope that someone from Instagram pops up and says they suddenly remember they had sex with Ida in 1951 just before she disappeared?'

Gloria snorted and Derek looked out of the side window. He

always did that when he felt uncomfortable, Gloria noted. She pushed her hands through her hair and pulled the sun visor down to look at her reflection in the mirror. It wasn't good, but there was nothing she could do about it now, so she ruffled it up as best she could and started the engine to warm up the car. Her powder compact was in her bag, but she decided not to fix her face. She couldn't bear the judgement from the back seat. Why Bridget was so disparaging she didn't know. What did it matter to her that Gloria took pride in her appearance? Gloria had always wanted to look her best. Tim had been pleased she'd taken so much care of herself. He'd always been proud of her. She liked the appreciative glances both men and women gave her. It was a much-needed boost for an older lady. She hadn't had any surgery, never touched Botox, but equally wouldn't rule it out if she felt she needed it. Bridget was just a typical, unhappy old woman who'd forgotten how to have fun. As she thought this, Gloria acknowledged the word *forgotten*. Perhaps Bridget had every reason to be unhappy and joyless if she thought she was going to end up in the same place as her father. She made a mental note to be a little kinder, more forgiving – well, she'd certainly try.

'For now, we can just send the photos to Charlotte and see what happens,' Gloria said. 'You had a good feeling about this, do you remember, Bridget?'

Bridget didn't answer and Gloria wasn't sure if it was because she couldn't remember or that she was just quietly annoyed with her. She turned her attention to Derek.

'Can you find us a place for a light, late lunch, my navigating legend?' she said and was delighted to see Derek's shy smile.

'I wish I could, but I don't have signal at all. Let's just retrace our steps until I can start looking. We'll not get anything with regards to restaurants or cafés off my paper map.'

Gloria navigated the road back towards Uyeasound and the

car was buffeted from both sides. She hung on tightly to the steering wheel and didn't tell the others that even she was beginning to feel a little disconcerted at the worsening storm.

Once Derek had his signal back, he said that the options weren't vast if they kept to the south of the island and near to the ferry, but there was a café where they could certainly get a hot drink and a light snack.

'There's a loo too,' he said, and there was a collective sigh of relief from both Gloria and Bridget.

'We've got those brownies from the honesty fridge,' Bridget said.

'We won't want much anyway,' said Gloria. 'I don't want to spoil my appetite for those most northerly fish and chips.'

'If we can get back on the ferry, that is,' Bridget said. 'I think we should just go back now. Can you check to see if the timetable has changed, please, Derek?'

'My signal has dropped out again. We're quite near the café now; let's get a drink and then see.'

The café, it turned out, was another honesty box. It was outside a house, right on the seafront with a table and a couple of chairs tucked inside an old shelter. Gloria pulled up as close as she could and then got out to investigate. There wasn't anyone around, but maybe they were indoors keeping out of the appalling weather. There was a kettle sitting inside an upturned crate, plugged in and with a sign to an outside tap to fill it. Several other boxes had crisps and biscuits and cups with hot chocolate and coffee and there was a drawer with a pot for coins and a large pebble with the word *notes* written on it in pen. There was a five-pound note tucked underneath and a good few coins in the pot. No one was around, so she filled the kettle and stuck her head back in the car to take orders.

'It's like a drive-through café,' she chuckled.

They all chose the hot chocolate option to keep them going. Derek handed her a fiver and she stuck it under the pebble to cover what they'd had. Then she noticed there was a notebook with a pen and she opened it to see that people had written a list of what they'd taken and how much money they'd left. There were little notes of appreciation too, which made her smile. She left her own and signed it from the best friends of Norman Knits. And that was when a little niggle started in her mind. She opened the car door and handed over the drinks, then she looked over Bridget's knees and into the footwell. Then, she glanced over the seats into the back.

'Where's Norman?' she asked. 'Did you put him back in my bag?'

Gloria had her bag in her hand now and was rummaging through the contents, but really, Norman's urn was substantial enough that it couldn't be hiding in the depths.

Bridget looked stricken when Gloria looked up and she knew straight away, before Bridget even said anything, that he was gone.

'I think we left him in the castle,' she said. 'I'm sure he'll still be there if we pop back.'

'You left him in the castle?'

'*We* left him. I don't remember being in sole charge of him.'

'Well, that's exactly what you were: in sole charge. And that's the trouble, isn't it? You don't remember.'

Gloria barked this out and could see that Bridget was taken aback.

'Let's just get back there,' Derek said. 'I'm sure he'll still be there waiting for us.'

'If he hasn't blown away,' Gloria said.

'I need to use the loo,' Bridget said, and Gloria had to bite back her response because she did too.

Once they had all relieved themselves in the dilapidated and incredibly welcome toilet, Gloria started the engine and turned the car around to head back the way they'd come, hopeful that Derek was right and that Bridget had popped him down somewhere dry and out of the wind, but it was quite the hope bearing in mind he'd been left in a roofless sixteenth-century castle.

'I can't believe you just left him behind,' Gloria started again. 'How hard is it to keep hold of an urn, for goodness' sake?'

Gloria didn't need an answer, which was good because it was clear she wasn't going to get one. Bridget was silent in the back of the car. Gloria had to hang on tight to the steering wheel as the car moved against the wind. It felt like trying to keep hold of a huge dog, pulling on a lead. If she let go of the steering wheel it really did feel as if the car would fly away.

They were back in sight of the castle within only half an hour and Gloria began to feel a little less uneasy. The rain had intensified and the wind was getting incredibly gusty, but if they could just have Norman back with them she'd feel even better still.

The lane was wet and the wipers were on their highest setting, frantically whipping back and forth across the screen, but even so, it was becoming increasingly difficult to see where she was going. Then, seemingly from out of nowhere, a motorbike appeared in front of her and Gloria swerved to avoid it. In doing so, she hit the front of the car on one of the large white rocks on the grass. The bike sped past them, and was gone but not before she'd registered that the colour of the rider's helmet was that unmistakable orange.

'Damn it,' she said as she righted the car back onto the road and carried on. 'I didn't see the bike until it was too late. The rain is making visibility almost impossible. How the rider is staying on that bike is beyond me.'

But something wasn't right with the car. She found that the

steering wheel was pulling to the left quite considerably. She managed to keep the car straight until they were right outside the castle and Bridget climbed out.

'I'll go,' she said. 'No need for us all to get wet and I know where I popped him down so I could pull on my gloves.'

Gloria opened her mouth to say something more, but when she took in Derek's firm expression, she closed it again. Don't say something you'll regret, his face said, and he was probably right. Gloria swallowed her frustration.

'That bike,' she said, turning to Derek. 'I think we might have to assume it's no longer a coincidence. I just don't know what their game is. What's the point of chasing us around the islands and not bothering to speak to us? Is it sinister? It's certainly incredibly annoying.'

'I don't know,' Derek said. 'I agree, it's very strange, but with all the social media attention perhaps they just wanted to come along for the ride, as it were. Norman was a big deal in his world.'

'I'm not sure,' Gloria said, folding her arms across her chest. 'Bridget's taking her time. I'm going to see what she's doing.'

'I'll come too,' Derek said, and Gloria knew it was to keep the peace.

Bridget was standing in the middle of the main part of the castle with her hands over her face. When Gloria approached her, Bridget lowered her hands and her expression was a picture of shock.

'He's gone,' she said. 'He's gone.'

## 20

### WHERE'S NORMAN?

*Derek*

Gloria looked as if she'd been slapped, her face as shocked as Bridget's. Derek searched the whole area, assuming that Bridget hadn't looked properly, but he wasn't there. Bridget was right, somehow Norman had vanished. Derek felt it was up to him to take charge, but he had no idea how. He decided that standing there and getting drenched was not the answer and urged them back to the car.

They all bundled back inside The Beast and Gloria turned the key to start the engine.

'We need to find the motorcyclist,' she said. 'That's who has him. That's who's kidnapped him.'

'Possibly,' Derek said. 'But possibly not.'

'Derek, we haven't passed another person or car for miles. That bike happened to be at the castle and now Norman is gone? No, we need to get him back. We have to find the bike.'

She began turning the car around, but it was clear something was wrong.

'I don't think we're going anywhere,' Derek said. 'I think that rock has done some serious damage to the wheel.'

He pulled his hood up again and got out to look. It was simple, the tyre was flat and there was a big dent in the underside of the bumper. He walked around to the back of the car and opened the boot.

'I'm going to change the wheel. It's completely flat. We can't go anywhere on it. Shit!' Derek said, which made both women turn to him in surprise. 'There's no spare, no puncture repair kit, no nothing, just a big space where it should all be.'

His words seemed to be whipped away in the wind, even though he'd been shouting.

'What do we do now?' Bridget asked. 'We need to get the ferry. We need to leave the island. We're supposed to be having fish and chips at six. We have to get Norman back. God, I'm so sorry.'

'Don't worry,' Derek said, but he was worried. They were in the middle of nowhere. Not a hope of getting back to the ferry before they stopped running. The last time he'd been able to look, when they stopped at the honesty café, the Met Office had raised the weather warning from amber to red. He'd not told the girls yet; he hadn't wanted Bridget catastrophising before they knew their options. Now, he was very concerned. This could be serious. He did not want them to bed down in The Beast for the night in this weather. They'd all perish. 'The only thing we can do is to get the car off the road, gather our essentials and walk down to the house at the end of this lane. Ask them if they can help us with the number for a recovery vehicle. Or take us to a hotel or B&B.'

Gloria had been oddly quiet for a while, which was disconcerting and unusual. Derek thought she'd be shouting at Bridget. He closed the boot and got back into the passenger seat.

'Do you want me to move it?' he asked her gently, but she seemed to rally then.

'No, I'll do it. I'll get it over and into that gap,' she said, pointing to a space at the end of the drystone wall that surrounded the castle.

It was obvious the tyre was flat as she drove. Derek's side was dipping low. Gloria parked as best she could and they gathered their things.

It was no fun whatsoever walking down the lane, but it was the only option available to them. Derek was in the middle of the group and it was awkward battling against the wind. They had their bags with them too, and Bridget's kept bumping into his side until she swapped it to her other shoulder and nearly lost it in a huge gust.

The house was a rundown-looking stone property with pallets stacked out the front with tarpaulin flapping where it hadn't been tied down properly. Derek didn't think any of it would be there in the morning. An old, battered car sat under a makeshift carport that had so many holes in the roof he couldn't imagine it gave the car much shelter. Other things were stored there under sheets, but probably not for much longer. They walked up to the front wall and could see a light on inside the house. He didn't relish the prospect of knocking on the stranger's door. He didn't really know why, but a sixth sense told him all wasn't as it seemed. And perhaps he would just always be that boy, a little bit frightened.

'I'll go and see if anyone can help us,' he said. 'Wait under the carport for me.'

They both dutifully did as he suggested and he was glad to see Gloria take Bridget's arm. Then he boldly walked up the front path and knocked loudly on the door.

The man that opened it was battered looking, like his car. He was old and grey with a ruddy complexion on a very lined face that told of a lifetime of outdoor activity. He swayed slightly on the doorstep and Derek wondered if he was drunk.

'Hello, I'm sorry to bother you, but we have a problem with our car and we need to find a garage that can come and recover us.'

'A garage? You do know where you are, don't you? This is Unst and we don't have a garage. There's a petrol pump at the Skibhoul stores.'

'We need a new tyre, not fuel.'

'You're out of luck then. You do know there's a red warning out for a serious storm? No one will be coming out to you until it's over.'

'We'll need to find somewhere to stay then. Just until the storm is done. We can phone for help from the mainland tomorrow.'

'We? Are you not alone then?'

'No, my friends are sheltering in your carport.'

'Not much shelter to be had there, I'm afraid.'

He stepped out of the house then and looked over to see the women huddled there.

'You can't leave your womenfolk out in this. You'd all better come in, get dry and warmed up.'

It felt very much against Derek's better judgement to go inside this man's house. He had such an uneasy feeling about it. And then he thought he was probably being ridiculous and this man was just being kind. Gloria and Bridget joined him on the doorstep after he beckoned them over and they all stepped inside.

They followed him down his hallway and into a shabby but surprisingly cosy kitchen. He had a stove lit and the warmth was welcome. He filled the kettle and set it to boil, then he encouraged them to gather around the stove while he made a large pot of tea. He introduced himself as Magnus.

'You're very kind,' Gloria said as he handed her a chipped mug.

'American?' he asked her, and she smiled.

'Yeah,' she said. 'But I'm one of the good ones.'

'My daughter lives in Seattle with her American husband. He's one of the good ones too,' he said and winked at her.

'Do you know of any accommodation around here?' Bridget asked him. 'We're going to need a hotel or a B&B for the night.'

'You're in luck,' he said. 'I run a B&B from here. I'm small, but I'm friendly and I cook a great breakfast. Let me go and get your room ready.'

He passed the last mug of tea to Derek and disappeared out of the room. The next thing they heard was a clattering and banging coming from above.

'I do not like this at all!' Bridget said.

'I don't see we have much choice now,' said Derek. 'How can we decline his offer and go out in that storm to look for something better? There might not be anywhere.'

'I think he's sweet,' Gloria said. 'We're all together and he doesn't look the type to murder us all in our beds.'

'I really wish you hadn't said that,' Bridget said.

'And I really wish you hadn't lost my dearest friend,' Gloria bit back.

Derek thought Gloria had forgiven Bridget. He was wrong.

Magnus returned and Gloria asked him if he had Wi-Fi. Magnus laughed and told her that he had a phone line and that was all he needed, but she could use his telephone if she needed to. It was by the front door and she could help herself.

'I need to call the car hire place so they can organise recovery, or a man with a wrench or something. Luckily I have the documents with me and all the numbers I need. Thanks, Magnus,' she said.

Derek asked Magnus what he charged a night for his B&B, not really believing that he ran a bed and breakfast usually. He wondered if the man was just lonely and his thoughts softened. His daughter was in the States and there was no sign of a wife. Maybe he was just pleased they had knocked on his door.

'I don't charge when there's a red weather warning,' he said, and Derek couldn't tell if he was joking or not. 'I only have the one room, but there's a big bed and a wee put-you-up. You'll have to toss for it.'

One bedroom. Derek had a horrible thought about snoring in the night and Gloria hearing him. He didn't question why he wasn't worried if Bridget heard him or not.

'Well,' Gloria said from the doorway. 'No one is coming out until tomorrow morning at the earliest and they can swing if they think I'm paying the excess on the insurance for that dent. They leave me with a car I don't want and without the ability to be able to repair it ourselves.'

Derek thought she was magnificent.

They'd settled at the table now they were dry and Bridget asked if she could use the bathroom. Magnus directed her to a toilet down by the front door. She looked terrified to be going on her own, but Derek could hardly go with her.

'So, you live here alone?' Gloria asked him.

'Aye, for near twenty years now since ma wife died. God rest her soul.'

'I'm sorry to hear that. How do you manage? It's so remote up here. I live in York and I can't imagine not being in a city and near to all my favourite shops and restaurants.'

'I like the quiet life on the whole,' he said. 'I'm not one for anything fancy. I like simple food and simple folk.'

He began rummaging in his cupboards and opened and closed the fridge.

'And you'll be needing your tea,' he said, looking at the clock hanging on the wall. It was nearly five, Derek was surprised to see.

'We booked into Frankie's fish and chips for six. It's safe to say we won't make it,' Derek said as Bridget arrived back looking slightly bewildered. She sat down next to Derek.

'Did you not have your dinner then?'

'No, we had some hot chocolate from one of those honesty boxes. They're great,' Gloria said. 'Bridget had brownies with her, but in the rush to find our friend, we forgot to eat them. But please don't go to any trouble.'

'I cannae rival Frankie's, but I do have some stew in the freezer. I'll get it out and we'll have a feast.'

He looked animated then and pulled a big plastic tub from the freezer. He took off the lid and slid the brown icy block into a large saucepan, then after lighting a flame underneath he took four glasses from the cupboard and an unopened bottle of whisky from a shelf.

'As no one's going anywhere,' he said, and without asking, he poured them all a glass.

Derek was surprised at the speed with which Bridget lifted hers to her lips and said, 'Cheers.'

'Slàinte Mhath,' Magnus said.

'Your good health,' said Derek.

'Bottoms up,' said Gloria, and they clinked glasses and laughed.

The stew was excellent. It was rabbit and the best Derek had ever eaten. He wondered if the two women might be squeamish about eating a soft fluffy animal, but Gloria didn't baulk when Bridget asked Magnus what the meat was and he told her. Derek had a feeling that Bridget would have stopped eating when she heard, but she had a couple of whiskies in her at that point and seemed keen to soak up the booze. He saw it in her eyes, though. She stopped eating with a fork halfway to her mouth for a moment and pondered her response. Luckily she just agreed it was delicious and kept eating.

After, Magnus found some sort of cake or dessert his neighbour had made him – a clootie dumpling, he told them. He served it hot with some cream. He asked if they wanted to settle in comfortable chairs in his living room, but no one was keen to leave the warmth of the kitchen. Derek noted, when he went to use the loo, that the rest of the house was quite chilly in comparison. The wind had been howling for hours now and the rain kept up a relentless battering against the kitchen window. The clattering sound of things being blown around outside made him twitchy. He'd been waiting for something to come through the roof. One thing was for sure, it wouldn't be a tree.

Bridget had her knitting with her and got it out. Neither Derek nor Gloria had theirs so they just sat back and watched her making a hash of it.

'My wife was a great knitter,' Magnus said.

'Much like Bridget,' said Gloria, laughing. It earned her a frown from across the table.

'It's why we're here,' Derek said. 'Our old friend, Norman, died recently and wanted us to scatter his ashes up at Muckle Flugga Lighthouse. He was a great knitter too. Made a business from it.'

'Why here? Was he a Shetlander?'

'No, he'd never been here,' Gloria said. 'Well, only as an unborn child, but he found out, before he died, that he might have family here. We're looking into that too, but we don't have a lot to go on. Here.'

She took the photo of Ida from her bag and slid it across the table to Magnus, who picked it up with grubby fingers. Derek hadn't really noticed before and wished he hadn't noticed now.

'This was his mother, Ida. We realised it was taken down the road at the castle. Well, it was pointed out as a possible place and we were delighted to find it was exactly where it had been taken.'

Magnus turned the photo over and looked at the date. For a mad moment, Derek imagined he was going to say he knew her, but he didn't.

'And you're off up to the lighthouse to scatter his ashes when the storm dies down?'

'Well, we were,' Gloria said. 'But we have a problem now. Norman has been kidnapped.'

Magnus choked on his whisky and put the glass down on the table.

'Kidnapped? How does someone kidnap ashes?'

'I left the urn in the castle, by mistake,' Bridget said, her words a little slurred. 'We've been followed for the last couple of days by a man on a motorbike. I left the ashes and when we came back for them, the motorbike ran us off the road. When I looked in the castle, Norman was gone.'

'Oh, aye? You've got yourselves a right problem. You can't scatter him if you can't find him.'

'You don't know anyone with a motorbike and a predilection for kidnap, do you?' Gloria asked.

Magnus laughed. 'I know a few people with bikes but can't imagine why anyone would want to steal a deceased knitter. That's mad, that is.'

'Oh, God!' Bridget suddenly moaned. 'Magnus is right. We can't scatter Norman's ashes if we don't have him. We can't fulfil his last wishes.'

## 21

### THE MOTORBIKE

*Bridget*

The night was not comfortable. The bed wasn't large and, to be fair, neither were Bridget or Gloria, but still, to be so close to a person that wasn't Graham made her feel anxious.

Derek didn't look that much more comfortable on what was little more than a camp bed, but he hadn't spent the night snoring like Gloria had. Although it was the sounds of the storm that had kept Bridget awake mostly. The constant groaning of the house as it was buffeted was disconcerting. It didn't look that sturdy and Bridget was convinced the roof would be ripped off and take them all with it.

At seven she had to get up to use the bathroom and she tried to do it as silently as possible. They'd all slept in their clothes, much to Gloria's disgust. Bridget knew she wanted to slip into her silky pyjamas, probably with a face pack on or some expensive night cream that she didn't have with her. She didn't have her extensive make-up bag with her either and Bridget was looking forward to seeing her face in its naked form when she got up. Gloria would hate it.

The bathroom smelled damp and she used the loo quickly before inspecting Magnus's toiletries cluttered around the sink. There was some toothpaste she'd used last night. She'd squeezed some out onto her finger and pushed it around her teeth. She did the same now and it made her mouth feel a whole lot better.

She didn't want to go back to bed so she made her way downstairs to see if she could make some tea, but when she saw the telephone on the table in the hallway she thought of Graham and decided to phone him. He picked up after a couple of rings.

'Graham, it's me,' she said and her voice sounded pathetic even to her own ears.

'Thank God,' he said. 'I've been so worried. The storm has been all over the news and I phoned your hotel as I couldn't get through on your mobile, but reception said you hadn't been back. I had an image of you stuck in the car somewhere.'

'Oh, Graham, it's been awful. We are stuck on the north island in this strange man's house who says it's a B&B, but I don't think it really is; it only has one bedroom and it's not very clean. The storm has been terrifying and I've not slept at all, and the worst of the worst thing ever is that I've lost Norman. I put his urn down somewhere – I forget where now – and when we went back it was gone and it's because we're being followed by a man on a bike and I thought Derek was going to hit him, but luckily he didn't, but he did run us off the road, well, Gloria ran us off the road really and the car's broken.'

'Take a breath, love,' Graham said, and Bridget did exactly that, but then she heard a cough coming from the kitchen. 'You're safe, though? You're with Derek and Gloria?'

'Yes,' she said, in a whisper now, acutely aware of Magnus just down the hallway. 'Gloria phoned last night for recovery. I think we'll be okay today.'

'That's good. Look, Bridget. Phone me when you've got the car back on the road. In fact, can you send me Gloria and Derek's phone numbers? I can't believe I didn't get them. I thought I could just be in contact with you, but I can see now...'

'Graham, I've got to go,' she whispered, aware that she hadn't actually asked if she could use Magnus's phone, just as he coughed again. 'I'll phone you later. I love you.'

Bridget hung up the phone and considered scurrying back to bed, but she couldn't live her life like a little church mouse. She also desperately wanted a cup of tea. Her head was thick from the whisky she'd drunk and rehydrating was at the forefront of her mind. She even wondered if she might still be a little drunk because she didn't really have as big a hangover as she normally would after drinking too much.

Magnus was in the kitchen, sitting at the table and reading a book. Bridget stopped in the doorway and almost reconsidered, but he'd looked up and seen her.

'I hope you don't mind, but I just made a quick phone call,' she said. 'You probably heard.'

'I don't mind at all and I didn't hear. I'm actually a bit deaf,' he said, patting his ear as if to confirm it. 'Cup of tea?' he asked her, and she nodded and sat down at the table.

Magnus left the book open, upturned, and she could see it was a copy of a book she'd read before. She picked it up, careful not to lose his place, and scoured her brain for a memory of the plot. She remembered a man walking a long way. She remembered his wife left behind and unhappy, she remembered crying as she'd read it. It seemed to her a most unlikely book for Magnus to be reading.

'My daughter's,' he said as if he'd read her thoughts. 'She left a few of her things when she went. It's been ten years now, but she would have gone sooner if it hadn't been for worrying about me. I told her she had to live her own life. She couldn't be worrying about her old Da.'

'My daughter lives in Germany, so I completely understand. We talk on the computer, though. It's not too bad. I'm not good at travelling so we tend to wait for her to come to us with her kids. I loved this book,' she said, putting it back on the table. 'The trouble is my memory isn't what it was and I can't recall all that happens in it. I do remember how it made me feel, though.'

'Well, that's the most important thing, isn't it?'

'I suppose it is.'

Magnus placed the mug down in front of her and sat back in his chair.

'Seems like you've travelled a long way to get up here. Maybe you're not a bad traveller at all. You three have been on a bit of a journey yourselves. Known each other long?'

'Yes, a long time. We all used to work together at a factory near York. Gloria's husband owned it and when he died she took it over. I was his secretary and then hers, Derek worked in the warehouse and Norman was an engineer. My husband actually worked there for a couple of years too – that's where I met him – but he left for another job as a salesman. I started there in the eighties. We were all so much younger then. We weren't really friends as such, just worked at the same place.'

'How did you end up from that to being all the way up here now?'

'Like we said, Norman asked us to scatter his ashes.'

'But why you three?'

'Believe me, I've been asking myself the very same question.'

Bridget sipped her tea and thought about that question again.

'Norman had an accident at work, ten years ago, just before he was due to retire, and was left permanently without the use of his legs. It was terrible. I used to visit him, every week more or less, for years. Really, up until his death.'

'If you weren't friends before, what compelled you to keep up the visits? Did you just feel sorry for him?'

'Guilt,' Bridget said without thinking.

Magnus just stared at her, not unkindly, and she decided to tell him.

'He fell from a platform, a cherry picker. It needed to be looked at. One of the young lads told me it had a fault, and it was my job to bring in an external company to fix it and to maintain all of the heights equipment. I didn't phone them in time. My father was ill and had just moved in with me and my husband as my mother couldn't cope. She got on a plane to Spain to live out her retirement in peace, but I'm making excuses. I had a job to do and I took my eye off the ball. Norman wasn't supposed to be in the factory that day, but he decided he fancied the overtime. The platform failed when it was at its highest and Norman fell thirty feet to the ground.'

Magnus whistled through his teeth before leaning forward with his arms on the table. Bridget noticed he had patches over the elbows of his worn sweater. It was an old fisherman's gansey, as Graham would call it, or a Guernsey as it was to her. Although she could see the difference. Magnus's was heavily textured with cables, but the one she had bought for Graham the last time she'd visited Guernsey was plain.

'A terrible accident, no doubt, but sounds to me like just that, an accident.'

'That's what Norman always said. Derek blames himself for

some reason too, even Gloria, but I assume that's just because she was the boss and it was on her watch. I can't really remember.'

'So you think he's got you three together so you can forgive yourselves?'

Bridget thought about this for a moment and then she smiled at him.

'That's very intuitive of you, Magnus. Perhaps you're right, but we haven't talked about it. We've been fixated on finding this family member and scattering Norman's ashes. Not that we can do that until we find him.'

'Now that is a queer one,' he said.

They finished their tea in a comfortable silence. The light was changing in the room as the day began to think about getting up. The storm had gone over now, moved on to some other poor unsuspecting place or hopefully fizzled out altogether. The sun hadn't quite made an appearance, but there was a slip of pink on the horizon that Bridget could see from the kitchen window when she went to wash up her mug.

'It's nice to talk to you, Magnus,' she said just as Gloria appeared in the doorway.

'Nice to talk to you too.'

'Morning, all,' Gloria said in an annoyingly chirpy tone.

The phone began to ring in the hallway and Magnus disappeared to answer it.

Bridget took a sneaky look at Gloria's face while she was looking out of the window. She didn't have her usual full face of make-up, but she did have a little powder on her cheeks. Her eyes weren't as open looking as they normally were without her mountain of mascara, but Bridget had to concede that Gloria looked good without it. It shouldn't bother her, but it did. Really, Gloria didn't seem to have lost her confidence, which meant that she didn't need her war paint as Bridget had suspected.

'So, what are we doing today?' she asked, and Gloria turned to her with a confused expression. For goodness' sake, if Gloria, the bossiest boss ever, didn't know what they were doing, how was Bridget supposed to? 'Are we scattering Norman's ashes?'

'Bridget, we have to find him first, do you remember?'

And she did then, she remembered the castle and the rain and the urn being in her hands one minute and not the next, because it was a lot warmer with her gloves on.

'That was the garage,' Magnus interrupted them. 'They'll be here in the next hour.'

He offered to cook them some breakfast once Derek came down, but no one had the appetite for a fry-up. Magnus suggested some porridge instead and they ate it together next to the stove. Bridget didn't really like porridge at the best of times when it was ladled with honey or golden syrup, but Magnus had put salt in his and she wasn't prepared for that taste sensation. She swallowed the large spoonful she'd pushed into her mouth and thought it best not to mention it. Then, not long after they'd finished, Gloria and Derek got ready to leave the house to go back to the car.

'Do you want to come with us?' Gloria asked, still with that furrow of concern in her expression.

Bridget felt comfortable with Magnus now and said she'd be happy to stay in the warm until they got back.

'We won't be long,' Derek said. 'Sit tight and we'll be back to pick you up once the car is sorted.'

Once they'd gone, Magnus said he was going to see what damage the storm had done now it was light enough and Bridget offered to wash up their breakfast things.

She watched him through the window poking around outside. It was impossible for Bridget to tell if Storm Beryl had done much damage because it had all been a bit of a mess anyway. She felt bad for thinking this; Magnus, it turned out, was a lovely man.

Then, as he prodded about his battered car, Bridget could see what had been under the flapping sheets that she and Gloria had stood next to while Derek had knocked on the door last night. The sheets had gone now, blown into the corner of the carport by the wind, and there, leaning against the wall of the house, was a motorbike, a black motorbike. She dropped the bowl she'd been washing into the sink and hurried to dry her hands on the towel.

It was Magnus that had been chasing them around on his bike, it was clear to Bridget, and she suddenly felt a rising panic at being alone in his house. She watched as he dragged the sheet back over it to cover up the evidence – and did he glance back at the house as he did it? Was he looking shifty? Did he now not seem like the lovely man he'd been at the breakfast table?

Where was Norman then? She was the one to lose him, it was up to her to find him and she had to find him before Magnus came back in.

She rushed through to the living room and scoured the place, looking behind the sofa and chairs, opening and closing the doors in his sideboard, but not finding Norman. She went back to the kitchen and opened the cupboards there, but nothing. Then she walked as quickly as she could back up the stairs and along the landing towards Magnus's bedroom. As she raised her hand to push his door open, she faltered for a second. What was she doing? This wasn't a Bridget thing to do, but the thought of telling the other two that she had an opportunity and didn't take it was not good. She had to show them she wasn't completely useless.

His room was surprisingly feminine. His bed had a floral blanket thrown over the top, there was a dressing table with pots of cream, a couple of books and a small jewellery box. The pictures on the wall were pretty paintings of cottages and seascapes. Bridget realised two things at once: one, that this was a shrine to Magnus's wife, and two, that she was very much intruding. Had she got this all wrong? She turned at once to leave, but Magnus was standing in the doorway and his face was as hard as ice.

## 22

### IS IT A DATE?

*Derek*

The storm may have gone, but the morning was bitterly cold and it was an effort to walk back to the car as the frigid air nipped at them. Gloria shoved her arm through Derek's and he didn't read too much into the gesture. It was for warmth and support, he knew that.

'What a night,' she said. 'And I won't tell Bridget, but she was probably right. Maybe I shouldn't have urged for us to leave the mainland when we did. I know I can be pushy, but I get an idea in my head and I like to get on with it. But now we have a broken car and we've lost Norman.'

'The car will get sorted, I'm sure, but I really don't even know where to start with Norman. I don't think driving around the island looking for bikes is going to work. Maybe we should get in touch with Charlotte and she can send out a message that he's gone, with a description of the man. Every time she's posted something it's had a great response. We should use that.'

'I think that's a good idea,' Gloria said. 'You know, Bridget was very confused this morning. She asked me what we were doing today and if we were going to scatter Norman's ashes.'

'Really? That's a bit odd.'

'You know her dad had dementia? I'm really not trying to be unkind, but do you think she has the same?'

'But why would Graham let her come without having a word with either of us? That seems a bit off. I mean, I get it, she's a bit forgetful, but being a bit forgetful when you're very much out of your comfort zone and having a dementia diagnosis are two completely different things.'

'I don't know, Derek, but I think we should keep an eye on her. We don't want her putting herself in a difficult or dangerous situation, do we?'

'I agree.'

The car was in sight now and there was a van parked up next to it. *Garage Repairs and Breakdown Services*, Derek read the words printed on the side. Once Gloria had given the repair man the keys, he suggested they waited in his van where it was warmer.

'I'm going to message Charlotte now,' Gloria said. 'Let's get this ball rolling.'

'Do you have a signal then?'

'I seem to at the moment, although I didn't at the house.'

Derek watched as her thumbs moved over the screen. Gloria messaged like a young person, he noted. He, on the other hand, used one finger and it took him ages to type out the shortest of correspondence.

He checked his own phone and found that he also had a signal and a notification from the Mature Companions website. Sherry apparently liked the look of his face and was interested in meeting up. Perhaps a meal, a trip to the theatre or a walk in the countryside. He left off reading the rest of the message to look at her profile picture. She was quite an attractive woman with a nice curvy figure and a warm smile. He could imagine a walk with Sherry. He went back to the message and continued reading.

> I'd like to be honest up front and tell you I've
> always enjoyed a rigorous sex life and would
> want that to continue. Is that something you'd be
> up for? You look like a lot of fun Del.

Derek jabbed at his screen to shut down the message as a heat hit his cheeks. Gloria was too engrossed in her own phone screen to notice, he was glad to see. Was Derek up for a rigorous sex life? The thought made him feel a little queasy. He didn't know Sherry. How much walking would they do first, or theatre trips, or meals out before she wanted to start getting vigorous or rigorous? Either way, he decided, he couldn't possibly date someone who called him Del. It was another non-starter.

'Derek,' Gloria suddenly said, pushing her phone towards him. 'Charlotte has been in touch and said that she had a private message from someone who thinks they could be Norman's nephew. Not the guy with the dog, he was a time waster apparently. This is a Cameron Ramsay.'

'But Norman didn't have any brothers or sisters.'

'Yes, but he might have had a half-brother or sister. Just because Ida didn't have any more children doesn't mean his father didn't.'

'Yes, that's obviously a good point.'

'Well, anyway, he wants to meet up with us. Charlotte has passed on my number and he's going to be in touch directly.'

'That's amazing. The power of social media. You don't look as pleased as I thought you would, Gloria.'

'Don't you see? How on earth are we going to meet up with Norman's nephew and have to tell him we've lost his uncle?'

They were silent for a while and Derek searched his brain for some nugget of wisdom but he didn't have one. Honesty was all he could consider. If the man was indeed Norman's nephew, they really would simply have to tell him that his long-lost uncle was in fact lost again.

'Gloria, can I ask you something personal?' Derek said.

'Ooh! Ask away, I'm intrigued.'

'How do you find dating as an older person?'

'Now, that's quite a question. After Tim died it took me a while to even consider starting something with someone else,' she said and then stopped.

Derek realised she'd slipped up. She'd forgotten she was talking to him and he was back in time suddenly, back to that moment in her office on that terrible day. He had no idea if there had been anyone else in her life after Tim, but he knew there had been himself, one time when he'd felt that finally all the stars were aligned and it was really going to happen for them. Gloria had been very clear she wanted him and there was no question he felt the same. He wondered, if it hadn't been for Norman's accident, would he and Gloria be together now? He pushed the thought away. It was too painful.

'But I realised I'm not great at being without someone in my life,' she continued quickly. 'I'm fine living alone, don't get me wrong, but sharing a meal, a conversation, a bed with another human is something I like to do occasionally.'

Derek tried not to dwell on the word *bed* as he thought about what she'd said.

'So, you never thought about getting married again, making those things you like permanent.'

'Not really, no. I know it sounds selfish, but I want those things when I want them, not because they're there all the time. It keeps things fresh.'

'Paul didn't sound that fresh,' Derek said and felt he was pushing his luck with this line of questioning.

'No, well, that was a mistake and one I won't be repeating.'

'My sister's put me on a dating app. I keep getting messages from frisky women.'

Gloria threw back her head then and laughed.

'Frisky women, hey. Lucky you.'

'I don't respond to them and I've not been on a date in years. I'm not sure how to do it any more.'

He stopped talking as he realised that he was making himself sound like a loser. Why had he even started this conversation?

'Would you like to go out for dinner with me when we get back? I can coach you in brushing up on your skills.'

'Oh, I'm not sure about that,' he said quickly. The thought of going on a non-date with Gloria was almost too much to bear.

'I understand,' she said, but when he looked at her he thought she seemed a bit put out.

'It's not that,' he said. 'It's just... well... I don't know. I wouldn't want to impose myself upon you.'

'Oh, Derek, don't be silly. We should do it; it could be fun.'

He didn't think it would be fun; he thought she'd likely break his bloody heart. He was saved any further thought by a knocking on the window. The car was fixed.

They drove back to Magnus's house with the heating on full. Gloria said she was keen to get Bridget and get back to the hotel to freshen up. Then they had to try to find Norman. Derek's lack of dating wasn't mentioned again.

'I've given Charlotte a description of the bike and the rider, in particular the orange helmet. Really hoping that social media does what it does best and finds him.'

She pulled up behind Magnus's battered old car and switched off the engine. Then they walked up to the front door and Derek turned the handle to open it. He assumed they were still guests of Magnus and it was okay to walk in. He didn't really think Magnus ran a B&B, but he was going to have to discuss with the other two what they should leave him in payment. He'd been the perfect host in the end and Derek was grateful for his generosity.

Bridget wasn't in the kitchen where they'd left her. She wasn't in the living room or the downstairs bathroom.

'She must be upstairs. Let's go and get her and our things,' Gloria said. 'I'm keen to get going while the car's still warm.'

But Bridget wasn't in the bedroom or the bathroom either and Derek suddenly had an uneasy feeling.

'Bridget?' he called out and heard a muffled response from Magnus's bedroom.

Gloria looked at him in alarm and he strode forward to open the door. Bridget was sitting on the bed surrounded by photos. Magnus was perched on the dressing table stool, looking animated.

'Hello,' Derek said warily. 'The car's fixed. All okay in here?'

'All is fine now, but I've made a bit of a fool of myself,' Bridget said, and Magnus chuckled. 'I accused him of stealing Norman's ashes, but he was very good about it, once he'd got over the shock of finding me snooping in his bedroom.'

'Oh, Bridget,' Gloria said. 'What are you like?'

Derek didn't think Gloria needed that question answered, but Bridget did regardless.

'I'm like a bit of an idiot,' she said.

'No, you're not,' Magnus said. 'You just made an honest mistake.'

Derek noticed Magnus was looking at her quite earnestly.

'Anyone can make a mistake, you know,' he said and turned his earnest gaze on Derek and then Gloria.

'Magnus has a motorbike,' Bridget said. 'I saw it in his carport.

The sheet that had been covering it had blown off and I just assumed he was our mystery rider.'

'He would have had to have driven like a maniac to have run us off the road, get back to his house, light the stove – because don't forget we saw him on the ferry and I doubt that fire would have kept itself lit for all that time – park up, cover up and get back inside before we knocked on his door,' Gloria said. 'Plus, one rather large hole in your plot is that there is only one road and the rider was going the other way.'

Derek was hugely impressed with Gloria's rundown of events and her attention to all of the details. He warmed to her all the more.

'One other very large thing is that the bike hasn't been ridden for twenty-odd years and it belongs to my wife. I've never ridden a bike, ever,' Magnus said.

'See, I told you I was an idiot,' Bridget said. 'But we've been having a lovely time looking at Magnus's old photos of Shetland and his family.'

'That's great, but we really need to go now,' Gloria said. 'We really appreciate your hospitality, Magnus, and you'll need to let us know what we owe you for bed, breakfast and for that excellent evening meal last night.'

'You really have to go?' Magnus asked, and Derek could see how disappointed he was.

'Once we find Norman and his family we'll be back up here to scatter his ashes,' Bridget said. 'We could pop in for a cup of tea.'

'I'd very much like that,' he said. 'And I said, I don't charge in a red weather warning.'

Derek noted his wide grin and thanked him for helping them out. And then they were on the doorstep and Bridget and Magnus were hugging like long-lost friends. It made his heart swell to see Bridget so relaxed and comfortable.

The journey back to Belmont to catch the ferry was quiet. They were all tired and looking forward to getting back to the hotel in Lerwick. Derek thought about his date with Gloria, and had she really asked him out, and had he really turned her down? Nothing more had been said and now he really didn't know where he stood. He was also getting increasingly irked that they didn't have Norman with them. He wasn't cross with Bridget. As Magnus said, accidents happen, but it seemed that just as they were making progress with the family connection, they had another problem to deal with. He couldn't wrap his head around why someone would even be interested in taking the ashes. What on earth would they do with them? As Gloria said, how could they possibly try to reconnect Norman with one half of his family when he was AWOL?

There was quite a queue for the ferry. He wasn't surprised. Everyone who'd needed to travel last night would be getting the early ferries this morning. Except, he realised that this wasn't the earliest and he imagined a motorbike would have been on that one. Not that they could have done much about it. He just hoped that Charlotte would have some news for them soon.

One thing was for sure, they were all looking out for the bike through Yell and on the ferry from Ulsta to Toft, where they'd first seen him. But as they drove into Lerwick, with the hotel a welcome sight, they all had to admit they hadn't seen a single motorbike.

## 23

### OLD LOVE

*Gloria*

Charlotte messaged them that afternoon. She suggested that they look at Instagram and see the responses to the post she'd made about the missing ashes and the description of the bike rider. Norman's fans had made several suggestions about who the biker might be, even offering up addresses, which was too much for some. Messages were coming back from people defending themselves as innocent with comments like *I don't even have an orange helmet* and *In this weather? You're kidding, haven't been on my bike for weeks.* Charlotte suggested that until an address was offered up more than once they should hold fire on knocking on doors, something none of them were that keen to do anyway.

Once they'd got back to the hotel, the three went to their rooms after pulling straws to see who would get the bathroom first. Derek said he was happy to go last and Bridget disappeared inside without a backward glance at Gloria.

Gloria relaxed back on her bed and went through Norman's Instagram account. She could see that Charlotte had posted all of the photos Gloria had sent her. Looking through the images of their trip so far brought a smile to her face. She enlarged the picture of them with Shona, ostensibly to admire the view, but really she was taking a closer look at Derek. She hadn't been joking when she suggested they have dinner, but she got the distinct impression he wasn't interested. She enjoyed his company, his steadiness, his ability to keep calm in most situations. She was probably too much for him, too brash, too American. Did she fancy him? She thought about how close they'd been as they walked down the lane that morning, her arm linked through his, the side of her body pressed against him. Yes, of course she fancied him, and the thing was, she always had.

Of course, something had actually happened that one time, at work. They'd been skirting around each other for weeks. Tim had been gone for over two years and poor Liz, Derek's wife, for many, many more than that. He cut a lonely figure, Derek, but somehow with Gloria he came alive. Something fizzed between them, but every time she had tried to take it a little further, to press him and see if he'd consider dinner or a drink, a walk in the park after work even, he always held back a bit. She asked him once if he missed his wife, to see if that was at the root cause of his reticence, but to her surprise he said that, no, he didn't think about her that often anymore. Gloria never found out if it was because he didn't want to upset himself or if he didn't actually care – although she'd have been surprised about that – because Derek astonished her by coming to her office to find her. There were no words exchanged, but it was obvious that he'd changed his mind about wanting to start something with her, because he walked straight up to her, wound his hand through her hair and without any hesitation at all brought her face to his. Gloria hadn't the time to be surprised, Derek had lit something up inside her and she responded with everything she had.

But the cruel hand of fate had been waved at them and Norman had his accident. Gloria and Derek would never forgive themselves for being so wrapped up in her office that day, they didn't even realise Norman was injured. She shuddered at the memory, still so raw. How could she and Derek enjoy time together with that hanging over them? They had tried it once and look what had happened.

For years after, Norman had tried to make her see that he didn't blame her, even though she'd been completely honest about where her head had been in the weeks before the accident and that she and Derek had shared a passionate kiss that same day. Fundamentally she was the boss and should have been in charge of more than Derek's lips.

'I wasn't supposed to be in work that day. I should have checked if the cherry picker was working properly. I'd heard that there might be a fault and I chose to use it anyway. I should have made sure I wasn't the only person in the warehouse too,' he'd said. 'Do I care that you and Derek were snogging? Of course I don't. What happened to me was nothing to do with either of you.' Again and again, Norman had repeated himself, but Gloria couldn't really hear him. All she could see was her and Derek in her office with their lips pressed together when poor Norman was sprawled on the floor with his spine in tatters.

She considered luxuriating in the bath for a while until she remembered that Derek would need to get in there after her, so she resorted to a quick wash, a good brush of her teeth and some dry shampoo. She'd get her straighteners on her hair to get rid of the windswept look. She tapped on Derek's door and called out that the bathroom was all his.

'Thanks,' he called back.

Then she hovered for a moment, wondering if she was brave

enough to walk in and tell him how she felt, but she imagined his startled face and scurried back to her room.

Gloria was just putting the finishing touches to her make-up and feeling all the better for it when her phone rang and an unknown number came up on the screen. She wasn't the sort of person not to answer unknown numbers; she picked up her phone to anyone. Maybe that was half the problem, she thought, as she accepted the call.

'Is that Gloria Taylor?' asked a man with a soft Scottish accent.

'Yes,' she said.

'My name is Cameron Ramsay and I think I might be the nephew of Norman George.'

* * *

Gloria met the other two in the bar once she was ready. Bridget and Derek both had their knitting with them, but Gloria hadn't taken hers out of the bag more than a couple of times since she'd got the kit. After one interesting knitting session at the Sunday tea where the chat had been more fun than the yarn, she realised it really wasn't her thing and even though she told Bridget she'd be awesome at it, she wasn't actually. She was a terrible knitter and that was mostly because she wasn't interested. Bridget, on the other hand, who'd worried about not being any good, had kept at it and knitted every opportunity she could get. The ribbing was now complete and she'd moved on to the main body of her hat. Gloria's was buried at the bottom of her suitcase.

'I just felt so inspired after talking to Magnus about his wife and her knitting heritage,' Bridget said. 'He lent me one of her pattern books to look through. I think he did it so I'd have to go back to return it, but that's okay.'

'That's really sweet,' Gloria said. 'Can you see yourself knitting one of the patterns?'

'God, no, they're all lace and very intricate, but it's a nice book to look through.'

Gloria ordered coffee and they all decided on what they fancied for their late lunch.

'I've just had an interesting conversation with Cameron Ramsay,' she said once they'd put in their order for food. 'He wants to meet up with us. I've said I'd talk to you both and get back to him with a time that works.'

'Who is Cameron Ramsay?' Bridget asked. 'Do I already know this?'

She looked so confused and worried that Gloria instantly felt terrible. They hadn't told her. They'd forgotten to include her in the latest information.

'No, you don't and that's on me, I'm sorry. Charlotte sent a message this morning to say that a man who thought he might be Norman's nephew had been in touch and wanted to meet up. That was him on the phone.'

'Nephew? Norman didn't have any brothers or sisters,' Bridget said.

'I said exactly the same thing when Gloria told me,' said Derek.

'Oh, so you both know and it's just me who's left out again,' Bridget said and put her knitting down so she could fold her arms across her chest in annoyance. 'Guess after losing Norman, I'm not in your hallowed circle any more.'

'That's not how it is at all,' Gloria said. 'Derek only knows because he was with me when the message arrived. And then we were rushing back to the house to get you, so it got a bit forgotten. You can read all the messages too, you know. They're all there on the WhatsApp group chat. Not my fault that you choose not to look.'

Gloria's thoughts about being kinder to Bridget were spoilt only by Bridget herself. She could be impossible sometimes.

'It's true,' Derek said, looking like he wanted to be anywhere but there. 'I mean, the bit about me knowing because I was there when the message came through.'

They were saved any further uncomfortableness because their food arrived. Gloria, having missed Frankie's, the most northerly fish and chip shop, had chosen the fish and chips and was delighted to see it was a huge portion. Derek tucked into his steak and ale pie and Bridget unfolded her arms in favour of the salmon she'd chosen. They ate in silence.

A slice of cheesecake for dessert seemed to soften Bridget up.

'So, when does this Cameron want to meet up with us?' she asked.

'Ideally as soon as possible, but we've got to make a concerted effort to find Norman first,' Gloria said.

'Or we tell him the truth and see if he can help us find the urn,' said Derek. 'It's not like we're criminals or anything. Someone stole him from us.'

'I assume he already knows. He's contacted Charlotte through Norman's Instagram account and would have to be blind to have missed the post about Norman's disappearance. I just meant that it would be good to have him back when we meet, but I'm guessing that's unlikely to happen in time. He seems keen to meet up pretty soon,' Gloria said. 'I think we should just get on and arrange it. He might not even be a family member and then we'd have to start looking again.'

'I agree,' Derek said. 'Set it up, Gloria.'

## 24

### CAMERON RAMSAY

#### *Bridget*

They were on the Toft to Ulsta ferry by ten the next morning and the three were sitting upstairs and watching their progress across the water. There had been a flurry of snow as they reached the north of the mainland, but for now it had stopped.

'The thing that annoys me is that Norman's fans were so happy to see his urn travelling around the islands and now he's not with us at all and they can't join him in his final journey,' Gloria said.

'I have to be honest,' Derek said. 'Things seem to have taken a bit of a turn in the comments. They're not all positive now that someone has come forward as a potential family member. They're starting to question why we should have him at all, and now we've lost him, they've jumped on that too.'

'Should we be worried?' Bridget said. 'Are they looking for us?'

The thought of vigilante knitting fans out for blood was not as funny as it might seem. 'And what if we never find him? Do we just go home?'

'Let's not think about that yet,' Derek said. 'Let's just keep positive for now.'

Bridget spent most of the journey looking out for the bike, but she supposed if his objective was to get the ashes, he had no reason to keep trailing them. What she'd most like to do is pop back to Magnus's and hear more of his tales. His wife sounded like an amazing person, someone who didn't worry about the things in her life she had no control over but embraced what she had and what she could do. Imagining the tiny woman from the photo on her motorbike was impressive. Bridget watched out of the window as they drew closer to Yell. The water was still but looked perishing. She shivered at the thought of falling in. And that was typical Bridget. She was on a warm and sturdy ferry. Why was she thinking about falling in the water? She glanced over at Gloria and wondered what she might be thinking about, but Gloria was staring at the side of Derek's face as he watched the water below. She looked so intently at him; Bridget wondered why he couldn't feel it. Was something actually going on between the two of them? And then she had another thought, the way those chunks of information she held in her head came back to her sometimes, in fractured pieces.

'It's a woman,' she suddenly said. 'The biker is a woman.'

Gloria's and Derek's heads both turned at the same time and Bridget scrabbled to organise her thoughts.

'The Knitting Warrior,' she said and silently congratulated herself on remembering the name. 'I think it's a woman and I also think she's got Norman.'

'Because?' asked Gloria.

'Think about the biker in those leathers,' she said and then dismissed Gloria and turned to Derek. 'Derek, you're a man.'

'Last time I looked.'

'So, I assume you'd recognise a woman's figure if you saw one.'

Derek looked incredibly uncomfortable at Bridget's line of questioning, but she wasn't deterred.

'Lots of men are slim and small,' Gloria said.

'Yes, but not with hips like that,' said Bridget.

'I agree,' Derek said. 'You know, I even wondered the same thing. I mean, I don't usually go around looking at women's hips and I didn't want to make a sexist comment. It's hard to gauge what's the right thing to say any more, so I usually stick at saying nothing.'

'How did I not notice this?' Gloria said. 'Because I do go around looking at women's hips. That's usually the first thing I'd see.'

'I thought it when she approached us on the ferry,' Bridget said. 'As she walked past me, I thought, he's got some hips on him. But you know me, I forgot almost as soon as I saw it. Plus, we were in a bit of a predicament after that, what with me losing Norman and the car crash. It went out of my head.'

'Well, this is a starting point at last,' Gloria said. 'We need to see if Charlotte can contact The Knitting Warrior directly and see if it's the same person.'

Bridget felt the full force of admiration coming from both Gloria and Derek and she basked in it until they were driving off the ferry.

They followed the same road north, the only road north on this side of the island, and Bridget kept her vigil going. She hoped they'd just see the bike and be able to speak to the rider, to appeal to their sense of what was right and get Norman back. Bridget was gripped by a sudden fear that the ashes had already been scattered and that it was too late, but she pushed the thought aside because another fractured memory jostled for position. It was something about the bike, something Bridget couldn't get a grip on. She closed her eyes and tried so hard to grasp hold of it, but it was already slipping away.

* * *

The café was in Mid Yell. It was a lovely find, seemingly on a road to nowhere. A building that looked as if it could have formerly been a village hall but had been repurposed. Bridget wondered about that. Did it suit the local Shetland people as much as it suited the tourists? She made a mental note to ask Norman's nephew. Unfortunately, along with a lot of other things, his name had slipped from her memory. Gloria parked up and they got out into a howling wind, all hanging onto their doors and then onto their hoods and hats. They were almost at the top of a hill, so the squall shouldn't have taken them all by surprise. They really should have been used to it by now. Bridget suddenly felt very nervous walking in. What on earth would they say to this man? She couldn't think of a single question to ask him. She'd have to leave it to the others.

There was a man sitting in the corner of the café with a coffee and the remains of a cooked breakfast on the table in front of him. It was safe to assume it must be Norman's nephew as there wasn't anyone else there. He looked up as they came through the door and Bridget could see he appeared as nervous as she did.

'Cameron?' Gloria asked him and he stood up with his arm extended.

'Aye,' he said. 'Cameron Ramsay.'

He pulled out the chairs next to him and suggested they sit down for a chat. Derek went up to order drinks for them and Bridget and Gloria sat down with Cameron.

'I have to say this is all very strange,' he said. 'I'm not sure if

I'm sad my grandfather won't know he had a son. He slipped away a couple of years ago. This would have been a lot for him to take in. He was ninety-three.'

'What was his name? What did he do?' asked Gloria.

'He was called Ivar, a fisherman all his life. Hard working, good family man and good husband. I guess he must have had a fling with Norman's mum when she visited the island. Of course, it was long before he married my grandmother, though.'

Bridget noticed that Cameron seemed very proud of his grandfather and she felt terrible.

'Oh, my goodness. This makes it all the worse that I've lost his son then,' Bridget said, and Gloria sighed.

'Well, that was a nugget of information we were gonna hold back a little longer,' Gloria said as Derek arrived with coffees and pastries.

'What have I missed?' he asked.

'I read about the missing ashes,' Cameron said. 'I thought it was a publicity stunt or something, not that you really have lost my uncle.'

'Half-uncle,' Gloria said, as if that softened the blow of the loss, but Bridget winced.

'Look, it's all my fault,' she said. 'He was taken from us and we're trying to find him.'

'Who takes ashes?' Cameron said. 'That's really weird.'

'How did you make the connection? How did you know you might be Norman's nephew?' Bridget asked, to change the subject.

'It was my sister, Esther. She asked me if I'd heard about you three coming to the islands. She's a big knitter and she'd mentioned Norman to me a couple of years back. She thought she might do something with her own knitting and got me to watch a couple of his videos. She wanted me to set her up on

YouTube so she could create her own content. She did and she's good.'

Bridget could see how proud he was of his sister too.

'So, she followed Norman and then saw his post about him being ill and she seemed to get a bit obsessed with him then. I mean, in a healthy way,' he clarified, although Bridget wasn't sure there was such a thing as a healthy obsession. 'She's into alternative therapies and was convinced she could help him. She was so upset about him dying as he'd been such an inspiration to her. She'd done some live classes with him during Shetland Wool Week the year before last, online. Anyway, she seemed really affected by it all and then she came round to show me the Instagram posts of you three and about the scattering of his ashes. She'd gone back to watch his early videos where his mother, Ida, featured a few times before she died, and then Esther said she'd been digging around in the loft and found some things of Grandad's. He had a letter from an Ida. She wrote about how sorry she was to be leaving Shetland, how much she'd loved spending time with him, but that she needed to get home, get back to her reality, she said, that this had been a dream, but she needed to wake up. There were a couple of photos too. One of her on her own and one of them together. My sister was convinced Norman was our half-uncle. Personally, I thought she'd lost it, but then, when you shared the photo of Ida on Instagram, it was clearly the same woman. I had to agree with her. To be honest, I think it's a bit off of her to disappear like that, without telling him he was going to be a father.'

'Maybe she didn't know at that point,' Gloria said.

'Hmm,' said Cameron, seemingly unconvinced.

Bridget got the distinct impression he wasn't happy about them being there. She decided to move the conversation along.

'And what about your parents?' Bridget asked. 'Are they interested in knowing about their half-brother? Would he have been your mother's or father's relation?'

'My mother's, but both of my parents died in a boating accident in Greece, many years ago.'

'I'm so sorry, and is your grandmother still alive?'

'No, she died a few years back. We're such a small family now. Me, Esther and her husband and kids.'

Bridget understood why he seemed so protective of his sister, now. She was important to him.

'What's your sister's YouTube name?' Gloria suddenly said, and Bridget thought it was the oddest thing to ask until Cameron replied.

'The Knitting Warrior,' he said.

## 25

### THE KNITTING WARRIOR

*Gloria*

'That's it then,' Gloria said. 'It's gotta be her.'

'No, it can't be. She isn't the sort of person to steal ashes,' Cameron said. 'She doesn't even ride a bike. You put on Instagram about the thief being on a bike. That's not her.'

'Does she have a friend who rides a bike?' Derek suggested.

'We will go and ask her,' Cameron said, 'but I know you're wrong.'

'If she has taken them,' Bridget said, 'she'd have every right, more rights than us, if she is Norman's family. It would be her half-uncle, after all.'

'That's true,' Gloria said. 'But Norman entrusted us with his sacred ashes. Not anybody else.'

'And look how well you have kept them safe and sacred for him,' Cameron said, and Gloria couldn't really blame him for the sarcasm. How inept they seemed.

The conversation was a little one-sided after that. Cameron was obviously offended they'd blamed his sister and all they could really do until they finished their coffee was for Bridget to remark on the beauty of the island, Derek to engage him in the history of various places and Gloria to ask how hairdressers managed their businesses in all this howling wind. By the time they were ready to leave, Cameron could not have looked more relieved.

His van was in the car park and he suggested they follow him out to the house to talk to Esther.

'She runs a bed and breakfast in West Sandwick, near the beach. There's nowhere quite like it in the world,' he said. 'It's only down the road.'

They followed him out of the car park and back in the direction they'd come. Gloria had to put her foot down to keep up with him.

'He's not impressed about Norman, is he?' Bridget said.

'Well, I'm not going to be too apologetic until we know for sure he's really Norman's nephew. It might turn out to be a hoax or something. I'm beginning to wish we'd just scattered Norman's ashes as soon as we'd got here. All this doing nice things for him hasn't got us very far at all,' said Gloria.

'That's on me,' Derek said. 'I'm the one who pushed to look for family.'

'And the sightseeing trip,' Bridget reminded him. 'In fact, most of it was down to you and Gloria.'

'And you're the one who lost him,' Gloria retorted.

'It's all done now, though,' Derek said. 'There's no point playing the blame game, again. It's now up to us all to work together to get Norman back and up to Muckle Flugga Lighthouse as soon as we can.'

Cameron was indicating to turn off up ahead and Gloria followed him onto a narrow road that looked as if it ended in the sea. It didn't quite. There was a property off to the left with a big sign telling them that West Sandwick Bed and Breakfast had vacancies. They pulled up outside and watched Cameron jog to the door and walk straight through.

'I'm not happy about this,' Bridget said.

'Well, you're not happy about anything and you said that about Magnus and he turned out to be a sweetheart,' Gloria said.

'That is true,' said Bridget. 'I just won't be happy until we've got Norman back.'

Gloria leaned round in her seat and patted Bridget's leg.

'Me neither,' she said kindly, just as her phone pinged with a message. Derek's did the same so Gloria guessed it would be from Charlotte. Hopefully with some good news.

'Charlotte has an address for the thief,' Derek said. 'Someone has tipped her off quietly apparently. She feels it's more legitimate. That does sound better than splashing it all over social media. The whole thing has been a circus and we somehow need to claw back a bit of sanity. It's not here though, so whoever sent it doesn't believe that Cameron's sister has the ashes.'

Cameron came back out of the house, but this time he was followed by a petite woman with a mane of dark curls that were being whipped around in the wind.

'She's got Norman's hair,' the three said, almost at the same time.

'Well, sort of Norman's hair,' Bridget said. 'He didn't wear his like a catwalk model.'

'No, that is true, but I have a feeling if he'd grown it long it would have looked exactly like that,' Gloria said.

'I think that's why I had my reservations when I first saw Cameron. I was expecting some sort of family resemblance, but there was nothing. I know we're talking a half-relative situation, but even still, I'd have never picked him out in a lineup of possibles,' Derek said.

'Unlike his sister,' said Gloria and opened her door into the wind to greet Norman's niece.

* * *

Esther's home was beautiful inside. It was cosy and welcoming, but also had some modern touches in the art that hung on her walls and the minimalist way it was devoid of clutter. When Gloria said as much to compliment her, she laughed and suggested Gloria take a look in her kids' bedrooms.

She offered them champagne because, she said, this was a huge celebration.

'It's not every day you learn that you have family you've never met,' she said. 'I knew I was onto something when I first contacted Norman. Unfortunately, he was too ill to engage. Whoever runs his account didn't relay my messages, because he never got back to me. No one here took me seriously either and it was too late to ask poor Grandad any questions.'

'So, you're The Knitting Warrior?' Gloria asked her. She couldn't wrap her head around the fact. This woman was beautiful, engaging and not remotely threatening, but that was the impression Charlotte had given. Gloria thought back to the messages and wondered if they could be read in many different lights with a bit of understanding.

'That's me. I was so inspired by Norman's ability to turn his unfortunate situation into a positive business. I just wanted to do the same. My kids are quite young and my husband is away with work a fair bit, so I'm pretty housebound myself. Please don't think I'm comparing having children with a life-changing injury. I don't mean that at all. I just empathised and also wondered what the hell I was moaning about. Nothing was stopping me. So, we converted part of the house for a B&B and I run that, but I do still have some spare time when the children are at school, so I turned to knitting. It's always been a passion, and historically Shetlanders have made money from their knitting skills.'

Gloria didn't know she was crying until Esther stepped forward and wrapped her arms around her.

'I wish he had known you were his niece. You're really a chip off the old block,' Gloria said as she sniffed. 'He'd have loved to have known you.'

'And you three are such amazing friends to make this journey and scatter his ashes,' Esther said.

'If only we knew where they were,' said Cameron with that sarcastic tone again.

Gloria felt that the nicest part of their conversation was probably over. 'Champagne would be fantastic,' she said.

They took their glasses out to a conservatory that overlooked the sea. Esther had comfortable sofas with blankets and cushions. The floor was covered in a brightly patterned rug, and books and magazines littered the large coffee table. Gloria imagined how much light would come through the glass in the summer months, but even now, with the squally clouds scudding across the sky and the waves crashing against the shore, it was a cosy place to be. Esther shared the photos she had of Ida with her grandfather and there really was no question at all; the connection had been made.

'You know we've lost Norman's ashes, don't you?' asked Gloria.

'They were stolen,' Bridget clarified.

'Yes, Cameron told me and he said you think it was me.'

'No, we thought it was The Knitting Warrior, but that was before we knew they were you. We don't think you personally have taken him,' Derek said.

'We'd like to be there, when you scatter him – after you've found him, that is – wouldn't we, Cameron?' Esther said.

Cameron nodded without much conviction.

'Aye, I suppose. It's off Muckle Flugga where he wanted to be scattered? That's where our grandad's ashes were scattered too. It's quite a coincidence, isn't it?'

'It is,' Gloria said. 'I'm beginning to wonder if Norman had some kind of special sixth sense or something. Perhaps he was a wizard in a former life.'

'Well, practically we might just have to do it at the end of the land. I don't think we'll be able to get out on the water,' Derek said.

'We can take Grandad's boat. He left it to me when he died,' Cameron said. 'I did the same trip for him.'

'And you're happy on the water after what happened to your parents?' Bridget asked.

'Bridget!' Gloria reprimanded her. 'I don't think that's appropriate.'

'It's okay and a fair question,' Cameron said. 'I don't believe in dwelling on things that are out of your control. Just because they had an accident doesn't mean that I will. We were in our teens when they died and our grandparents looked after us until we were old enough to look after ourselves. Our parents had always instilled a sense of love and security for us and encouraged us to do whatever we wanted. I believe they would want us to live a full life without fear. And that's what we're doing, regardless.'

Esther took Cameron's hand and squeezed it in hers. They shared a smile that showed how close they were and Gloria wanted to take Derek's hand at that moment. She pushed her own into her pocket to stop herself.

'Wise words,' she said. 'A sentiment that we should all live by.'

She did glance at Derek then and he was gazing straight at her.

'But first we have to find him and we think we have a lead, so

I'll contact you once we have him back in our possession,' Gloria said.

As they left Esther's place, Gloria's phone began to ring and after checking her rearview mirror she pulled over at the side of the road to answer it. She nearly handed it to Derek so she could keep driving. She was keen to get to this house and get Norman back, but the idea that a teary Paul might be on the other end stopped her.

'Hello, is that Mrs Taylor?' It was Lachlan from the hotel.

'Yes, it is,' she said.

'Good, I'm trying to get hold of Mrs Scott; I don't suppose she is with you, is she?'

'She is, yes. I'll hand you over to her. It's the hotel, for you, Bridget,' she said, passing the phone back, and then she hissed, 'Why isn't your phone on?'

'Hello, yes. Oh! Really? What? Really? We'll be right there. Well, we have to get a ferry, but then we'll be right there. Okay, goodbye.'

Gloria found it infuriating listening to a one-sided conversation, especially on her own phone. What on earth did Lachlan want with Bridget? Surely it was clear Gloria was the person in charge of this trip.

'Well?' she said.

'Graham has just arrived at the hotel.'

'Has he? What on earth for?'

'I suppose he wants to be with me,' Bridget said a little sharply.

'Of course,' Gloria said quickly, although she did wonder why he hadn't bothered to accompany his wife at the start of this trip. 'Okay. Well, Derek and I will drop you back and then we'll go on to the address Charlotte has given us for the person who supposedly has the ashes. If the tip-off is right and Norman is there, it will make the perfect end to this day. We really do need to find him and time feels a bit pressing now that his family knows we're here. It would be nice if we can get their uncle back as quickly as possible.'

'Fine with me,' Bridget said. 'I don't mind admitting that the thought of going to this house doesn't exactly fill me with joy. You won't get into a fight with the motorcyclist, will you, Derek?'

'Of course not. Especially if you're right and it's a woman. We'll knock on the door and ask politely if we can have Norman back,' Derek said.

'And if she says no, I'll kick her ass and take him anyway,' said Gloria.

Bridget laughed from the back seat and Gloria pulled away, feeling a bit like she was always stuck being the boss, but wishing someone else would take the reins for once. She held back a large sigh that she knew would make her feel better but wouldn't make her sound kind.

'Gloria, I know I lost Norman and I'm sorry for that, but I do appreciate you going to get him,' Bridget said from behind her. 'Please don't kick anyone's arse.'

'You know, I could go alone,' Derek said. 'I could drop you both back at the hotel and go on by myself.'

Gloria glanced across at Derek and then at Bridget in the rearview mirror and smiled.

'Thank you both,' she said. 'Bridget, you need to go to Graham; he's travelled a long way to be with you. And Derek, thank you, but I'm the only one insured on this car and I think we should go together.'

# 26

# NORMAN'S HIDING PLACE

*Bridget*

They dropped Bridget at the door and she tried hard not to read too much into how quickly Gloria drove away. They probably wanted to be alone. It was quite clear to Bridget that they should just get together and put each other out of their shared misery.

Anyway, she was very keen to see her husband and was delighted he'd finally relented and flown out to be with her. The words 'better late than never' rattled around her mind, but in truth she just didn't understand why he'd not come with her from the start. Graham had known Norman for a couple of years when he'd worked at Taylor's and of course he knew Gloria as the wife of his boss and Derek as that nice chap who worked in the warehouse. Their paths had crossed in later years at the odd Christmas do, but she supposed he was never really their friend. After Graham left the factory for the sales job at a pharmaceuticals company he only had Bridget's chat about the people at work to keep him up to date with what was going on. Was Bridget friends with Derek and Gloria, though? No, she wasn't really.

They'd never socialised out of the work environment and yet she'd known them for over forty years. How was that possible? But then, she'd known Graham's sister for the same length of time and she wasn't particularly friendly with her either. They were colleagues, not friends, and the only reason they were here together was because Norman had asked them. Plus, she'd never really liked Gloria, although she couldn't remember why, now.

And then she flushed at a sudden memory, a very personal conversation she'd overheard between Mr Taylor and Gloria. Husband and wife having a very public row in his office. Except Bridget was the only one there to hear it.

She stopped in the hotel reception as she realised *that* was what Derek had been talking about the other night. How could she have possibly forgotten? Tim had duped Gloria. Bridget remembered being at her desk and listening to Gloria shouting. It was his fault she couldn't have children; he'd not told her he'd had the snip before they were married. And what had Bridget done with that information? She'd told Derek.

Graham wasn't in the reception area or the bar of the restaurant and he wasn't in her room either, but then perhaps the staff were careful about who they handed out keys to. He could just be pretending to be her husband, after all. How would they know? She made her way back down the stairs and found Lachlan on the reception desk speaking on the phone. She waited until he'd finished the booking and he turned to her with a smile.

'Apparently my husband has arrived,' she said. 'Thank you for finding me through Gloria.'

'Ah, of course. He arrived about an hour ago and because you wouldn't be back for a while he decided to take a walk around Lerwick. He said he wouldn't be too long, though.'

'Thank you,' she said and wandered over to take a seat by the window.

She realised very quickly that her phone was dead when she found it in the bottom of her bag. She couldn't even remember the last time she'd charged it up and decided to just sit and wait for Graham to get back. She could see the length of the street from this vantage point and felt happier waiting than going upstairs to find her charger and possibly missing him. Irritatingly, her head swum with thoughts about the factory and about Gloria and Derek, but it was such a long time ago now and she pushed those thoughts away and turned her attention to her husband. Her heart hammered with excitement. She and Graham had been married for over forty years and it pleased her that she still felt this way. She began to question exactly where this excitement originated. Was it her deep love for him or could it be simply that her constant fear of losing him made her want to be near him all the time? She chose not to think further about any of it. Deep thinking seemed to unsettle her these days. She concentrated on the fact that if Graham was here with her, she wouldn't have to feel like a gooseberry in the back seat of the car.

She wondered how Derek and Gloria were getting on finding Norman. Having just come back over on the ferry to drop her off, they had to retrace their steps. The address was for a house in Unst, so they'd have to get the second ferry too. She was actually amazed at Gloria's stamina, all this driving back and forth. For a woman in her seventies, she had energy. Bridget crossed her fingers in her lap as she continued to look out for Graham. Hopefully it would be as easy as them knocking on the door and the person – the woman – handing Norman over.

Then something else sparked in her mind. What on earth was happening to her? She grappled with it for a moment, like a slippery fish on the end of the line. She closed her eyes to shut out the scene from the street, trying not to distract herself. She had seen the bike on numerous occasions. Plenty of times when it had been following them. But there were other memories of it now. She'd seen it parked up near here. Back down towards where Gloria parked behind the hotel. Had it just been hovering and waiting for them? But those spaces were for residents of the row of flats. Gloria had pointed that out when she first parked. And twice, Bridget had seen the bike parked up with a chain around its wheel and without the rider. You wouldn't do that if you were hovering. You'd only do that if you lived in the flats.

She reached for her phone again, but of course it was still dead. She stood up to go to her room, to find her charger and get some life in her phone to call Gloria, to tell them they were on the wrong track, travelling towards the wrong house. She raced for the stairs and got up them as quickly as she could. She was in her room and had her phone plugged in within minutes. That painful wait for the phone to switch on seemed interminable and when she finally had enough charge to phone Gloria, the call didn't go through. She tried Derek but got the same.

'Damn,' she said. They must be in a black spot. She'd have to wait for them to get back, but that could be hours; they were all the way up in Unst and it was gusty, maybe too gusty for the ferry.

She felt herself dithering and needed to focus. The priority was getting Norman back and what was stopping her doing it herself? Obviously fear was a big factor, but firstly, all she needed to do was check if the bike was even there. She might have it wrong; she often did. In a moment of bravery, she pulled on her coat and hat and left her phone charging in the room.

She walked out of the hotel and round to where she'd seen the bike parked. It was tucked away and she assumed the only reason she'd seen it was because when Gloria had reversed out of her space, she would have had her eyes on her mirrors, Derek always had his head down in his phone for directions and Bridget would have been looking out of her window. That's when she'd seen it, but not registered it. Certainly not the first time, before she'd realised it was following them. Then, without the rider and that orange helmet, she wasn't sure she'd noted it. It was just a black motorbike, after all.

'There,' she said under her breath, with a feeling of being right, but without anyone there to witness it. There was the bike parked in its spot. It had the security chain around the wheel again. Behind it was the number six painted on the wall and above that, up some steps, was the row of flats. She could see they all had numbers on the doors and so all she had to do was knock. Suddenly Bridget felt sick, but she was determined to do this, to make amends. She could wait for Graham so he'd come with her, but what if she missed the opportunity? What if she did wait for her husband and they found the bike gone? She was here now and she would do it on her own.

She made her way tentatively up the steps and along the walkway until she was standing outside the door with the six painted above the letterbox. Then she raised her hand and, after a moment of hesitation, she knocked.

Bridget held her breath while she waited, but the sound of footsteps could be heard inside and then the door was opened. A woman was standing there. She was younger than Bridget, but not by much. Her grey hair was flat, as if she'd just pulled off a helmet. Her expression was resigned.

'I want Norman back,' Bridget said, and the woman didn't say a word, but she stepped to one side and invited Bridget in.

# 27

## THE STAKEOUT

*Derek*

The sun had spent the day skimming the horizon and was now beginning to set as they pulled up outside the house. It was making Derek feel as twitchy as he'd felt knocking on Magnus's door, but then that had turned out okay in the end. He hoped this was going to be the same.

'I have to be honest; I don't like this at all,' he said.

'You're beginning to sound like Bridget. Look, all we're gonna do is knock on the door and ask for him back. Think of him like a football kicked over a neighbour's fence. Any sign of trouble and we're out of here. I didn't mean what I said about kicking ass. Norman wouldn't have wanted us to get in a scrape,' Gloria said.

'No, that's true.'

'Are you doing the honours again?' Gloria asked him, and he swallowed his concern and said that yes, of course he was, and then Gloria reached out and touched his hand.

'What would I do without you?' she said, and she didn't sound like she was taking the piss. He saw genuine admiration in her eyes, or it may have been the last of the sunrays coming through the windscreen. It was hard for him to tell. Either way, his legs were wobbly when he got out of the car.

He walked into the front garden, glancing around him as he went. The house was on its own out here. It was so remote, in fact, that for once you couldn't see the sea, although he knew it wouldn't be far. There was little garden, but then why would you worry about that when you had miles of that view in front of your house? It wasn't as untidy as Magnus's, but it wasn't exactly kempt like Derek's own pristine garden. This had weeds rather than plants and they had grown over old pots and paving slabs and a bit of trellis that had been abandoned before it had made it to the top of the fence. He picked his way to the door and raised a hand to knock. Was he hoping it was the wrong house and he could scuttle away? Yes, he was a bit, but then he looked over his shoulder at Gloria with her nose pressed up against the glass and he took a breath and then knocked.

He wasn't sure if he was relieved or not when no one answered the door. He'd talked himself into being the big man here, he had his witness in the car and he was going to have to turn around and walk back to her. He decided to go up to the front window and have a peep in, so it would at least look as if he was doing something.

He raised his hands to his face and leaned into the glass, feeling his heart hammering inside his chest. He imagined a face leering at him from inside like it would if he was in the middle of a horror film. His breath misted up the glass, so he wiped it away and leaned in again and this time he held his breath.

The room was shabby and Derek felt bad for that thought as soon as he'd had it. There were boxes and bags piled up in every corner of the room. The sofa looked worn and grubby. There were no bookshelves or ornaments, nothing that made the place a home. It reminded him, with a stab in the heart, of his uncle's place before the intervention. He'd been a lifetime hoarder. It had started with a collection of this and a collection of that until it was a collection of everything. Anything taken into his house would never be taken out again. It had been impossible to clean his place because no surface was visible to run a vacuum cleaner or a cloth over.

This place looked to be on its way to the same end. He decided to go round the back and see what he could find there, but other than a yard full of rubbish, there was nothing. No motorbike, no woman in an orange helmet, and most importantly, no urn. Then he noticed the back door had a padlock on it and when he walked back around to the front there was one on the front door he'd not noticed. The place was abandoned. He felt less terrible about the house knowing no one was in it.

'Empty,' he told Gloria when he got back in the car.

'So much for the information. Whatever Charlotte heard, it was clearly wrong. What a wasted journey.'

Derek didn't think it was a waste. He decided he liked being in the car, just him and Gloria. It was fast becoming his favourite place to be.

They set off again and Derek did feel a little deflated at not having found Norman. After all, that was what they'd set out to do.

'Do you want me to drive for a bit? I'm feeling a bit emasculated being driven around all the time.'

He'd meant it as a joke, but Gloria didn't laugh and he realised it had fallen flat.

'You're every bit the man, Derek. Not something you have to worry about.'

A flush of something pleasant flowed through him at her

words and he was glad it was dark in the car so she couldn't see the silly grin on his face.

'Derek, can I ask you something?' she said.

'Go on then, ask me what you like,' he said, wishing he had a drink in his hand to boost the confidence of his words.

'A long time ago, at work, I thought there was a spark between us. I'm not talking about that last time in my office when poor Norman... well, you know. I'm talking way back. Look, I know I was married then and that is wrong in itself, but I got the impression you were interested in me and then suddenly it was like a switch went off and you avoided me all the time. I really want to know what happened.'

'It wasn't about Tim; I could see things weren't good between you. It was what Bridget said to me.'

'What? Bridget said something to you?'

'She said you had an agenda to have a baby.'

'She said what?'

'She told me that Tim hadn't been honest with you before you married him and that he couldn't offer you a family of your own.'

There was a lengthy silence in the car for a while then, and Derek wasn't sure if Gloria was going to explode or break down in tears. He wished she'd pull over, but before he could suggest it she started talking again.

'So, you thought I was after you to get me pregnant?'

'I did a bit, yeah.'

'Oh my God! No wonder you backed off. You must have thought I was out to trap you.'

Derek thought about that time and what Bridget had said. He hadn't backed off because he thought Gloria was trying to trap him in some way. Christ, he'd have cut out his heart and offered it up on a plate if she'd asked. He'd definitely have given her a baby. But he was being careful with *her* heart, and he didn't really think he was good enough for her. He'd give her time and if it was meant to be, it would happen. But she seemed to back off herself and make a go of it with Tim.

They were nearing the ferry now and the atmosphere inside The Beast was loaded.

'I would never have done that; I hope you know that. I was interested in you, not what you could give me,' Gloria said. 'And frankly, Bridget's got a fucking nerve. Oh, that's why she doesn't like me, isn't it? The randy wife of the boss trying to cop off with the staff. It all makes sense now; that's what she thinks of me.'

'I think she actually meant well,' Derek said, quietly. 'She tried to remind me I had a job to keep hold of.'

'Well, it worked, either way. You made it clear you weren't interested in me and I decided to make a go of my marriage to Tim and it wasn't so bad in the end.'

'Not interested in you? My heart has been bloody pining for you for nearly forty years, Gloria,' Derek said, and he was appalled to hear his voice break.

Gloria manoeuvred The Beast into the right lane and switched off the engine. Derek wanted to open his window and let out some of the intensity. Instead they sat in their own world of thoughts until he decided he'd try to lighten the mood.

'What you said the other day about going on a fake date to give me some practice. Don't suppose that's still an option, is it?' he said and laughed, but it sounded wooden.

'No, Derek.'

'Oh, okay,' he said quickly. 'I understand.'

'I don't think you do understand what I'm suggesting. I don't want a fake date. I'm all in, if you want it.'

Derek gulped and tried to pick apart what it was she was telling him.

'Gloria, can you not be American for a minute and tell me

exactly what it is you're saying? Because I think it's clear I like you, a lot, what with the old pining heart thing, and I always have done. So, what is it you're saying to me?'

She looked at him for so long it was almost as if all the air had gone from the car, and then she unplugged her seatbelt and closed the gap between them.

And she gave him the sweetest kiss of his life.

# 28

## THE RETURN OF THE ASHES

### *Bridget*

The flat was quite dark and for a moment, as the woman shut the door behind them, Bridget thought she'd made a terrible mistake. Then, as she was shown down the hallway into the living room, light was everywhere. There were spotlights in the ceiling, table lamps on most of the surfaces and a welcome fire crackled in a hearth. There was a huge window with the most amazing view over Lerwick harbour. Even though it was now dark, the lights twinkled on each of the boats and the streetlights made pretty reflections in the water. Bridget thought that if she lived here she'd spend all of her time in the window seat watching the boats out on the water coming and going with the tide.

The woman clearly had a passion for houseplants because they were everywhere: on every surface, shelf and even hanging from the ceiling in those old-fashioned-looking macramé potholders that Bridget remembered making at school. She had brightly coloured paintings and vividly patterned soft furnishings. It wasn't at all what Bridget had been expecting after the dim interior of the hallway. The place had a tropical feel and it was an interesting contrast to the glacial view through the window. Surely serial killers didn't care for houseplants.

Then, as Bridget turned around and dragged her gaze from the view, she could see Norman's urn sitting in pride of place in the middle of a polished dining table. She was in touching distance of him and for a second she did consider snatching him up and running back to the hotel, but this woman could be unpredictable.

'I'm sorry,' the woman said. 'I mean, I'm sorry for your car going off the road, although I'm not entirely sure it was my fault. It wasn't easy to handle the bike in that storm. I'm not sorry for taking Norman, though. He should be with his fans, not with a group of people who didn't know him as well as we did. And you just left him there. How special could he possibly be to you, left abandoned in the grass?'

'He was our friend,' Bridget said simply. 'And leaving him was a huge mistake of mine.'

'Well, he was our friend too. Do we not get to go on this final journey with him?'

Bridget didn't know what to say and then she remembered she had his letter in her bag.

'He asked us to come here. He clearly loved his fans and was so happy making his knitting videos. He planned to come here too and made a list of the places he'd like to visit. I expect he'd have been in touch with his fans and I'm sure you may very well have met him. We thought by documenting his journey we would be sharing his final steps with you.'

The woman, who had yet to introduce herself, seemed to consider this.

'I went to his funeral,' she said.

'Oh, goodness, that was a long way to go. He'd have appreciated the support.'

Bridget wondered why she was pandering to this woman who had stolen Norman's ashes. Partly she was concerned she might turn nasty, but it wasn't just that. There was something incredibly sad about her.

'Your friend, the American, was very rude to me.'

'Was she? Can't say I'm surprised, she's quite often rude to me too,' Bridget said and watched as the woman's lips twitched. 'When was this?'

'At Norman's funeral. All I wanted to do was to take a closer look at the knitted blanket on his coffin and you'd have thought I was running off with it.'

Bridget glanced at Norman's urn on the table and wanted to roll her eyes at the irony.

'My name's Bridget and I used to work with Norman. I've been his friend and he mine for many years.'

'I'm Nicole,' the woman said and sank down onto her sofa.

Bridget eyed the urn and reconsidered taking it, but Nicole's expression seemed so dejected.

'Why don't you tell me what compelled you to take the urn? It was my fault it was left at the castle. I just put him down so I could pull on my gloves and my memory isn't very good. I left him there. I'm grateful to you for picking him up, keeping him safe.'

She was pandering again, she realised.

'My father died when I was working away in Norway. I had a residency teaching textiles in a summer school. My mother had his funeral and scattered his ashes before I could return. The speed with which she did this was phenomenal. I know I'm grieving and feel so furious with her for taking that away from me. I think I saw your journey with Norman, who was a huge influence in my life, and I had a mad moment. I didn't mean to take him. To start with I was just following your journey with interest and I nearly spoke to you on the ferry, but changed my mind, decided you'd probably think I was mad. When I stopped at Muness Castle to see if it matched the photo you'd shared online, I saw him there, abandoned in the grass. I was going to return him, but then I began to feel a bit cross that you had the opportunity to say goodbye and I didn't. Saying it out loud now, I know it sounds a bit mad.'

Bridget had perched on a dining chair to be nearer to Norman, but she no longer felt the need to pick him up and run. It was unlikely Nicole would stop her.

'Where are your friends?' Nicole asked.

'They're trying to find Norman's ashes in Unst. We had an address come through from his assistant as a possibility. Clearly it was wrong.'

'That was me,' Nicole said. 'I thought I'd send you off in the wrong direction, sorry.'

Bridget sighed. 'I'm sorry about your father. My dad had dementia and came to live with us, so I had the completely opposite experience from you. I found it incredibly hard to watch his demise, but I also see it was a privilege and did give me some sort of closure.'

'Yes, I can see that, but hard too. Dementia is a terrible thing.'

'Hmm,' Bridget agreed noncommittally and swallowed.

She wanted to go now. She didn't want to listen to this stranger's pain.

'Have you thought about talking to someone?' Bridget asked her, and it wasn't lost on her that Graham had been asking her to do the same for ages.

'I might,' Nicole said.

'I'd like to show you something,' said Bridget, reaching into her handbag. 'I have the letter that Norman sent me, to be read after he'd died.' She handed it over and after a moment's hesitation, Nicole read it. Then she folded it up and handed it back.

'You should take him. He calls you his dearest friend and clearly wanted you to look after his ashes.'

'Thank you for looking after Norman while I couldn't,' Bridget said, rising from her seat. She picked up the urn and clutched it to her. 'I think it might be an idea to get a photo, actually. There's been a lot of unpleasantness on Instagram surrounding Norman's disappearance. We could clear up any misunderstanding.'

'That's probably a good idea,' Nicole said, looking contrite. 'I do seem to have caused a lot of trouble.'

She had, but Bridget didn't want to make things worse than they were. She had Norman back and that was the main thing.

'Why don't we stand in front of your window with that stunning night-time view behind you?'

Bridget felt this was a sensible gesture to calm Instagram down. Perhaps also a bit of closure for Nicole. Despite the fact that she'd taken him in the first place, Bridget couldn't help but be moved by her sad story. Nicole stood in front of the window with Norman in her hands and then Bridget remembered she'd left her phone at the hotel.

'I'll have to use your phone,' she said. 'I don't have mine with me.'

Bridget stood next to Nicole and they took the picture. Nicole showed her the image and Bridget thought they just looked like a couple of friends. It would certainly calm things down if they were careful with the wording.

And then with Nicole behind her she walked to the front door with Norman tightly in her grip. There were no more words, and after leaving Nicole her phone number so she could share the photo, Bridget left.

\* \* \*

Norman sat on the table in front of Bridget and she watched over him as if her very existence depended on it. She was so proud of herself, and when Gloria and Derek came back she knew they would be too. She looked up briefly and her eyes went to the window. She had completely forgotten about Graham in all the excitement of getting Norman back, and then he appeared. He was walking down the street towards her, looking very handsome in his navy winter coat and a wool hat that Norman had knitted him a couple of years ago.

She rushed to the door and threw herself into his arms, much to the surprise of a young man cycling past.

'Graham, you came!'

'I didn't have much choice. You tell me you're stuck in a house with an odd man, that you've lost Norman, that someone is following you and Derek nearly got in a fight. That Gloria's crashed the car. Then you say you'll phone me back and you don't. Of course I was going to come.'

'Oh, yes, sorry. It's all sorted now, though. Come in, I can't leave Norman unattended for long.'

Graham looked bemused and then he smiled. 'I've really missed you,' he said and kissed her in front of everyone.

Bridget didn't care, she was delighted.

They ordered coffee in the bar and Bridget filled Graham in on all that had happened. He sat in a stunned silence while she told him all about their antics. About their visit to the mill, the Sunday tea, ferry crossings, dear Magnus and lovely Shona. Most importantly about Cameron and his sister – The Knitting Warrior. Losing Norman and then finding him again.

'That wasn't the cleverest idea to go and get Norman on your own,' he said. 'You didn't know what you could have been getting yourself into.'

'I know, but I just had to try. Now we have him back we can finish what we started.'

Once they'd checked Graham in properly, Bridget took him up to their room and he unpacked his few bits while she tried to phone Derek and Gloria again, with no luck. Nicole had sent through the photo and Bridget decided to take control for the second time today and she sent it to Charlotte on their group chat. She suggested she word it that this kind person had found Norman rather than taken him, and then she wouldn't get any hate.

'What a world we live in where the online community can be so cruel,' she said.

'That's why I usually try and avoid it,' said Graham.

'Gloria showed us a message someone had sent on Norman's page the other day that said, "If you can choose to be anything in this world, choose to be kind." Someone else responded underneath with some very colourful language telling her to get lost.'

Graham stretched out on the bed and Bridget lay down next to him. He put his arm around her and she snuggled into him.

'I'm very happy you came, but I don't understand why you didn't to start with,' she said.

'I thought you needed to do this on your own. To show yourself how capable you are. I've been worried lately that you've begun to limit yourself. I think you're concerned about your memory and have stopped almost everything you did before.'

Bridget thought about how true this was, but it wasn't the whole truth of the matter.

'I'm more worried about you,' she said.

'I'm fine, there's no need to worry about me.'

Bridget leaned back so she could look at Graham. He was still a very attractive man despite the years they'd both seen. He had more hair than a lot of men his age and yes, his face was lined, but it was because he smiled so much and that made him all the more appealing. She sighed. It was time for some truth.

'You know how my mother left when things kicked off with Dad?'

'Of course I do, I was right there with you.' He laughed.

'I'm worried that I'll get too much for you and you'll disappear like she did.'

'Bridget, that won't happen.'

'You don't know how you'll feel, though.'

'Listen to me. Firstly, I made a vow to you when we got married and that was in sickness and in health. We've had a long time of health and if there is sickness to come, I'm ready for that. But this isn't about duty. I love you. I would never do what your mum did. Secondly, you've not spoken to anyone about this occasional memory issue. There could be a number of reasons behind it. Did you know that a urine infection can cause dementia-like symptoms?'

'I don't have a urine infection, though.'

'Well, no, but I'm just using that as an example. Until we go and get you checked out, there is no point playing guessing games.'

'But today I'm just someone with a terrible memory. If I go and get checked out, tomorrow I could be someone with dementia.'

'Yes,' he said calmly and clearly. 'You might be and if that's the case we will deal with it, but one thing is for sure: no matter what happens, I'm not going anywhere. I can promise you that.'

Bridget buried her face in his chest and swallowed the lump in her throat.

'I thought you'd sent me off up here alone to get me used to being without you.'

'Not at all. I just wanted you to see how much you were capable of, and look at what you've done.'

'I can't wait to see Gloria's face when she realises I've got Norman back.'

'Shall we book a table for dinner and we can all catch up?' Graham suggested.

'The way those two are beginning to behave, they might prefer a table for two, with candles.'

'Oh, are they getting close?'

'Gloria looks at Derek like a lovesick schoolgirl and I think the feeling is mutual.'

'About bloody time. I was always surprised they didn't get together romantically way back. But I suppose Gloria was married then.'

Bridget shifted her position and swallowed.

'I think I might have been partly responsible for that,' she said.

'Oh, I doubt it. I think it's always been a case of wrong place, wrong time with those two.'

'Well, this trip has certainly given them the opportunity to revisit that.'

'I'd be very happy for them, Derek particularly. He confided in me many years ago that he was in love with Gloria. He deserves some happiness.'

## 29

### TIME TO FORGIVE

*Gloria*

They held hands on the ferry back to Yell and again on the ferry to mainland Shetland. Gloria didn't think she'd ever been as happy as this at any point in her life.

On paper they weren't a match. Derek was a home person with a joy for the quiet life, a love of his allotment and everything ordered. Gloria was impulsive and had a love for her city centre: shopping, eating and the theatre. Right now, though, Gloria didn't want to think about how they might make this work, because, quite simply, it felt so right.

She parked up behind the hotel and she took his hand as they walked round to the front. She wondered if he might be embarrassed and drop it when they walked in, but he didn't. Neither of them wanted to lose the other, it seemed.

Bridget and Graham were sitting in the bar and still Derek held onto her. Graham smiled broadly, Bridget just widened her eyes and Gloria thought, You see, Bridget, despite everything, here we are.

When Bridget stood up, though, Gloria's thoughts strayed away from Derek momentarily because Bridget was holding Norman's urn.

'Norman!' cried Gloria. 'How on earth did you find him? How did you get him back?'

'I wondered if you'd see on your phone,' Bridget said. 'I sent a message to Charlotte with a photo to post on Instagram.'

'My phone's still in the cradle in The Beast,' Gloria said.

'And mine's in the side pocket,' said Derek.

'You had your thoughts on other things,' Graham stated matter-of-factly.

Gloria watched as Derek offered up a shy smile, but she was grinning.

'I think this calls for a round of drinks,' Graham said, getting his wallet out. 'I'm so happy for you both.'

He patted Gloria's shoulder and shook Derek's hand so enthusiastically that Derek stretched out his fingers and massaged his knuckles once Graham had let go.

They settled with their drinks and Bridget regaled them with the tale of Norman's return and Nicole's part in their wild goose chase.

'I don't even mind now,' Gloria said. 'It gave us a chance to chat. I have to say, though, it was very brave of you, Bridget. Good for you.'

Gloria was feeling generous, despite what Derek had told her in the car. Was it best to forget the past and just to move on? The trouble with that was it was impossible. Festering resentment and judgement about others ate away at you. Perhaps it was time for a heart to heart. She needed another drink first because this one seemed to have evaporated.

'Bridget, as you've proved yourself incredibly capable, will you come and get a round of drinks in with me?'

Bridget hesitated and glanced at Graham for a moment as if she knew Gloria had an ulterior motive, but then she stood and nodded with an expression of resignation.

'So,' Gloria said as they walked towards the bar. 'I really want to clear something up with you.'

'Okay, but before you do can I just say how very sorry I am for the way I spoke to you the other evening. I should never have judged you on your family situation. I'd forgotten why you didn't have children. It wasn't your fault, it was Tim's.'

Gloria took Bridget's elbow and led her over to a small table in the window overlooking the harbour and they sat down.

'It's not a case of fault, Bridget.'

'But Tim had a vasectomy without telling you. I overheard you both talking, well, shouting.'

'Yes, that is true and I was angry for a very long time. But I could have divorced him, I had grounds. I could have remarried and had a family with someone else potentially, but I didn't. I could have adopted, had a sperm donor – although I imagine Tim may then have divorced me – but I didn't. It turns out I didn't want a family as much as I thought I did. That's the truth.'

'And I told Derek. I thought you were trying to use him.'

'I wasn't. I'm not gonna lie, I was attracted to him and in those early and difficult days with Tim, maybe I was looking for something else, but I would never have used him in that way.'

'I'm sorry,' Bridget said, and Gloria took her hand across the table.

'Is that why you don't like me?' she said. 'Because you thought I was trying to extract Derek's sperm?'

Bridget dropped Gloria's hand and her own flew to her mouth. Gloria laughed.

'Oh, come on, Bridget, don't be such a prude,' she said, and Bridget smiled.

'It was a bit of that, yes. Derek is a nice bloke and I didn't want to see him taken advantage of, but I shouldn't have interfered. It was more than that, though. I've always been a bit intimidated by strong women. I feel inadequate. Sounds pathetic, doesn't it?'

'I always admired you and envied you too,' Gloria said, and she thought back to the Bridget she knew in the office. How well she juggled everything: her job, her family, her marriage. 'I used to watch you leave work and skip out into the parking lot when Graham picked you up at the end of the day. I thought, there are two people who have that rare thing: a happy marriage. I made the best of it with Tim, but in truth, I was never really truly happy. I was the second wife and I never felt like I was number one to him.'

Bridget looked a little tearful for a moment, but then she sat forward and took a breath.

'Derek told Graham he was in love with you when Graham still worked at the factory. The past is the past, but I say get hold of that future with both hands and don't let it slip away again.'

They stared at each other for a moment until a smile broke out on both of their faces.

'Best advice ever,' Gloria said.

Just then Derek and Graham appeared.

'Dry old bar,' Graham said. 'And our table for dinner is ready.'

* * *

'So, what are the plans now?' Graham asked as he tucked into his steak.

Gloria thought about how much she'd like to ditch dinner altogether and whisk Derek up to her room, but she knew that wasn't what Graham was referring to.

'Now we have Norman back, perhaps we could think about

scattering him?' Bridget said. 'I'm quite keen to go home, to be honest.'

'I think we've done good by Norman. He's seen some of the island, we've found his family and maybe it is time to say goodbye,' Derek said. 'Having said that, I'm keen to spend some more time here.'

Gloria's heart sank a little at that. Did Derek want to go off on his own?

'What do you say, Gloria? Once we've said our goodbyes to Norman, do you fancy taking The Beast for another spin around? See if we can get into some tucked-away corners?'

Graham snorted and Derek blushed. Gloria hoped he'd never find a way to stop that colour flooding his cheeks.

'I think that sounds fantastic,' she said.

'There is one thing that I feel needs addressing,' Graham said. 'Now, you might not think this is my place, but I'm going to say it anyway. Norman loved you three and he never thought for one minute any of you were responsible in any way for his accident. He's said it enough times, but I hope you really heard him. I hope you can scatter his ashes with peace in your hearts.'

'I did blame myself for ages,' Gloria said. 'If I'm honest, I still feel terrible about that day. While Norman was lying there, injured, I was thinking only of myself.'

She glanced across at Derek, who just sat looking at his seafood pasta.

'So, you two were snogging. So what, neither of you were supposed to be in the factory that day. You could have been snogging at home, in your car, behind the bloody bike sheds. It wouldn't have made any difference. Norman knew that cherry picker was faulty, everyone knew it was faulty, Bridget told me, but he was reckless. Do you remember how reckless he used to be? Do you remember when he did that bungee jump in the pub car park off that crane? That was a dodgy set-up and no mistake. I thought he was gonna smash his head in. And what about when he knocked himself out after mountain biking through the woods? No one else tried that steep descent, but Norman did. I think you lot have forgotten what a bloody thrill seeker he was. All you remember was him knitting in the comfort of his own home, but he'd have done it on a bloody roller coaster given the opportunity.'

'But it was my job to get it fixed,' Bridget said.

'Yes, and you made the call. They were coming out the next week. All Norman had to do was stay away from the bloody cherry picker, but no, he thought it would be okay. And he knew this, he knew it was on him. The only thing he was gutted about was his accident wasn't skydiving,' Graham said.

'Well, it sort of was,' said Bridget, and after a long moment of silence they all began to laugh.

Gloria leaned in to Norman's urn and touched the golden wings on the front.

'Norman, we think it's time to forgive ourselves. What do you say? Give us a sign.'

And it was at that moment that Gloria, Derek and Bridget's phones buzzed simultaneously. It was a message from Charlotte to say she'd posted a compilation of their photos on the Norman Knits YouTube channel and it had had thousands of views.

Charlotte's last words were:

He'd have been so proud of you lot.

# 30

# GOODBYE NORMAN

## *Bridget*

Gloria took the turning onto the track leading to Muckle Flugga Shore Station and parked in one of the few spaces by the water. There was a large shed with a track leading from it down into the sea, but Bridget was happy to see that Cameron's fishing boat was already out on the water at the end of the jetty. She didn't fancy a bumpy ride into the Burra Firth.

'The conditions seem perfect,' Graham said as they all got out of the car.

Gloria held onto Derek's arm with one of her hands, the other clutching firmly onto Norman. She clearly had no intention of losing him again – Norman, or Derek for that matter.

It was bitterly cold and the possibility of snow hung in the air, but for now it was pretty perfect. There was barely a breeze and with all their layers they wouldn't freeze to death on the water.

Bridget and Graham had booked flights back to the mainland, with Bridget insisting she'd need a large gin and tonic to get her on board, but that she'd prefer it to the vomity ferry. Graham's car was waiting at the airport where he'd parked it, anyway, so it was the perfect solution. They were leaving the following morning. Bridget had phoned Magnus to say they'd pop in for that cup of tea so she could return the knitting book and that was where they were heading next. He'd seemed delighted to hear from her.

Derek and Gloria had booked into Esther's bed and breakfast after one more night at the Harbour View Hotel and planned to stay for another few days at least. Derek had a lot of places he still wanted to visit, but Bridget got the impression he was stringing this out. She thought that maybe he didn't want to go home to reality and burst this Shetland bubble he and Gloria had created for themselves.

'Looks like we're finally doing this then,' Gloria said. 'It feels so much more real than it did at the beginning of this trip. It really will be saying goodbye now.'

'I'm just so glad that we found his family,' Derek said. 'It's more of a fitting tribute to Norman, to say goodbye this way.'

His voice caught on the last words and Bridget watched as Gloria squeezed his arm. She surprised herself with how happy it made her to see them together. All those years wasted on miscommunications and misunderstandings, not helped by her own interference.

'Come on,' she said. 'Let's go and do this properly.'

They all walked out to the end of the jetty and Cameron stepped off the boat to greet them.

'Hello,' he said. 'Welcome aboard the *Faith Emily*. The weather is good for now, but a squall is forecast for later so it's best if we get going right away.'

He helped them all aboard one at a time and Bridget was just settling herself on the wooden bench that ran the length of the boat when she caught sight of someone waving madly from the car park. It was Esther and she was running down towards the jetty with a basket swinging from her arm. She was out of breath and panting by the time she reached them.

'I'm sorry,' she said. 'I took so long making the food, I thought I was going to miss you.'

Cameron rolled his eyes at his sister and nodded at her to climb aboard.

'I hope you've got some goodies in there,' he said, pointing to the basket.

'Yes,' she said, grinning. 'Champagne and some canapés.'

'Oooh, very posh!' Cameron said, taking the basket from her and rifling through it as she stepped on board.

'I feel like we're in the way now,' Bridget said. 'You're his family. We're just his friends.'

'Which means so much,' Esther said. 'You have come all this way out of love for him. That is everything. You are his family really.'

'Oh, I nearly forgot,' Gloria said, reaching into her handbag. 'He wanted you to have this. Apparently your grandfather gave it to Ida, but it belonged to his grandmother.'

She handed over the box with the ring that had been with the photos and letters. Esther took it out. It was a pretty gold band with a mother of pearl wrapped in spirals of gold. She pushed it onto her finger and smiled.

'Thank you,' she said. 'It's lovely.'

They settled in and Cameron navigated along the Burra Firth round towards Muckle Flugga. His skill at avoiding the rocks was definitely put to the test. They followed the coastline heading north and Bridget's eyes were firmly on the land.

'Who would have thought that such a bleak landscape could be so stunning,' she said. 'The way the cliffs seem to fold in on themselves is fascinating.'

'It's beautiful,' Gloria agreed, but she wasn't looking.

'How are you doing?' Derek asked her.

Gloria had made it clear on several occasions that she wasn't happy in small boats and Bridget admired her for pushing herself to get on board.

'Not as bad as I thought it would be,' she said.

'Have a nip of this,' Esther said, handing Gloria a hipflask.

She didn't ask what was in it but put it to her lips and tipped her head back.

'Thanks,' she said, wiping the back of her hand across her mouth.

As they rounded the top of Unst, the lighthouse came into view and the wind began to pick up. The little boat began to lurch as the waves hit the front of it and Bridget watched Gloria reach out for Derek. He wrapped an arm around her shoulder and whispered something into her ear.

As Bridget looked back towards the land she noticed a figure standing on the cliff top. They were wearing black leathers. She stood up in the boat for a moment and peered back. The figure raised a hand and waved. It was Nicole, Bridget knew it. She smiled to herself, waved back and then sat down. Nicole was saying her own goodbye. She wasn't a bad person, just a woman that was grieving.

'I'm going to circle the island so you can get a great view of Muckle Flugga Lighthouse, but I'm not going to land there. It wouldn't be safe getting you all on and off the boat. To be honest, if Norman asked to have his ashes scattered at the northernmost point of the UK, that is actually Out Stack. You see that rocky outcrop?' Cameron said. 'That has never been inhabited, but if you head north from here, there's nothing until you reach the North Pole. We are at the full stop at the end of Britain. Perhaps you should scatter his ashes just off the north of Out Stack. That's where his father went.'

'I think that's a great idea,' Derek said, taking the urn from Gloria's hands. 'Come on, old friend, you're nearly there.'

Bridget wiped a tear away from her eye. She accepted it was going to be an emotional experience.

'We need to take one last photo,' Gloria said. 'All of us with Norman and the lighthouse if we can do it.'

As they posed with Norman for the last time, Esther pointed out the seals that were on the rocks, and just before they slipped into the sea Gloria took the photo. After, when she enlarged the image, you could clearly see them in the background. Bridget was delighted that Gloria got her wish.

Cameron kept the boat as steady as he could in the worsening weather and they skirted the lighthouse.

'It was built in 1854 by Robert Louis Stevenson's father and uncle. The island of Unst is said to have been an inspiration for him writing *Treasure Island* after he visited. Don't know if that's true, but an interesting fact if it is,' Cameron said.

'A man after my own heart,' said Derek. 'I love hearing about the history of a place, don't I, Gloria?'

'You do indeed,' she said, clutching onto Derek and the side of the boat. 'It's getting a bit rough now, isn't it?'

Cameron nodded at her. 'Do you know that the lighthouse sits two hundred feet above sea level, but in the depths of a bad storm the waves crash up the side of it? It's a mere wisp of a breeze right now and no trouble. We won't be long getting to Out Stack.'

Gloria set her lips into a tight line and nodded also.

And it did only take a short time to motor out to Out Stack and once they were there, Cameron cut the engine and it was over to the friends to say their final goodbyes.

The three stood with Norman between them resting on the side of the boat.

'I would just like to say,' Derek began, 'that I will be eternally grateful to Norman for showing me what it was I was missing in my life and putting me in a position to go for it. God speed, my friend.'

Derek lifted the lid of the urn and poured a little of Norman's ashes into the water that lapped around those northernmost rocks. Then Graham got up and held Bridget's hand.

'Norman, you were a wonderful man with so many people that loved you, even people that never met you. That's something we should all try and aspire to. I will miss you and I thank you for being my friend,' Bridget said, and then she and Graham tipped the urn together as Graham said a quiet goodbye of his own.

'Did you want to say something?' Gloria asked Cameron and Esther.

'I'll keep the boat steady,' Cameron said, but Esther came forward.

'I just wanted to say to you, Norman, what an inspiration you were to me, and I might go so far as to say you changed my life when things were not easy. I'm so sorry I never got to meet you, but I'm very happy you sent these three on your behalf.'

Gloria stepped forward after Esther had scattered a little more and picked up the urn and looked inside.

'I hope you've all left some of him for me,' she joked. 'Norman, you were definitely one of the best people I've ever known. Your enthusiasm for life in whatever form it took was infectious. That old saying about life giving you lemons then you make lemonade was written for you. I believe I will see you again in a better place and I hope you'll have the drinks on ice and the bar stool ready for me. Oh, and just so you know, I'm not knitting that damn hat.'

She upturned the urn and the rest of the ashes slipped into the water. Esther handed Gloria three white roses.

'I picked these up, thought you might want to have them.'

'That's really thoughtful,' Bridget said, and one by one the three friends threw them into the water.

As they motored back, they shared their personal stories of Norman while Esther handed out the champagne. They celebrated the man they had all come to love.

# EPILOGUE
## BRIDGET

'Come on, Graham,' Bridget called up the stairs. 'We can't be late.'

She turned to the mirror hanging on the wall by the front door and adjusted her hat. She'd gone for a peachy pink-coloured dress and matching hat as suggested by the woman who had done her colours. Bridget hadn't even known having your colours done was a thing until Gloria had a friend of hers come round to Bridget's, sit her on a dining chair and wrap swathes of different-coloured fabric around her neck. She had to admit, it was a revelation. Now she knew she was officially *spring*, she'd treated herself to a whole new wardrobe in warm greens, yellows, orangey reds, peachy pinks and every shade of light brown from tan to the palest beige. She'd never felt so good in her life and what with a new haircut too, she was happy. Not only that, but she'd also booked flights for her and Graham to Hamburg, to stay with Imogen and Jamie, to go and see their gorgeous grandsons. Graham's face when she'd shown him the booking was a picture and only slightly spoilt by his insistence on checking through all the details. She didn't really mind; let's be honest, it was highly likely she'd made a mistake.

'I'm ready,' Graham said, dashing down the stairs in his navy-blue suit. He'd not wanted to have his colours done when Bridget suggested it. He'd said he'd not be buying any new clothes, so what was the point in knowing which season of the year he was supposed to be?

Navy didn't really suit him, but Bridget decided he still looked quite handsome all dressed up, so it would have to do. Maybe she'd stand in front of him for the photos.

'All set for your appointment next week, love?' Graham asked her when they were in the car and leaving Bridlington for York.

'Can we just enjoy this weekend first, please?'

He'd been reminding her every day and she knew why; he didn't want it to come as a complete surprise when they left on Tuesday morning for the hospital. A gentle daily reminder, but she hadn't forgotten, not yet anyway. It was one of the biggest reasons she was happy. It wasn't really the haircut, the colour swatches and an imminent holiday with her family, although they were all very nice things to do, it was the fact she'd finally made a decision. She was going to the memory clinic. There would be no more burying her head in the sand about it. She'd heard about new treatments to help with the symptoms of dementia, and ways she could help herself also. Now she knew for sure that Graham was on board too and wasn't about to do a disappearing act like her mother, she felt in a better place to face her future, because she wasn't alone: she had Graham, their daughter and now she had two of the best friends possible in Gloria and Derek.

'I'm sorry, Bridge, of course we can enjoy the weekend. I just want you to feel comfortable and safe, that's all.'

'I do,' she said.

'I think you've just stolen Gloria and Derek's line,' he said, and she smiled all the way to York.

* * *

*Derek*

Derek was having a drink with his brother-in-law, Bert. They were in the bar of the hotel in York and he only had half an hour left of being a single man. It felt like the longest thirty minutes of his life.

Ever since he'd asked Gloria to marry him he'd been convinced she'd change her mind. She was happy on her own, only wanted something casual. Isn't that what she'd always said? And then he'd taken the plunge and asked her, and to his utter amazement and joy she'd said yes. They'd talked long into the night, on several occasions since, about how it would change both of their lives, but in the end they agreed it could only be for the better. It had been a long time in the making and they both felt that, since Shetland, they had Norman's blessing. It was their time.

Bert finished his pint and Derek his lemonade, and they left their glasses on the bar. They walked out into the hotel gardens and the marquee the staff had set up in the grounds. Gloria had chosen a champagne-coloured theme that was in the flowers that had been hung up in cascades from the lining of the marquee and the arrangement sitting on the table at the business end of things, where the registrar stood. The chairs were covered in champagne-coloured silk and the guests were beginning to sit down. He walked down the aisle with Bert and he said a few hellos, got a few pats on the back and when he saw Bridget and Graham he got the warmest of hugs. He really needed to hold it together. He didn't want to be crying when Gloria arrived. And then he saw Moth and his wife and children. He walked over to shake his hand, but Moth pulled him in for a manly hug that

involved strong back slapping. Gloria had been delighted when
her stepson had accepted the wedding invitation and they'd all
met up for dinner so Moth could meet Derek. Derek had been so
nervous, which seemed silly now he knew how personable Moth
was. He'd not wanted to take on the factory after his father died
and had been happy for Gloria to take the reins, something his
mother, Brenda, had been furious about, but they didn't talk
about it. It was history.

'Right then, you ready, mate?' Bert asked him as they took
their positions at the front.

'More than,' Derek said.

His fingers went to the flower that sat in his buttonhole.
Bridget had knitted them all, for him, Bert, his nephews and
Graham. She'd used some of Gloria's champagne-coloured wool
that Shona had given her. Gloria had never finished her hat and
had no intention of ever picking up her knitting needles again,
but Bridget had become quite proficient over the last few months
and when she'd offered to knit for their wedding, Gloria had
been delighted. It somehow felt as if Norman was there with
them.

* * *

*Gloria*

Gloria checked her face one last time in the mirror on the
dressing table. She didn't look too bad for a golden girl, she
thought. Her hairdresser, Gillian, had done a fabulous job.
They'd discussed options for a formal up-do and soft curls
pinned at one side, but in the end Gloria went for a more natural
look without involving a can of hairspray. She'd said she would
want Derek to be able to run his fingers through it later without

getting them stuck. The girl who had done her make-up had made her skin glow in a soft, peachy tone and Gloria had joked about taking her on their honeymoon with them.

They had a week in Vienna booked and Gloria couldn't wait. It had been Derek's idea and even though she'd imagined they'd be spending a week on a beach somewhere, to see the itinerary he had planned had turned her head. Art and culture, palaces and museums, champagne cruise on the river and the cakes and desserts in the cafés looked like they were to die for. He'd done his homework and she was impressed.

This felt like the most grown-up thing she'd done in the last twenty years and she realised how good it felt to belong with someone again, with someone she loved with everything she had. They'd discussed the mechanics of living together and decided to both sell their houses and buy a place together; their forever home, Derek had called it, which made her laugh. Derek had told her all about his needs and what he'd like from their living arrangements and it hadn't bothered her at all. She loved how house-trained he was and the fact he wasn't looking for someone to look after him. They would share the cooking, the cleaning, the washing and the shopping, fifty-fifty. He said she wasn't his mother and he didn't expect her to pick up after him, which was music to her ears.

Gloria knew it would take some adjusting to get used to this new normal they found themselves in, but she was prepared for it. For Derek she was happy to push herself to be more emotionally intimate, to give more of herself. She felt excited about her future for the first time in a long time.

She turned away from the mirror and picked up the brooch Bridget had lent her – something borrowed. Her simple peach dress was new and she decided she was old enough to cover that angle of the saying. The something blue came in the form of a knitted garter that Derek had made for her. He'd unravelled some blue wool from the first scarf Norman had ever knitted him and turned it into something blue for Gloria's thigh. They'd had a lot of fun when he measured her for size.

They'd forgiven themselves in Shetland and were no longer weighted down by their collective guilt. Gloria would never forget Norman, the man with the hugest of hearts and the capacity for love that reached so many.

She picked up her posy of roses and opened the door to the hotel room. She took a breath and, knowing she had Norman's blessing, she made her way to marry the new uncomplicated man in her life. Her soulmate.

* * *

## MORE FROM KATE GALLEY

Another book from Kate Galley, *Old Girls Behaving Badly*, is available to order now here:
https://mybook.to/BehavingBadlyBackAd

# AUTHOR'S NOTE

A few years back I was listening to the radio in the car on a long journey and was glued to a programme about women in the Shetland Islands knitting fishing ganseys. When I arrived home I went straight online and read everything I could find about the subject. I wasn't a knitter; I'd never picked up needles in my life, but these women and their stories really captured my imagination.

I turned to a knitter on YouTube and after watching their videos I taught myself to knit. I now regularly knit jumpers, cardigans, hats and scarves, but I have yet to attempt an epic fisherman's gansey. One day I will.

# ACKNOWLEDGEMENTS

Here I am having finished my fifth novel!

If someone had told me a few years back when I first started on this writing journey that I would now be typing the acknowledgements for book five, I don't think I would have believed them.

It's not a solo journey, though. There are many people behind the scenes that work to get the best book out there.

I want to thank my amazing editor, Rachel Faulkner-Will-cocks, for her invaluable input, from first idea to finished book and most steps in between. She saw something in my words right back at the start and took on my debut. I'm so happy to still be working with her all these books later.

A big thank you to everyone who works so hard at Boldwood. You are a fantastic bunch of people and make every step of the process both manageable and enjoyable. You really do deserve your recent win at the British Book Awards: Independent Publisher of the Year! Congratulations!

Thanks so much to Hazel Tindall, who agreed to feature in my Sunday tea with Bridget, Gloria and Derek. You are such an inspirational knitter.

Thanks also to Lynn at the Jamison's of Shetland shop in Lerwick for answering my questions about their mill in Sandness.

Thank you to the brilliant Patricia Gallimore, who reads my audio books. You really do bring my characters to life.

This book is dedicated to my husband, Richard. He is the

hardest-working person I know and I aspire to work as hard as he does.

Last, but by no means least, I want to thank my readers. A lot of you have been on board with my stories from the start and I appreciate your kind words and wonderful reviews. Whether you read on your device, pick up a paperback, listen on audio or borrow from your local library, I am so grateful.

Thank you x

# ABOUT THE AUTHOR

**Kate Galley** is the author of uplifting golden years fiction, including *The Second Chance Holiday Club*. She was previously published by Aria, and is a mobile hairdresser in her spare time.

Sign up to Kate Galley's mailing list for news, competitions and updates on future books.

Follow Kate on social media here:

- facebook.com/Kate-Galley-Author-100083291782773
- x.com/KateGalley1
- instagram.com/kategalley1
- threads.net/@kategalley1

## ALSO BY KATE GALLEY

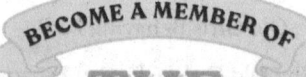